RISE OF THE
SHADOW

R. A. MAYES

For the women out there who don't know their own strength.
Caeli wants you to know that you should never doubt yourself again.
It's what she kept telling me through the process of writing her story... and we've only just begun.

CAELI'S PLAYLIST

for when she needs to remind
herself she's a badass

Bad Girls || M.I.A	3:48
Blood // Water || grandson	3:37
Burn Your Village || Kiki Rockwell	4:05
Bury Me Face Down || grandson	3:52
COFFIN || PLVTINUM	1:42
Daisy || Ashnikko	2:27
Devil Is A Woman || Cloudy June	3:12
F.W.T.B - grandson remix || YONAKA	3:19
Glass Houses || Bad Omens	4:01
Goddess || Jaira Burns	3:08
Lion || Saint Mesa	2:51
Little Girl Gone || CHINCHILLA	3:09
Own Me || bülow	3:29
Play with Fire (ft. Yacht Money) || Sam Tinnesz	3:01
Siren || Kailee Morgue	3:20
Survivor || 2WEI	3:15
Tantrum || Ashnikko	2:20
Vendetta || UNSECRET, Krigarè	3:34
What's Up Danger || Blackway, Black Caviar	3:42
You Can Run || Adam Jones	4:00

"Trust is the easiest thing in the world to lose, and the hardest thing in the world to get back."
- R. M. Williams

RISE OF THE
SHADOW

R. A. MAYES

EIGHT YEARS AGO

Sirens echoed through the hallways.

Red lights flashed in concordance with the grating sound.

Bodies scattered the floor, and their blood coated the polished concrete.

I ran my hand over my face at the carnage. Screams ricocheted through my ears, as if the corpses still had their voices and needed to make their fear known. This had ended in a far worse massacre than I could have imagined.

"She's gone?" I flinched at the voice next to me, and caught a glimpse of green eyes before I turned towards the still open door. My stomach turned and threatened to bring up everything I'd eaten over the last twenty-four hours, but there wasn't much there. Eating hadn't been on my list of priorities of late.

"Yes." Short and simple; over the span of twenty-three years, I'd learned it was the best way to communicate with Victoria Ashford. Any more words than necessary and she'd get bored. Her boredom always evolved into anger, and that had a history of escalating to violence.

"I'm aware this wasn't easy for you." That couldn't be further from the truth. It was easy for me to let the kid loose from the compound—to let her go free. "But this was necessary."

"How so?" It was best to ask questions after a plan's completion. If you did so beforehand, then you'd be accused of doubting leadership or Victoria's intelligence. I'd learned it was best to avoid the punishment for doing that.

"Because we need her strong enough for an incitement, and we need the best circumstances possible for her to survive it. I've already made the plan." Victoria crossed her arms over her chest as she spoke, and the words made my uneasy stomach churn once more. "Templum Gratiae, they have a few conduit children... one of them is a guardian."

Shit. A guardian was all we needed to ensure the kid's survival. The Entity demanded balance, and it was only happy when its demands were met. We wanted it to be happy, so it wouldn't turn her to ash during her incitement.

"I've made a deal with Ryne. When their guardian is fifteen years old, they'll track down One and get her in for her incitement. They'll give her back afterwards." It sounded so simple, as if One wouldn't be so overpowered that there'd be no chance of controlling her.

I looked over my shoulder at the bodies she'd left in her wake. She was only fifteen, but she'd dealt this much destruction within twenty minutes of me leaving her 'bedroom' door unlocked. Of all the shit I'd had to do in this fucking organisation, this was the most painful. Not because of what I'd done, but because of how it would come back to bite me in the ass later.

The kid trusted me. If she ever found out that what I'd done had been an order, I'd be worse off than the guards she'd killed.

"Do you trust them?" I asked. She shook her head, which made her strawberry-blonde ponytail swing behind her.

"No, but it's the best option we have. Finding our own guardian will be too hard, and Ryne won't let his go since she's the daughter of the love of his life or some shit. I don't know the details and, frankly, I don't care." That made sense. It was information that wasn't important to the plan. "Even if they don't cooperate, we'll still get her back."

"They outnumber us," I uttered. Her green eyes were sharp enough to cut through my skin, but I didn't so much as flinch. I couldn't. It would be a sign of weakness, and fragility was prohibited in the Order of Shadows.

"But we have more conduits, ones that know how to use their power. Ryne's faction is still new, and they won't stand a chance against us, or against *you*. Besides, I doubt she'd let them control her." Her voice was as pointed as her eyes, and so I nodded my apology. "Remember, this is a test more than anything else. We've taught One everything we can; she has to find her own way in the world now."

Right, *her own way.* I already knew that part of the plan. They hoped she'd form attachments out there, ones that could be used against her when the time came to imprison her again. If I could, I'd have gone with her, to make sure she didn't fall into that trap...

"You made a mistake with her." Victoria's eyes focused on me as I looked down at her.

"And what would that be?" I needed to know what she knew—I was either in trouble or I wasn't.

"You thought of her like a daughter, Aric." Shit, that meant she knew nearly everything, but not enough to want me dead. Not *yet*, at least. "She's not. She's property that cost us millions of dollars to create. I understand she has your DNA, but she is not your child. She's a weapon." I nodded once again, even though I disagreed. How could they reduce the kid to nothing more than a fucking *weapon*?

I should have done more to ensure One's safety, but I had more important things to focus on here—more plans that needed to be enacted within the Order. More people that needed my protection.

"Tell me you'll rectify that mistake."

"She's not my daughter. She's a weapon." I stopped myself from tensing my jaw, from giving away the fact that I didn't believe a word I'd said.

"Good, then let's move forward. We have research to get back to." I took a final look through the open door as Victoria walked away.

The plan would take at least five years to come full circle, which meant it would be at least that long before I'd see One again—at least *five years* that she'd have to survive alone for.

Taking a final breath, I closed the door and stepped back. The alarms and flashing lights ceased the second it clicked shut, and then I followed Victoria back into the compound as I prayed that the Entity would spare One...

Even though I knew it wouldn't.

Chapter One

THE AMERICAN AND THE PRINCESS

He held a dagger to my throat. The flat of the blade both cooled my skin and served as a precious reminder that I'd become complacent.

This wasn't how the night was meant to go. It was supposed to be an easy break-in, followed by an even easier getaway. Instead, I was pressed between two walls, one made of plaster and the other of taut muscle. And it was too late for me to back out of the situation...

Not that I wanted to.

This gorgeous, but dense, man was nothing but an amateur. That much was obvious from the way his golden eyes watched me, and how tense his body was against mine. I wouldn't need to back out of the situation. The way the flat of the blade sat against my neck instead of the edge told me I had the upper hand... and this was supposed to be an *unfavourable* situation. Even so, it would still be easy enough to get what I wanted and leave in one piece. I just had to play my cards right.

"What's your name?" I asked as I tilted my head back. The movement was to help see his eyes without my eyelashes obstructing the view, and it worked. It allowed me to watch as he glanced down; I assumed to check where his dagger rested against my neck. I could barely feel the blade anymore, which was another indication this beautiful idiot had no idea what he was doing.

"I'm the one with a sharp object, so maybe I'll ask the questions." Of course his voice was as pretty as his eyes. But we'd been standing here for the better part of two minutes. If he was going to ask a question, he would have done it by now.

Not being able to move always made me a little twitchy, and it was getting difficult to resist doing something stupid for the sake of getting away from him.

His gold eyes lifted from my neck to stare directly into my soul, and I held that gaze. If I kept his attention on my eyes, then he wouldn't see my hand as it inched towards the sheath on my right thigh-

"Don't." The warning came from his throat as he dropped his hand from the wall next to my head and caught my wrist.

He pinned me to the plaster, and it took everything in me not to snarl at him. Soon enough, and he would regret ever touching me. *Patience.* "You had plenty of opportunity to get that out before we ended up here, *Princess*." Wow, how original. It was almost like he heard my British accent and thought of a fun nickname for me because of it... just like everyone else did.

Although, what he'd said was true, and that didn't sit well with me. There'd been ample opportunity to unsheathe my dagger before he'd pinned me against the wall; but like I said before, I'd been complacent.

What I'd expected to happen was to come across some museum guards, take them down, bag what I wanted from the glass cabinets and disappear into the night. I hadn't planned on being attacked by someone with half a brain, so I'd walked into the unguarded museum thinking I'd been stupidly lucky. Instead, I now knew there weren't any guards because this idiot had likely already disposed of them, and I'd allowed him to throw me against the wall with a blade to my throat. The artefacts I was after were just out of arm's reach, and they mocked me from behind their glass shields.

Why'd you let him get the upper hand on you, Caeli?

Why didn't you pay attention to your surroundings, Caeli?

Fuck, Vince would never let me hear the end of this.

Okay, *think*. Some men liked to talk when they had control. They liked to gloat and prove themselves even though they already had the upper hand. The smart ones kept their mouths shut until they had a blade to their throat.

So that's all I had to do—swap our positions.

Maybe because he'd cleared the guards for me, I could be courteous. Instead of just attacking, I could give him a warning to prepare himself for the onslaught.

"This'll hurt," I whispered as I tilted my head to the side.

"What?"

This would be far too easy.

I tucked my left foot behind his right and threw my elbow up to knock his arm away from my chest. With the hit, I pulled my head away from the stray knife, but the point of it nicked my chin. Alright, I'd let that wound go. It was my fault I was in this situation in the first place, so it was a fair punishment.

There would only be a small window before he'd start fighting back, so I had to utilise it.

Before he could think about striking me, I ripped my right wrist free from his grasp and jabbed him in the throat. But I couldn't let it end there. I had to make him realise just how big of a mistake he'd made.

The onslaught continued as I threw my knee into his stomach, forcing him to stumble away from me. Good, I could use a little space.

"What the fuck?" He whispered as he staggered backwards. The hand that held my wrist captive now rubbed his throat.

Oh, he thought this was over.

"You want to know how I can tell that you're an amateur?" I stalked towards him as I pulled the dagger free from it's sheath on my thigh.

The knife in his hand caught the harsh fluorescent lighting. Did he think adjusting his grip would help him out here?

"It's because instead of slitting my throat like you should have, you attempted to intimidate me." I ran my fingers over the edge of my knife and watched as his tongue licked his bottom lip. "That was a huge mistake."

Overpowering him would be easy. It would only take three steps that I had practiced and perfected over the years. Three easily defensible moves that he couldn't win against.

I closed the distance between us in five running strides and went through my three actions.

The first was a fake swing, which he fell for as planned. It was easy enough to know he'd take the bait. My prey never looked at where I'd placed my feet—their focus was always on the imminent threat of my blade swinging towards their face.

The second action was a simple duck to avoid his baited counter attack. Although he had moved a little faster than I'd expected, it still wasn't fast enough to make contact.

The final move was a swift punch to his already bruised throat, which forced a piece of gum to shoot out of his mouth. The hit was hard enough to shock his system, to make him gasp for air and drop his blade, but soft enough not to shatter his windpipe. I could have done that if I wanted to, but something told me to pull my punches with him.

Not that I knew what that something was.

With his weapon on the floor and him struggling to breathe, I kicked him hard in the chest. Watching him tumble onto his back made something warm spark in my chest.

That was how you got someone out of the way, and maybe this American could take some notes on it.

I tucked my dagger back into it's sheath. "Don't move," I instructed as I pulled my backpack off my shoulder and walked towards a cabinet.

The display room was painted a light grey. The bland colour forced your focus onto the artefacts inside of the black metal framed glass cabinets—artefacts that I would take for myself soon enough.

Both myself and the American stood out in the pale room, since we were both dressed head to toe in black. Did the fact we were both wearing black long-sleeved shirts and black cargo pants mean he was just as prepared as me? Did it mean he was maybe a little smarter than I thought he was? I knew it meant he looked more attractive than he should have.

"What happens now, *Princess*?" I rolled my eyes and set myself up in front of a cabinet. It had a damned alarm installed. If I broke the glass, then sirens would be set off, and I'd have to deal with law enforcement. That inconvenience was something I'd like to avoid. "You going to kill me?" I only killed people for a reason, and I didn't have the time to waste on him.

I stood up and scanned the room to map the order I

needed to take things in. Vince gave me a prioritised list in the car, and I had to weigh up whether I should waste the time picking the locks on the cabinets or just smash and grab everything as fast as I could.

What would be of benefit was a second pair of hands. One set to unlock the cabinets and the other to take what I needed...

Maybe I could be nice, for the second time in my life.

"There are two ways this can go, and it's not the ways you think." I turned to look at the American as I spoke. He hadn't moved an inch yet, which was a good thing. It meant my attack had scared him into temporary submission. "You can sit up." He followed my instruction, his eyebrows furrowed. "The choices you have are to run, and I'll pretend I never saw you, or you stay."

"Why would I do that?"

"Because if you do, I'll make sure we both get out of here alive so we can go our separate ways." I thought that was a reasonable offer, especially since it was more than I had ever offered anyone else in the same position before. Although it seemed the American didn't realise the charity I'd handed him on a silver platter. "All you have to do is be my second set of hands."

"And I leave with nothing?" Why did they always want to bargain? Why was leaving with their lives never enough?

"Well, I'd argue that me not killing you would be payment enough." He smirked, which I didn't like one bit.

"If I'm going to be your second set of hands, then it feels

fair to get a piece for myself." I rolled my eyes. "And maybe I could get your name as well." Oh, for the love of fuck, *no*. I sighed and shook my head.

Telling him my name wasn't an option. It was far too risky to hand it to people just because they asked for it. I'd only told one person what my name really was, and that was only because I'd been around him for months before I gave it. Although, just because I agreed to something like that didn't mean I had to follow through.

"That's all you want?" I asked, and he nodded his response. It wouldn't be the first time I'd lied to someone I'd just met, or made a deal without a single intention of following through. It also wouldn't be my last. "Do you know how to pick locks?" I couldn't have him taking the artefacts. It would be too hard to make sure he took the right ones and didn't steal any for himself.

"Yes," he answered.

"So you can open these cabinets for me?" He nodded. Okay, I could work with that. My fingertips curled to run over my palms as I looked over my shoulder at the cabinet I needed to get into first. "You best start moving then."

"I-"

"Move. We only have a few minutes before the guards wake up," I said. Something acidic settled in my gut as I spoke, but that was something I had to ignore. Second-guessing my decision wasn't an option, I could rectify leaving him alive if it turned out to be a problem.

"Where do you want me to start?"

13

Chapter Two

AN INTERESTING PIECE OF INFORMATION

He worked on the lock to the first cabinet, and to avoid standing over him, I paced the room. Everything in the cabinets was of notable value, which could be expected from a high-end private museum. Most were made of precious metals, others were objects of interest, like ancient tools. They'd reserved this display room for Incan artefacts, and I'd take as many as I could carry.

Vince and I picked our targets carefully, and this museum had a history of stealing from the people of Peru. It was due time they got a taste of their own medicine.

The American opened every cabinet with patience and

focus, and I followed behind him. With each new cabinet, we moved faster, became used to each other in proximity, and the both of us fell into a flow of movement.

"You want that too, don't you?" The American asked as I stared at one extremely interesting thing that hadn't been on Vince's shopping list.

A golden statuette, no larger than my two fists stacked on top of one another. My stomach turned to ice as I looked at it, but the feeling only encouraged me to inch towards it. It was something I couldn't explain, but I knew I needed to get my hands on it. Whenever I got that feeling, it meant I was on the right track.

"We're running low on time, the guards-"

"Then move faster." I heard him run towards the cabinet, and no sooner than he'd placed a knee on the ground did I hear footsteps echo down the hallway. The guards were coming, but I wouldn't leave without that damned statuette.

If I waited for the American to pick the lock, the guards would reach the room and we'd have to fight our way out; but if I smashed the glass, we'd be out in a matter of minutes. Sure, alarms would reverberate through the night and police would rush to the scene, but I would be long gone by the time they arrived.

"Get out of my way." I pushed him aside—without a care that he ended up on his ass—and smashed my fist through the glass. Shards shattered to the floor around my feet, and the skin around my wrist stung as the sharp edges cut through me. I could deal with the injury later.

The alarms made my ears bleed as I wrapped my fingers around the gold idol.

"Great, now what?" The American seemed to be in a panic, not that I had the patience or time to care as I slipped my new statuette into my bag. "I can't go back to jail." Now, that was an interesting piece of information.

"Window," I said as I swung the bag back over my shoulders.

"Window?" For fuck's sake.

"Get to the window." Silence hung between us as I took my handgun out from the back of my pants and he stared at me with an empty expression. He was going to get us killed; I could feel it in my bones. "Go!" In an attempt to get him moving, I pushed past so I could smash through the glass with my fist.

"Now what?" Fuck, I did not have the patience...

"Jump or climb," I said. His eyes turned towards me, widened and blazing. Seriously, what was his problem? What was he even doing in a place like this? What was his plan to get out of here? "Fucking choose."

"Uh, jump?" Well, that sounded confident.

"Good choice." I threw my bag out the window, the trajectory landing it on a shrub below. "Once you land, head for the gate. When you see a black car parked, get into it; my partner is waiting for us." He rubbed his arm as I spoke. His breaths seemed slow but forced. "We don't have time for this."

"I'm sorry, but this jump could *kill* me." If he didn't hurry, he wouldn't have to worry about the jump killing him, I'd take care of that myself.

We were only on the second floor. If he had any kind of experience with urban climbing, then he should be fine.

"Then climb," I hissed through my teeth. We were running out of time.

"How?" Fucking *what*? What the hell was this guy doing trying to steal from a high-end museum without a proper escape plan?

We had to move, and soon. If he wasn't going to do it by choice, then I would have to force him. It would be easy enough.

"Roll on your landing. It'll ease the impact," I said as I walked behind him.

"What the-"

I kicked him square in the back, forcing him through the window. His descent was... *unrefined*, to say the least, and so was the roll at the end of it. But he hadn't broken his neck, even though he groaned as if he had.

I checked over my shoulder once again for guards and saw shadows in the doorway. Well, that was my cue. I had to jump, whether or not the American was out of the way.

So I did.

My feet landed an inch away from his head, and I rolled before my full weight hit the ground to deter any shock from setting into my bones. I twisted my body to face the window, propped myself up on one knee and pointed the barrel of my gun directly at the hole we had just jumped through.

"Any broken bones?" I asked as I clicked the safety off my Glock. My eyes locked on the space above us where a guard was likely going to stick their head out to look for us.

"You kicked me out of a fucking window!" Well, at least he was observant. But if he had any broken bones, he wouldn't shout at me like that. He'd be too busy screaming in pain, or cursing.

I glanced down at him and saw he wasn't so much as grasping any part of him that could have been in pain. He was fine, or he *would* be.

"We need to move, so get the fuck up," I said as I looked back up at the window.

"Head for the gate?" He hissed through his teeth. "Black car?"

"Yes," I hissed back as a guard poked his head out of the shattered window. There wasn't any time for him to make a sound before I squeezed the trigger.

The body tumbled to the ground and landed in the bushes next to my bag. The empty brown eyes of the guard stared right through me. Maybe it should have made me feel sick or sent a shiver through my body.

It didn't.

"Holy shit." The American's voice shook as he spoke. With the guard's back on top of the shrub, his head lolled backwards towards us. It made for good viewing of the perfectly placed bullet hole in his third eye.

I picked up my bag from next to the body and flung it over my shoulder. We had to move or we'd be just as dead as shrub guy. "Move." My voice echoed through the night.

The warning was enough to send the American to his feet, and I waited for him to sprint before I followed him through the garden towards the gate.

I was barely two steps behind him, and all I could hear was my own heavy breathing as I checked over my shoulder for any guards on our tail. There weren't any... for the moment. It didn't mean we were in the clear.

We reached the only black sedan on the quiet street, and the American jumped in the back as I opened the front passenger door. The echo of footsteps followed me, and I looked over my shoulder one last time to see four guards running towards us.

"Vince..." I slipped into the seat and locked over at the blue-eyed blond in the driver's seat. "Fucking drive."

Chapter Three

HONOUR AMONG THIEVES

The passenger door was still open as I slammed my foot on the accelerator.

The car shot forward without a second to waste, and in that moment I was more than glad that I'd insisted on an electric car. Caeli thought it was... I think she'd used the word *superfluous* to describe my choice, but with the non-existent wait time between planting my foot and the car reacting, I think it was perfectly *fluous*.

"Can I ask..." I trailed off as I looked over to Caeli, who had just slammed the passenger door closed before she did her seatbelt up. "Who the fuck is in the back seat?"

"Well, he hasn't told me his name yet, so I can't really answer that for you." *What?* Since when did she let fucking strangers into our car? Since when did she let *anyone* into our car? I ran a hand through my hair as I took a calming breath. What the fuck had the kid done now?

"Then why is he in my car?" I had to keep myself calm, since I was the one who was supposed to have a level head. But Jesus, she liked to push me to my limits.

"Because I helped her." Now that was interesting...

I slowly looked towards the rear-view mirror and took in the newbie. Gold eyes, dark hair, light cool-brown skin... New Orleans accent.

"*He* helped *you*?" I had to clarify the situation, because the kid had a tendency to avoid working with people at all costs, with me being the exception.

I raised an eyebrow at Caeli. We had discussed expanding our operation with people we trust, but I never thought she would actually agree to it.

"He was in the room when I got there," Caeli said, and I noted the dark tone behind her words. The good mood she'd begun the night with had definitely withered away. For once, however, it wasn't because of me, so I would take that as a win. "I gave him the option of staying or running. He bargained to help me in exchange for getting an item for himself." That was out of character for her, to say the least. "He knocked out all the guards. I didn't know how long I'd have before they'd start waking up. The extra set of hands was the only way to get everything you wanted me to take."

"We also agreed on you telling me your name," the newbie said. Caeli's silver eyes turned towards the back seat, most likely to send a crippling glare towards him. I'd been on the receiving end of that look more times than I cared to count.

"Jesus Christ..." I whispered as I glanced at Caeli once more. All I saw was her ponytail as she turned to face the window, and her near-black hair blended with the night outside. "Are you serious, kiddo?"

"You have heard of lying before, haven't you, Vince?" For the love of God, this kid would be the death of me.

"Wait..." the newbie leant forward, propped between the two front seats like a golden retriever. How had his belt let him move that far forward? I looked in the mirror and saw he'd tucked his belt behind his back. That was a bad idea considering the fact I was contemplating throwing my foot on the brake to send him through the windshield. "You aren't Vincent Sinclair, are you?" Perfect, just fucking *perfect*.

"Now you've fucked us," I said as I looked to Caeli through the corner of my eye.

What if this newbie sold us out? What if he sent people after us? And what if he took my daughter from me? My chest tightened.

Maybe I should hit the fucking brakes and deal with him now before he became a problem. Or is that something that Caeli would do? Would that action be too impulsive? Maybe I needed to give this newbie the benefit of the doubt; Caeli had already done it and it had to be for a reason.

"You're the Shadow," the newbie responded. Okay, that was a good sign. He wasn't after Caeli, or he would know the truth.

"I sure am," I said. A tight smile graced my lips as I looked over at Caeli; her normally warm, tawny appearance had paled slightly.

Her bright eyes only briefly met mine, which meant she was aware of exactly what she'd done by uttering my name before. We could have gone through this without anyone knowing it was us, but her need to say my name in warning had taken away that option.

"So who are you?" He was clearly speaking to Caeli.

"Who I am doesn't matter," she responded, as blunt as ever. This conversation was going to make my hair finally turn grey. That was the only possible outcome.

"What about honour among thieves-" Yep, definitely going to send me grey.

"How about we make a new arrangement? We drop you at whatever cheap fucking hotel you're staying at and you don't mention us being in Lima to a single soul. In return, you can take one piece from *my* haul and keep your life." Damn, this newbie really had no idea what he'd walked into. If he was smart, he was probably piecing it together. "Honour among thieves implies a preconceived notion of trust. There is none between us."

This was one of those moments when I was in conflict between whether I'd raised her right or wrong. On one hand, she was protecting us both, and on the other, she was threatening someone with death. Although, perhaps the murderous side wasn't my fault, that damage had already been done by the time I found her. But maybe I could have worked harder on softening it.

"The honour I will uphold is not killing you. But if anyone ever finds out that we were here tonight, I won't hesitate to throw that honour out the window like I threw you. Understood?" Jesus Christ, had she actually thrown him out of a window? And he was still trying to get on her good side? Did he have any self-preservation in his body at all? Even just a drop?

"Why are you so protective of your identity?" This newbie really didn't know when to stop. It kind of reminds me of when I first found Caeli, when I didn't give up on her until she opened up to me.

Maybe I could use that to my advantage.

"Because I have people pursuing me, and I would prefer they never found me. You got me on a good night because I don't typically leave witnesses. I'm starting to lament that decision." Silence encased the car for a few seconds. The weight of it landed on my shoulders and pressed on my chest. I was about to make an impulsive decision, one that I would probably regret.

If this kid was as curious as he seemed, and stubborn enough to compete with Caeli's own will, then maybe he was the only option we would come across that could join us. There had to be a reason Caeli had stumbled into him tonight, and that reason had to be why she hadn't killed him. I wasn't one to argue with fate.

"Don't mind her, she's just wary. It's not necessarily a bad thing in this line of work," I said. A chill ran down my spine as Caeli glared at me. It was something only she could do. I really had to learn how she did it so I could use the technique myself.

"I understand. It's the same reason I don't want to give you my name." That was a fair reason to hide your identity, and I wouldn't blame him for it. But if this was going to work, he was going to have to open up and he'd have to do it before we dropped him at his hotel. Otherwise, Caeli would never agree to let the newbie join our enterprise.

"Well, you know my name. The vow of secrecy would go both ways." I looked over to Caeli and saw her hands moving in understated, but familiar, motions. She was stressed, maybe a little scared, even though she would never admit it. "*Honour among thieves*, and whatnot," I added as I looked to the newbie through the rear-view mirror.

This would either end the way I wanted it to or in a trash fire. Honestly, it was far too early to tell which, but I knew there was no in between.

"My name is Hunter Black."

Okay, that was *believable*. Caeli inhaled like she was going to say something, but I shot her a warning look before she could open her mouth. If he wasn't comfortable giving his real name, then we would work on building trust first. She, of all people, should know how important trust was in our world.

"It's nice to meet you, Hunter." I turned my attention back to the mirror, watching as the newbie's golden eyes focused entirely on me. "Now, where am I dropping you off?"

Chapter Four

THREE GOOD REASONS TO NOT GIVE A FUCK

I could hardly believe Vince.

We'd left *Hunter* at his hotel, where he gave his phone number to Vince in hopes we would contact him if we needed an extra person to work with. Apparently, he was desperate for money and willing to pass his phone number to strangers for a lead.

It didn't add up to me. If this *Hunter* was so protective of his so-called name, why would he give us his phone number? I'd threatened to kill him; to me the risk didn't outweigh the reward. I'd never give a stranger my phone number—would never risk someone being able to trace me through it. Aside from that, there was the disconcerting conversation that Vince had led on the way to the hotel.

He'd built a fucking rapport with the American, and it made me both lightheaded and itchy just thinking about it.

"You alright, kiddo?" Vince asked, likely because he'd noticed how often my fingers were trying to ease the pain at my temples. "Is this about-"

"If you do so much as *imply* you want us to work with that lying American, I won't hesitate to walk through that door and never come back." That was a lie. I would hesitate, but I'd still do it.

"Caeli-"

"Come on, Vince. His name is *Hunter*, for fuck's sake." I collapsed onto the edge of my queen sized bed and wrung my hands together. "If he is a treasure hunter, don't you find it a little suspicious that's the name he gave us? We can't trust him." My eyes dropped to focus on the bandages that were wrapped around my wrist. The cuts were the least of my worries, because I knew they would heal quickly. I *always* healed quickly.

"Look, we both know your intuition is pretty shit when it comes to other people. I can list out evidence on that front if you need me to." *Asshole.* I crossed my arms over my chest and stopped my leg from bouncing. He was right, but he didn't need to know that I agreed.

"There's no need to do that," I hissed through gritted teeth. What I needed right now was a potent drink, not a damned lecture. Although, judging from the look on Vince's face, it was the latter that I'd be receiving.

"Well, then I won't. I'm just saying that we can't really hold his name against him." I really hated it when he made a good point.

"If you're implying that I should give him the benefit of the doubt, I won't." I furrowed my eyebrows as my mouth went dry. Leaving the American alive had been a bad idea. I should have killed him the second I found him in that museum. "We don't know a thing about him, and his name-"

"You remember when we met, right?" My face fell slack. He surely wasn't about to compare this situation to back then. "I stumbled upon this kid who saved my ass by killing seven people in the space of three minutes. It took six months of being around each other every minute of every day for her to give me a simple name." It took me that long because I didn't have a name—or I *did*, but that's not what I wanted to be anymore. For the first time in my life, I wanted to be some*one* rather than some*thing*.

"I remember saving an old man who should have known better than to piss off an entire black market ring without backup." I uncrossed my arms and dropped my hands into my lap.

"I was only thirty-four, which is *not* old," he argued. When I looked up at him, I saw the small smile on his face. It was one that I had seen plenty of times before. It was never a good thing.

"What?"

"I'm just grateful you didn't kill me that night," he said as he sat next to me on the bed. "I mean, I should be dead, but I'm not. You gave me a chance, and I gave you one. We're both better off for it. Because of that night, I'm not going to die a lonely old man... or just a lonely man. I would definitely be dead by now if it weren't for you."

"What are you trying to say, Vince?" I looked up at him as he pulled me to his side. My entire body tensed at the touch, but slowly I made myself relax. It still felt alien to be held in a comforting manner, even after eight years of being stuck with Vince.

"I'm saying that we didn't trust each other to start with, but we moved past it and everything turned out okay." I sighed as I rested my head on his shoulder. It was the closest I ever got to hugging him back. Allowing myself to wrap my arms around him had always been too much, but this was good enough for the both of us.

"This is different..." I whispered, shaking my head. "He isn't a random kid on the street, and he didn't save my life. He's an adult we know nothing about, who also gave us a fake name. That can only mean he's hiding something." My voice indicated peacefulness, which completely contradicted the storm that boiled inside of me. That was the side effect of being around Vince—he somehow calmed me. "I'm not putting us at risk because you want to do your one good deed for the year."

Vince sighed. The heavy intake of air made his ribs expand and push into me, which was strangely soothing to feel. "Kid, if your ideas keep growing, we're going to need more than just the two of us." This was something we had talked about before, and my standpoint on it hadn't changed. "If he wants money, then he would be absolutely stupid not to join us."

"But-"

"I'm not worried about him lying, or whatever it is he might be hiding, and you know exactly why," he cut me off. I rolled my eyes and took a deep breath.

"Because you have me," I replied. He smiled as he squeezed me against his side. The weight of being his protector had recently grown heavier, but I wouldn't tell him that. He didn't need to know, because it wouldn't change anything.

"Because I have you," he confirmed before he kissed the top of my head. It was something he did to calm my nerves, which was easier said than done. "I have my little Demon to take care of me, so why would I worry about what some lanky boy is capable of?"

I had to physically bite my tongue, because the only thing on my mind was what Vince defined as 'lanky'. To my knowledge, *Hunter* had been exceptionally well-proportioned and muscled... but there was no way I could say that out loud. It would give Vince the wrong idea.

"I never said I was worried about him," I said instead. What I didn't need right now was Vince thinking I would toy with the idea of giving *Hunter* a chance. I wouldn't. It was too much of a risk to do so. "I said I don't *trust* him. I'm more concerned with the prospect that he's working for someone."

"And who do you think he'd be working for?"

"You know exactly who I'd be concerned about. If he's working for anyone else, then we'll be fine. It'll get messy, but I'll get us out alive. If it's the Order, then I won't be able to protect you from them."

"Do you really think the Order would hire an *American* to do their dirty work?" No, they wouldn't hire an American to do their dirty work. They would *force* an American to work for them if that American had some form of speculated power. That was just as reasonable a belief to hold as the fact that *Hunter* could just be faking the American accent. "There's no trace of you anywhere. We made sure of that. Everyone in our world thinks I'm the Shadow, not you. The Order doesn't know where you are, so if this *Hunter* does know you, then we need to look at the people who know *us*."

"The ones I've worked for," I murmured before a sigh left my lips. It was easy to tell exactly where he was going with this, and there was nothing I could do to stop him.

"Like I said before, your intuition with other people is terrible. You're inherently bad at knowing who you can trust." I grimaced at his words. He was right, of course, but it still hurt to hear them spoken. Especially when his screwup on who he could trust was so much worse than my own. There wasn't enough energy in me to have that argument again, not tonight.

"I trusted *you*," I said as I looked up at him. There was a grimace on his face as well, which wasn't the response I'd expected.

"That proves my point. You shouldn't have trusted me—I'm *not* a good person," he said as he let go of me and walked over to the unopened bag of artefacts. Even if Vince wasn't a good person in the relative standing of the world, he was still the best I'd come across.

"I think it turned out okay." I repurposed his words from before and watched as a ghost of a smile reached his lips. There were things that he'd trained me to do, and listening to people so I could use their words against them was one of them. I was nothing if not an attentive student.

"Yeah, I think so too." His voice was too quiet for him to believe was he was saying, and he completely avoided eye contact with me. The lack of attention meant he was lying, but I wouldn't push him for the truth. Beneath the tightness in my throat and my hardened stomach, I already knew why he rejected the idea that us finding each other had been a good thing.

"What's this?" He asked as he lifted the golden statuette out of the bag. I guess I'd allow the change of subject, only because I needed the tightness in my throat to fade away.

I walked over to him, a smile on my face as I took the artefact from his hands and pretended to study it closely. It was gold, the size of my two fists stacked on top of each other, and carved in the image of a human-like figure. I assumed it represented a god or a goddess, but I'd have to do research to figure out which one.

"I believe it's called a statuette, Vince." I looked at him

through the corner of my eye and saw the exhausted look that was on his face more often than not.

"Caeli..." apparently it was too late in the night for my antics... or was it too early in the morning?

"What makes you think I know what it is? I saw gold, thought it would be worth some money, so I took it." A slight omission of truth, but he didn't need to know about that icy feeling that convinced me to take the damned thing.

"Well, I don't know much but I know that's not heavy enough to be solid gold. That means it's not worth what you think it is." Vince had a very specific set of skills. That was flying our aircraft, driving cars, hacking computers and guessing the weights of precious metals for estimation before we sold artefacts. If he didn't think the idol was solid, then it wasn't.

I narrowed my eyes for a moment and processed the information. It wasn't necessarily strange for it to be hollow, but as I ran my thumb over the statuette's torso, I realised something else. Maybe this was the reason I'd taken it.

"This has a seam around the centre," I said as I moved the idol to see it's waist better in the cheap lighting of our double room. It was a single line, an extremely thin one that I should have noticed earlier. That seam ran around the circumference of the statuette, almost as if...

I walked over to the table, held the top of the statuette in my right hand and the bottom in my left. Without wasting time on questioning whether this was a good idea, I smashed the statue onto the table's edge and broke it into two pieces.

"Caeli, what the fuck!" Why was everyone being so dramatic today?

"This has been opened before," I said as my fingers ran over the new edges of the broken idol. There wasn't any point in looking away from it, in looking at Vince, because I could imagine the look of despair on his face already.

"Well, it's fucking open now, isn't it?" I glanced up to see his hands running through his blond hair. He'd get over this, especially when I investigated what was going on and why this was important.

The inside of the statuette was hollow, but that void wasn't the right shape for the statuette. That meant something.

"This had something inside of it," I said as I handed the pieces to him. Maybe he would calm down if he saw what I did. The hollow was tapered, unlike the shell, which was roughly the same width from top to bottom.

"Whatever was in it is gone..." his brow furrowed before he looked up at me. "On top of that, it's now ruined and we can't sell it." For fuck's sake.

"You're always worried about a quick buck, Vince." I ripped the pieces away from him and inspected them once more. That icy feeling came back to my stomach, and I knew that my interest was well-placed. "You're not even slightly curious about what used to be in this?"

Vince let out a slow breath while he shook his head. "No, why are you?" How could he not be interested in this? Did he realise the potential this thing held?

"It's Incan, it's gold, and it used to have something in it. That's three good reasons to be interested in what's missing from it." I thought that would be reason enough to get him to care, but I should have known better.

"We have no idea what this is, what it's related to or if it ever had any significance. That's three good reasons to not give a fuck," he said before he bit his lip. He gently took the pieces back from me, knowing that if he rushed his movements, I would involuntarily defend myself. "But I know what you're like. If you find something on this, we can follow it up."

I bit down a smile and clasped my hands together to stop them from flying around. "Really?" The word tumbled from my mouth at the same speed as my thoughts that raced a million miles a minute.

"Your intuition with people is pretty appalling, but when you get a hunch about this stuff, it usually means something big." He put the pieces down on the table and shook his head. "Whatever it is, we could definitely use the cash."

CHAPTER FIVE

DON'T BE SO OSTENTATIOUS

"Okay, I know you said that I had to do research before I brought this up again, so..." Caeli dropped a slew of paper in front of me. All I could do was hold back my tears, because I couldn't imagine reading that many words without going insane.

"I don't remember asking for a thesis on it." It was usual for Caeli to go in depth when she did her research, but this was no doubt the hardest she'd ever gone.

"Well, think of it as an early birthday present," she said as she placed a finger on the first piece of the forest-worth of paper. "I spent hours looking this shit up in the library, so you better appreciate the effort I went into." There were a handful of factors that would determine whether I would actually be thankful it.

"I think I'd be able to *appreciate* it a little more if we didn't have to leave Lima in the next hour..." I said, and I saw Caeli roll her eyes. She no doubt thought I was being overdramatic, but I knew what she was like. Assuming she'd visited the sites she normally did, my reaction likely wasn't dramatic *enough*.

"Don't be so ostentatious," she said as she sat down in the chair to my right.

"That was a big word," I quipped with a smile. She turned towards me with raised eyebrows. Maybe that was an unnecessary thing to say when she knew far more words than I did.

"Maybe for you." *Ouch*. That was uncalled for. "Look, I already have a heading for us, so you don't need to be so nervous. The sooner you let me catch you up, the sooner we can leave."

"Alright, but make it quick. We have bags to pack." I sat up straighter in the seat and prepared myself for the onslaught, which was no doubt going to hit me in the face.

She smiled as she pulled pieces of paper off the pile, which meant she was after something specific. If I knew anything—which she would probably like to tell me I didn't—then that detail was the reason we'd have to leave Lima in the next hour.

"Is that..." I trailed off as I picked up the piece of paper.

Although I could see the image from the short distance, I needed to be sure of what I saw.

"It's a collection of the exact same idol together. Some of them have been opened while others are intact. An anonymous source said an English museum broke one open to see what was in it. When I looked up the group of historians that opened it to plan some light interrogation..." she trailed off as she clasped her hands together next to the pile of paper.

"They were dead?" I assumed, to which she nodded and handed me another piece of paper. A newspaper report from a few years ago, detailing the deaths of the group of researchers. Theories ranged from coincidence to a targeted attack, but they never found evidence of foul play.

"I'd be more inclined to believe the coincidence theory if all the statuettes hadn't disappeared from the museum without a trace," she said. Her fingers tapped on the table-top as I read the article. The kid was right. The story would be more believable if the things these people were researching hadn't vanished.

"So it's important then..." I trailed off as I finished the article, and Caeli nodded with too much vigour, considering the report in my hand. "What do you think it's going to lead to, then?"

"I don't know yet. All I'm sure of is that it's Incan inspired, and there's a chance it could depict Inkarri." What the hell was that?

"*Inkarri*?" He asked as she let her dark hair out of her

ponytail.

"It's an Incan folk tale. I'll explain in more detail later, but he retreated into Paititi, their lost city of gold." Jesus Christ. Caeli had picked her words carefully, specifically to prevent me from getting too excited about the chance of finding a city made of gold. It was definitely too late for that precaution, because I'd already realised we wouldn't be able to do this alone. "I'm not really convinced that's what it will lead to, though. The carbon dating those researchers did proved the statuettes aren't anywhere near old enough to truly be Incan."

"How old are they, then?" I watched as she ran her fingers over her scalp and heard the sigh that left her.

"About a century, not the half-millennium they should be." That was only a *slight* difference. It had to mean something, but I had no clue what it could be.

"Alright, and what about this heading of yours?" I immediately disliked the look on her face, but I'd have to ignore it for now. The more she became excited about her plan, the better chance I had of making my own without her realising.

"Egypt," she answered. "There's going to be a black market auction in two days, and an item for sale is one of those statuettes. It's listed as completely intact, which means it hasn't been opened." Okay, so we were definitely going to need another person then, because there was no way we could afford to place a bid on it.

The last time I'd done something relatively similar to this,

I'd almost gotten myself killed. But surely this was different. What was the worst that could happen if I got the Hunter kid involved without telling Caeli? No matter how bad it got, it wouldn't come close to my screw up two years ago, so fuck it.

I would go with my gut on this. I would get Hunter involved and have a contingency plan sorted for when Caeli would inevitably try to kill me for making this terrible decision.

It wasn't anything I hadn't done before.

"You're sure it's going to be there tonight?" I asked as we threw our bags onto our respective beds. That meant she was closest to the door, and I was the furthest, because she preferred keeping me in the 'safe' bed.

"Yes," she said as she unzipped her suitcase and pulled out the dress I'd told her to wear tonight. It was dramatic, which was exactly what we needed for the plan to work. She was going to be the distraction—the magician's assistant—while the actual work went on behind her. As far as Caeli knew, I was the one who'd take the statuette from the front of the room...

My chances of seeing the sunrise tomorrow were fucking slim, to say the least.

"Okay, well, we don't have long to get you ready, then. Go get changed, then we'll get your hair and face sorted," I said as she nodded and folded the dress over her arm.

"Vince..." she turned to look at me and I felt a tingling in my chest. God, I needed to fucking breathe. I needed to breathe, but she knew. She had to know. "What are your plans for my face?" Oh thank fuck.

"I don't know yet, but we need to make it look nice." I looked at the dress. Her makeup would need to be dramatic to match, but not too dark or the black dress would be too much. "You'll need the full attention of the room for this to work." Yes, she needed to take the attention away from the front of the room where Hunter would take the statuette while I shut off the power so there would be darkness to work in. "We both know there's no money left to buy this thing, so this plan has to work."

Maybe it was my fault that we didn't have any money left, but our old plane had threatened to fall apart mid-air, so it was best to get a new one. After that hefty purchase, Caeli's income had gone right into paying back the bad debts we both racked up.

"How am I meant to get the attention of everyone in the room? There's going to be at least a hundred people there. Even my best distraction won't be enough to stop everyone from seeing you," she said. I bit my lip as I nodded. All I had to do right now was play dumb and pretend there wasn't an entirely different plan already in motion.

"I'll worry about being spotted, you worry about the distraction," I said in a last-ditch attempt at throwing her off the scent. "Surely there's someone on the guest list that you can use to your advantage." That was definitely too strong of a topic change. She'd furrowed her eyebrows, which meant she knew something was going on. *Fuck.*

"Well, I do have a half a plan..." she trailed off as her brow smoothed out once more. "I checked the list on the plane ride over and figured out my best option."

Okay, that was good. That would keep her distracted as long as Hunter's name hadn't been on that list. It shouldn't be. I paid good money to keep his ticket anonymous.

"And who would that be?" I needed the confirmation, because if his name had slipped through the cracks, then I would need to give him a warning; being a target of Caeli's never ended well for her prey.

"Dallas." I felt relief wash over me as she spoke, but I also felt my stomach twist into knots. Dallas Walker was not a safe option to use in this situation. But I couldn't tell her that. I had to push her towards figuring that answer out for herself.

"Is he the best choice? It might be better to leave him out-"

"If he's going to be there, then he's going to come to me, whether or not we want him to. It's best to have a plan for it, and I do. Involving him in my distraction is the safest possible route for all of us," she said as she walked towards the bathroom.

Maybe she was right; having a plan for someone as unpredictable as Dallas was a good starting point, even if he had intent of his own for the night. At least if our plan went off the rails, we were still taking him into account.

"I hope you know what you're doing kiddo, because if he gets the better of you tonight..." I didn't really know how to finish that sentence. We both knew what he was capable of, and how close he'd come to destroying Caeli.

She looked over her shoulder at me. "He won't." While her voice was calm, I still had to cover a shiver that ran through my body. Her silver eyes burned with the heat of molten metal, the expression present simply because she had *thought* about Dallas and his betrayal.

"Fuck," I whispered only after she closed the bathroom door behind herself. There had to be a better way to cover my discomfort from that stare, because in a handful of hours, she would direct a scowl much worse than that at me. I ran a hand through my hair as I took a slow breath.

God, I wasn't prepared for the consequences of my actions. Not even in the slightest.

CHAPTER SIX

A RUDE AWAKENING

The room echoed with the sounds of people talking about and exaggerating their lives. The only thing that cut through the monotonous voices was the occasional sound of champagne glasses clinking against each other.

I was used to the surrounding echo. I was beyond used to hearing the lies people told in desperate attempts to climb the social hierarchy. It was intolerable to hear, the efforts to sound like they were worth more than nothing.

If I had to pick the thing I hated most about these functions, being stuck in a room with vain—and yet somehow self-conscious—criminals who shamelessly overcompensated for their underwhelming skills would have to be it. The one thing I would never do in order to bring in business was lie, probably because I didn't need to. The only people I cared to work for were those who came directly to Vince for our services. Those were the ones who knew exactly what we were capable of doing.

"And who do we have here?" I looked over my shoulder towards who had spoken. Their voice was instantly recognisable, and I did everything in my power to avoid scowling.

"It's nice to see you, Dallas," I said as I turned to face him. The issue was that I didn't want his focus on my face yet. I needed him distracted. So I brushed the front of my dress, which hugged every shape of my torso before it flared from my hips. It was my signature colour, but the cut differed vastly from what I was used to.

Under normal circumstances, I would wear a dress with a plunging neckline for distraction purposes and risqué slits for ease of movement. This situation, however, Vince had decided against my usual attire. Instead, he'd opted for a gown with a floor-length skirt *lacking* a slit. While I had yet to work out the exact reasoning behind his choice, my working theory was that he didn't want me to kill anyone here at the auction.

"You don't need to lie to me," he replied as I looked into his brown irises... or, more accurately, his *one* brown iris.

The one on his left used to be the colour of damp earth until he fucked me over and I sliced a dagger from his hairline to his chin in retaliation. While I could have avoided limiting his vision, it was something he deserved. Now the milky colour of the eye reflected the silver scar I'd left behind. Honestly, I hoped he would lose the entire eye, but of course he got to the hospital soon enough to keep the organ; at least they couldn't save it's function.

"It's no lie," I told him with a soft smile. "I haven't seen you with a healed face, so it's nice to have the chance to admire my handiwork."

The scar was a mere fine line on his fawn coloured skin, hardly noticeable unless you knew to look for it like I did. If anything, he should be damned grateful I was so skilled with a blade. The scar could have been more jagged, more ugly and angry, but instead it looked like he'd been cut with a scalpel at the hands of an expert surgeon.

"You say that like this is a piece of art and not my fucking face," he hissed through his teeth. It was likely an attempt to keep the peace in the crowded room. Even though we were stuck standing on the staircase, it was still a heavy traffic area, and Dallas had a public façade to uphold.

"It *is* a piece of art," I replied as a smirk spread on my face and I tilted my head to the side. If he thought he could make me uncomfortable here—that he would have even the most miniscule chance of making me feel *threatened*—he was in for a rude awakening. "And now I know you're still bitter about it, would you like to tell me how long it took for you to get used to the lack of depth perception? A few weeks? Months?" His face hardened, and it made me let out a breathy laugh.

"Oh, you still aren't used to it, are you? It's been two and

47

a half years, Dallas, you should-"

"Maybe I should take one of your eyes. We can see how well you adjust and compare notes."

I snorted out a laugh and covered my mouth with my hand. Did he seriously think he could threaten me?

"You hold far too much confidence for your capabilities," I said as I dropped my hand and smiled at him once more. "It's almost adorable that you think you could take one of my eyes, especially when you couldn't win against me when you had both of yours. Or did you forget how I fucked your face up? Did you forget how that entire situation went down?"

He closed the distance between us, the point of his dagger rested against my stomach as he pushed me against the staircase railing. Maybe I should have been concerned about my survival instincts, considering the fact that my heart didn't so much as jump at the proximity of him or his weapon. Maybe I should be worried about the fact I wasn't the least bit concerned about his blatant and extremely real threat.

"You're forgetting something, Hailee..." Oh shit, I completely forgot I used an alias when I worked for him.

I had to hold back the next laugh that threatened to bubble from my throat. Letting it slip out with a blade this close to my liver had a higher chance of ending badly than ending well.

"What would that be, Dallas?" I asked as I hid the grin that wanted to spill across my face.

"I know who the real Shadow is, and there are people

in this mansion who would pay well for that information." While I knew it would end badly, I couldn't hold in my laughter anymore. Nor could I stand being pinned to the staircase railing for a second longer. A light laugh slipped past my lips before I moved.

First, I took hold of his wrist before I squeezed on his joint until his face contorted in pain and something popped in my grip. The weapon he'd held against me fell from his grip and I caught the falling knife before I turned it back against him, the point of the blade right under his ribs as he backed away and I let go of his wrist.

"It's interesting that you use that as a threat, because to give someone information, you need to have evidence. I can't imagine how difficult it must be to prove who the Shadow is when you don't even know my real name." His eyes widened for a second before his expression fell into an unbridled rage. Or maybe it *was* bridled, considering the fact he was now the one with a dagger pointed to his ribs.

"Did you honestly think Hailee Porter was my real name? Because it's not, Dallas, which means you unfortunately have no leverage," I said. The smile fell from my face as he took a step away from me, but I didn't let a gap grow between us. Instead, I kept pace with his every attempt at retreat, and it warmed me to see the panic settle onto his face. "Maybe you should quit digging yourself this grave while you still have the chance to climb out of it again. The issues between us were resolved the second I took a knife to your face, so maybe think twice before you try making new ones."

"Is everything okay?" Fuck, not that Southern drawl again.

I did *not* have the patience for this.

Chapter Seven

TELL ME YOU KNOW WHAT YOU'RE DOING

"Everything's fine, American. I was just catching up with an old friend," I replied. I couldn't risk looking over my shoulder at him, not when I had Dallas at knifepoint. Of the two men, the one in front of me *actually* posed a risk, so that's where I needed my focus to stay.

"You and I catch up with old friends very differently, Princess." The muscle in my jaw jumped at the nickname. "It might be best to put the knife away before security gets invested in this little reunion." There were three men clad in black at the top of the stairs, and as I risked a look at them, I saw all three of them staring right back, their hands resting on their haltered handguns.

"You're lucky I don't have the will to deal with other people today, Dallas," I said as I stepped away from him. My grip on his dagger tightened as I looked at it. "I'm keeping this as payment for the inconvenience you caused me." The blade fit nicely in a pocket in my dress, so maybe this was meant to be. "Threaten me again tonight, and I won't hesitate to gut you with your own blade."

"Do you really want to work with this bitch?" Dallas asked, his eye trained on the American. "She'll fuck you over like she fucked me."

"Where do you think the bruises on my throat came from?" Hunter asked. The question forced me to look away from Dallas to inspect the damage I'd done. There was indeed some light bruising on his throat, but not as much as there should have been. Maybe he healed faster than normal, like I did. The cuts on my wrist and my chin were almost closed over, and it had only been three days.

"And I think I'll be alright," Hunter continued, and I couldn't take my eyes away from him. I was too invested in what he planned to say next. "You definitely did something to earn that little scar on your face. Now, I don't plan on fucking her." A playful glint filled his golden eyes as he looked down at me, and the smirk on his face made my body warm. "At least, not fucking her *over*." He didn't. He did *not* just...

I turned to face Dallas again, mainly to stop myself from stabbing Hunter there and then. But also because if I kept looking into his eyes, the warmth that was sitting in my stomach would grow into a burn, and that burn would become obvious when it made its way to my cheeks.

Why did he have to be fucking attractive?

"Look, Dallas, if you want to have a casual conversation, I would be happy to oblige you. Otherwise, I don't want to see your fucking face again tonight, got it?" I asked, and he nodded his response. I noted the sharp look in his eyes and decided on one sure-fire way to make it worse. "Give my best to Elyssa." I said before I turned on my heels and walked away. Mentioning his sister was probably a bad idea, but I could practically feel his anger burning through the air, which thoroughly entertained me to no end.

"Wait up!" I heard shouted over the crowd, but I didn't look back. If I did, then I would start planning how to cut out his voice box, and I suspected this idiot was the reason Vince had put me in this glorified straight-jacket of a dress.

I scanned the room for Vincent then, because if he couldn't see me, then there wasn't anything stopping me from committing murder and pinning it on any of the other criminals present. Hunter was beyond annoying, and some people here were known for killing people who'd done less than he had. Vince would be none the wiser, especially since I couldn't find his bright blond hair in the room.

"Can I ask what the fuck was going on between you and that *old friend* of yours? Do I need to worry about it?" The American asked as I let out an old sigh. Why couldn't he just leave me alone?

"No, you can't ask me about it, and you don't need to worry either. My problems are none of your fucking concern," I answered as I looked over my shoulder at Dallas again. He was watching my every move, which was unsurprising. "I am going to ask what you're doing here though, because if I need to remove you as an obstacle, I would rather do it now so I don't have to keep listening to you talk."

"What? You don't like my voice, Princess? Could have fooled me. I made you blush just a few minutes ago." Maybe I could just remove him from being an annoyance. Surely Vince would understand. Desperate times call for desperate measures.

I didn't respond verbally. Instead, I simply turned my eyes towards him in a heated glare, and noticed that his jaw was continuously moving, like he was chewing on something. Was he seriously chewing gum right now? In a place like this?

"Fine. I'm here because Sinclair messaged me, told me you guys would need some help tonight. He offered me a cut of whatever this thing leads to if I stick with you until the end."

Well, how Vince had been acting suddenly made sense. I thought my dislike of the man next to me was obvious enough that Vince wouldn't ask him to join us. Maybe I should have known better, but I was always far too optimistic when it came to him.

"Did he now?" I asked as I crossed my arms over my chest.

While he might not know how to read my body language yet, it was something that was easy to pick up on. Restraining my hands was the only way to stop myself from running the repetitive motions that eased my anxiety—that helped calm my mind. It was something I hated to do, but I couldn't change the programming that the Order had drilled into me.

"He told me you might be on the path to something huge." Oh, for fuck's sake, Vince really didn't know when to keep his damned mouth shut.

"And how are *you* supposed to help *me* tonight?" I asked. It was best to save my sanity and move the conversation forward. That way I could keep control of my anger; losing it in the middle of the crowded hall would *not* be a good look.

"Well, if everything goes according to plan, Vince gets the lights, you create a distraction and I grab the statuette." Damn it. As much as I didn't want to work with the American, or accept the fact that a third person was going to be beneficial to us, the plan sounded much more realistic with the three of us. Being able to knock out the lights, even for just a few seconds, would help my distraction immensely and give us more time to work with.

"Please, just tell me you know what you're doing," I pleaded as the crowd parted for me. I would have to hand it to Vince. This dress worked exactly as he said it would. Everyone's eyes were on me, which meant the distraction should be easy enough to make work.

"I'm taking the little gold idol that looks exactly like what you took from the museum back in Lima," he replied in a whisper as we made it to the front of the room. They'd displayed the items for sale atop long tables separated from the crowd by bollards. "Which means I'm going to have to set myself up down at the right end of the tables, so I'm close when you and Vince do your things."

I looked to the right, and three items from the end was the Inkarri statuette. The same icy feeling from Lima settled in my stomach as I looked at it, and I wish I knew what that feeling meant.

"If Vince is getting the lights, you'll only have a few seconds before the generator kicks in. I'll create the most dramatic distraction I can, so no one notices that it's gone, but I'll only be able to buy you a minute or two. You need to have the statuette before the lights come back on, and you need to be gone before anyone looks away from me. I'm assuming Vince will be back at the car by the time we get out?" My voice was hardly above a whisper, but he nodded in reply, which meant he'd heard me. "Monitor the guards, and don't let them catch you. I have no qualms leaving you for dead, because I have a backup plan that I can go to. This isn't the only chance I have of getting one of these things."

"Right..." Hunter trailed off. Were my words a little harsh? No. They were accurate. I couldn't give a single fuck about him, and it was best he figured that out sooner rather than later. "What's your idea for a commotion?" He laced his voice with additional concern, probably because he'd just realised how much his survival relied on my *distraction*.

"How about I worry about getting my job done, and you

worry about yours?" I asked as the hairs on the back of my neck stood up. We were being watched. I looked over my shoulder and found the people staring at me without shame. A topaz-eyed girl and a familiar young man. "Shit," I hissed through my teeth as I turned back around. Those two complicated things, but not necessarily in a bad way.

"What?" If Hunter sounded concerned before, then this tone must be related to his panic.

"How long until Vince gets the lights?" I whispered. He checked his leather watch before his bright eyes locked on mine again. Fuck, I couldn't work with him. No, this was going to end badly.

"Four minutes, why?" He asked as I stepped away from him and towards the two watching us.

"You need to be careful when you run. There's a Templum assassin here, and their Priest would never let this one be alone in the field. There's bound to be an army hidden in the shadows." I moved to walk away, but he grabbed my wrist to hold me still. My skin burned at his touch, at least until I tore myself away from him. "Don't fucking touch me," I hissed.

"I'm sorry, I just... Templum?" So he knew who they were, good. Maybe that would keep him focused. "What if they come after me? How do I ask for help?" I laughed. This idiot had no idea what he'd walked into, and he was going to get me killed. I could feel it deep in my soul.

"If they come after you, there won't be enough time for you to say a damned word before you're dead. Like I said before, you worry about your job and I'll worry about mine.

Dealing with these assholes is on me. I'm just asking you to be careful when you run." I walked away before he could say anything else that I didn't have the patience for, and locked eyes with my new target.

Using Dallas as a distraction was no longer necessary. My new option was so much better than the first.

"Malakai," I said as I reached him. "It's been too long."

Chapter Eight

INSTIGATE PURE CHAOS

I split my focus between Malakai and the newbie with topaz-eyes.

"Too long since you left me for dead?" He asked, which made me smile. His dark hair fell in soft curls, long enough that they fell into his honey eyes.

"Saying I left you for dead implies I left you alone," I corrected him. Already I could see the anger flushing his golden neck. It was so easy to make him flustered. "I know there were at least six other assassins nearby supervising daddy's boy. It's due time you stopped playing the victim card on that one." I turned my attention to the front of the room, because, unlike Dallas, he didn't pose a threat to me in the slightest. "What are you after tonight?"

"My Priest is after some items, but I'd rather not give you the details." That was a smart choice, which was rare for Malakai to make.

"You don't want me to steal them from you?" I asked with a smirk. For the moment I had control of the conversation, and I wanted to keep it that way, so I changed topic before he could answer. "Who's your friend?" I asked as I looked at the girl.

"She's not my friend, she's my sister." Sister? Since when did Malakai Eldridge have a sister? "My Priest forced me to bring her along." So he wasn't happy about the situation. That was an interesting piece of information to hold on to.

"I didn't know you had a sister..."

"Technically Malakai and I don't share blood, but we *do* share a brother," the girl said as she looked at me. Her voice was calm and collected compared to the rushed rhythm that Mal always spoke in. She was careful, calculated... good. She might make for an interesting opponent.

"Ah, right, I always forget about the elusive Samael Eldridge," I responded playfully. That was someone I'd like to face. He was apparently the best that Templum had, but I knew he would go down as easily as all my other foes. It was a pity I hadn't come across him yet, because Malakai was a complete disappointment as an adversary. "I'm Hailee Porter," I said as I stuck out my hand for her to shake. Using my alias was important, considering that's what I'd used when I worked with Malakai two years ago. Consistency was key.

"Nylah Dawson," the young woman replied as she shook my hand.

"So, if you have no relation to Mal here, then that means Ryne isn't your father," I stated, and Nylah nodded her confirmation. "That's fortunate. I've seen how he treats both his assassins and his children." Nylah—being a girl—wasn't an assassin. The misogyny was one of the many reasons I hated Templum Gratiae, but it wasn't the most important one either.

"That doesn't mean I'm treated well," she replied. Her accent was hard to place. Some vowels were extended, but others weren't, almost like she'd moved countries before her ability to speak had completely settled. I couldn't put my finger on it, but something about it was familiar.

"Well, I never said that," I said as I thought about what she'd said. There was a reason she'd made the clarification, but I couldn't tell why.

"Who's your partner?" Nylah asked, and I raised my eyebrows in question. "You left someone at the front of the room." Okay, so the girl was observant. That was good to know.

"I don't think the word 'partner' fits this situation in the slightest," I replied as I turned to look back at Hunter, who stared right at me and my companions with concern on his face. So much for being subtle...

"You're working with him, aren't you?" She asked, and I shook my head.

"I'd also use the term 'working with' very loosely right

now." I smiled before I could give too much away. All they needed to know was that this wasn't my choice, but anything more than that would be a liability.

Before the interrogation could continue, the room plunged into darkness—that was my signal to instigate pure chaos.

I took out Dallas' dagger and let out a quick breath before I plunged it into my stomach. I'd chosen the placement carefully, since I knew how to avoid my organs and make for an easy patch-job. Once I'd sunk it to the hilt, I moved closer to Malakai, and at the same moment the lights turned back on, I let loose an ungodly scream.

I staggered my breathing as everyone in the room turned to see what the fuss was about, and the lights let them see the perfectly placed betrayal on my face.

"What the fuck, Malakai?" I shouted. While few people in the room knew who I was—or even knew *of* me—everyone knew Malakai Eldridge. Getting their attention was as simple as shouting his name. "I trusted you!"

And for dramatic effect, I stumbled away from him and stared at the wound in my stomach. My blood leaked between my fingers, and I had to refrain from smiling. My distraction had worked perfectly.

A swarm of criminals ran towards us, because even in a place like this, the idea of a helpless girl being stabbed by a well-known assassin didn't sit well with anyone. For that reason, Malakai didn't even try to divert the blame—didn't even plead with the ring of criminals that now separated me from him.

I slipped through the cracks as his own hidden protectors came out of the woodwork; the Templum assassins were only recognisable because of their black cloaks.

I caught Malakai's eyes through the cracks in the crowd, and smirked pure anger lit up his honey-brown eyes.

I caught a flash of Nylah next. She'd put some distance between her and her brother, but she didn't seem angry at all. If anything, the girl seemed entertained at the idea of her brother being framed so easily.

And as I finally reached the edge of the crowd, the edge of freedom, I glimpsed Dallas. He split his focus between me and the now missing statuette.

Fuck, he'd surely put it all together. He was smart. It wouldn't be too hard for him to realise that this had been a not-so-elaborate ploy to take the statuette; one that involved the American he'd talked to on that staircase.

I could resolve that issue later.

For now, I had to focus on sneaking out of the mansion before anyone realised the statuette was missing and would piece together the pieces just like Dallas had.

I sprinted from the room, and slipped between people to reach the shadows. I also had to be careful of the dagger still in my stomach, because if it moved so much as a millimetre it was going to nick an organ I didn't want touched. Once I reached the car Vince and the American were waiting at, I stopped running.

"Tell me you fucking have it," I hissed. Hunter smiled as

he pulled the statuette from his jacket and held it in front of himself.

"Taking it was as easy as stealing candy from-"

Hunter was cut off as the statue shattered in his hands. The echo of a gunshot rang through my ears and I immediately turned to see where it had come from.

Malakai walked towards us, with his gun pointed directly at me. Why had he chosen to shoot the statuette instead of killing one of us? Instead of killing *me*? What was so important about this damn thing? There wasn't any time for me to ponder the answer as Vince pushed me into the passenger seat of the car.

I opened the glove box, removed the stashed Glock, and pointed it right back at Malakai. I smirked as he froze. The warning that I would shoot was enough to instigate a stalemate. We were both good shots, but I was better. I was *always* better.

"Give me a reason..." I whispered as I shut the car door and Vince turned over the ignition. If he took one more step, then I had reason to shoot him, and I would give anything to kill this fucker.

"Did you stab yourself for the distraction?" Hunter asked, but I didn't reply—the answer seemed obvious enough to me. He'd settled himself into the back seat as I adjusted my grip on the gun with one hand and stabilised the dagger in my stomach with the other.

Fuck you, Malakai mouthed as the car rolled away and he lowered his gun. I smirked as I let go of the dagger, lowered my gun, and replaced the weapon with a bloodied middle finger.

Fuck you too, I mouthed back.

Killing Malakai Eldridge wasn't in the cards for today, and while that disappointed me to no end, it was something I could live with. I'd get another chance, and I wouldn't let it slip through my hands.

CHAPTER NINE

YOU DULLARD

"Are you going to talk to me?" I asked once we made it back to the hotel room. The car ride over had been quiet, but the weight of that silence was heavier than I'd expected.

Having to explain to Caeli that I hadn't just let Hunter join us, but that I'd also paid to get him here, was... *fun*. But I couldn't blame her for the anger; not when I hadn't given her a single heads up over what would happen and I'd spent the money she'd made us in the process. In this case, a double negative didn't make a positive. It kind of just made an even *worse* negative.

Her silence was her way of telling me just how pissed she was. It was a response to let me know that if she said anything, it would be something she'd regret. The stupid part was that I knew this was exactly how she'd respond, that she would shut down on me. There were things I knew she could forgive without question, but making decisions for her wasn't on that list.

Well, that and ignoring her when she warned me against doing something stupid.

"Kid..." my chest tightened as she busied herself with taking out her earrings.

She then turned her attention to the dagger in her stomach. I let her continue to ignore me as she walked into the bathroom to change out of the dress and into sweatpants and a sports bra. When she came back out she had a towel pressed to the now open wound on her stomach.

"Caeli..."

All I needed was for her to look at me. That way, I could gauge just how badly I'd fucked up. If her eyes were cold, then it was forgivable, but if her eyes looked like molten silver, then I was screwed. And I needed her to let me stitch up that wound before she bled out on me.

But I wouldn't move closer to her until she told me it was okay to do so. I wouldn't move closer. Not even when she picked up one of her own daggers and walked over to the gas stove and turned it on. I wouldn't even budge as she held the blade over the flame until it was red hot. Even though I knew exactly what she was about to do, I didn't move a god-damned muscle.

"Caeli, don't do that. I'll stitch you-"

I cut myself off as her eyes finally looked at me and she

placed the scolding metal against her wound. The sound of her skin sizzling at the touch of the burning blade made me wince, even though I knew she hadn't so much as blinked. From what she'd told me, emotions were the first thing they taught her to compartmentalise, and pain had been the second. At times, I wondered if she felt any of it at all.

She just stared at me as she took the blade from the cauterised wound and slammed it onto the bench next to her. Her eyes were cold, which meant I had a chance to unscrew myself here.

"I'm sorry," I whispered, unsure of where else I could even start. Her jaw popped as she turned off the gas cooker.

"What part are you sorry for?" She asked. I was all too aware of the fact that she was acting far too calm for what she likely felt. I was lucky, because if I was legitimately *anyone else,* I would be lying dead with a dagger in me. "Because, honestly, I don't think you're sorry for the part you should apologise for. I think you're sorry that the best way out of the situation that you put me in without my permission was to frame someone for stabbing me."

That was something I didn't agree with. Of all the drastic measures I thought she would take, that hadn't been one of them.

"Was that really the best way?" I was already in the wrong, so what difference would it make if I dug in my heels and stood my ground? "The plan didn't have to change just because we had *help.*"

"Yes it did, Vincent, because I not only had to deal with

Dallas but Malakai and his sister as well, which meant that Templum was there. On top of all that, the three of them realised I was working with Hunter." She replied as she pushed away from the kitchen bench. "It was just supposed to be Dallas, and I was only supposed to worry about you." She reached into her bag and pulled out a sweater. "The distraction was just meant to be a screaming match with Dallas, but that wouldn't have kept the attention of Malakai or Nylah or any of the Templum assassins that were there."

As she pulled the sweater over her head, I took the moment of silence to think. Maybe things could have turned out differently if I'd let her in on my plan. Maybe it could have turned out better than it had. But I knew it would have turned out worse. Caeli would have threatened to kill Hunter before we even began and he never would have agreed to help us because of it. We would have gone in alone.

What I did was the right thing, even if it didn't feel like it.

"You know who wasn't on the guest list?" She asked next, her head tilted to the side as she stared at me. The cold in her eyes faded, but that didn't mean I was anymore comfortable under her gaze. No, instead of the bitter anger she couldn't control, there was just disappointment, which was arguably worse than the other option. "Mal, Nylah and fucking *Hunter*. I assume I have you to thank for that last one."

She was right. I couldn't have her knowing he would turn up. It had to be a surprise or she would've fought against it. There wasn't a whole lot I knew, but I knew my kid, and I

69

always would.

"You aren't sorry you put me in that position. You're just sorry about how far I had to go in order for the plan to work with all the new variables. All you're sorry for is that it was all a waste of time. Mal shot the statuette, so your lies were all for nothing."

My chest tightened at her words. She was right. I wouldn't apologise for not telling her about Hunter. I knew I'd done the best thing I could for all of us. But the rest of it... the rest of it felt like my fault, too.

"Caeli-"

"Unless you're going to apologise and tell me you'll never do that to me again, I don't want to hear it," she cut me off again, and I looked to the ground. I wouldn't apologise. In time, she would come to understand what I did and why. I just needed to give her some space to think it over. Even if it was going to hurt to have her look at me with nothing but anger for a little while, I wouldn't do it. I *couldn't*. "Right, got it."

She pulled her hair out of the delicate bun I had crafted for the auction and threw it into a ponytail. She put on a pair of skate shoes and walked towards the door. Although it might not seem like it, this was a good sign. It meant she didn't want to tear me to shreds.

"Kid-"

"Don't wait up for me," she said as she walked out and slammed the door behind her.

I ran a hand over my face and accustomed myself to the

new silence. While that had gone better than I thought it would, it still hadn't gone overly well. If she was going for a walk, then that meant I had plenty of time to talk to Hunter and figure out a way forward, one that wouldn't involve Caeli stabbing anyone.

But before I could do anything else that would raise my blood pressure, I needed a god-damned smoke.

———◦———

"I just need to double-check this... you *want* to talk to Caeli?" I asked, to which Hunter nodded as he chewed on some gum. Jesus, this kid had a death wish.

"That's what'll get her to trust me, isn't it?" Hunter replied from across the small table. I shrugged my shoulders and leant back in my seat.

"I wouldn't say 'trust', not yet at least. It might put you on the right path to it, but you won't get close for..." I trailed off as the door opened and Caeli walked into the hotel room. Her free hand flexed while the other held tight onto the door handle, strong enough that her knuckles turned white. Her body tensed, and I knew she was going to run.

"Kiddo, please sit down." She was just as stubborn as I was. It was how I raised her to be.

There was every chance she'd walk out of the room, even after my request, but she should know that I wouldn't let this go. She surely knew that if she walked out now that I would only orchestrate another situation to bring us to this same point. Maybe I just needed to convince her to do this now, to save us both time that would otherwise be wasted.

"I know you weren't happy about me bringing Hunter in without you knowing." The look in her eyes told me all I needed to know, they showed me exactly what she was thinking without her saying a damned word; *no shit*. "I think we need to talk it out and see if working together is a viable option. We could use the extra hands." And her eyes once again spoke for her; *for fuck's sake, Vince*. "Just hear him out, please."

Caeli walked over to the table and sat down, her focus completely on Hunter before she finally spoke. "I'm listening." Her tone made the otherwise regular words sound like a threat.

"I don't know if I trust that tone," Hunter said. I couldn't blame him, but I needed this conversation to move forward, no matter how much he trusted it or not.

"Ignore the tone," I told him. And right about now was the moment I realised I'd pulled a third stubborn asshole into our group. This would either end well or end badly.

"I wish I could, but the way she's staring at me is mildly terrifying." Hunter would have to get used to that stare if he wanted to work with us. He would also have to understand that no matter how often he looked at me for help, there was nothing I could do to stop her from doing it.

"I would rather it was completely terrifying instead of just mildly," Caeli replied in a monotone. Her accent always made her words sound more polite than intended, which was why when her tone dropped to something completely threatening you had to watch your back. "I would rather you walk out that door right now instead of continuing to work with us, but knowing Sinclair, he's convinced you to be all in on this. And it seems you need a big payday no matter the cost."

I flinched as she called me Sinclair instead of Vince. That was how I knew I was most definitely in the bad books. Hunter looked over at me once again, and I shook my head. I couldn't help him. He'd have to work this out on his own.

"Stop looking at him like he's going to help you," Caeli said, and Hunter looked away from me again. "Part of the cost you're going to have to pay is working with me, whether or not you want to."

"Take it easy," I whispered as I heard a familiar venom slip into her tone.

"No, why would I?" She asked as she looked at me. "We have no idea who he is. How can you trust him?" I took a breath to answer, but Hunter spoke before me.

"At least you know my name, I don't know yours." Jesus, this kid *definitely* had a death wish. Caeli let out a low laugh as she turned back to Hunter. And to say I was glad she wasn't focused on me anymore would be the biggest understatement of the century.

"I don't believe, for a single god-damned second, that your real name is *Hunter*. Now, because of that, I would like to keep my name close to my chest," Caeli replied.

"Kid-"

"Don't." Caeli cut me off as she stood up from the chair and ran a hand over her ponytail. This was not going the way I had intended. I should probably do something to calm the situation. "You know what... *fine*. You want to let this stranger into our lives, Sinclair? *Fine*." Why did I feel like this was a bad thing? Was it the glint of pure anger in her eyes? And the fact she was about to let that anger override her paranoia? Yeah, that would probably be it. "But he needs to know exactly who he's working with, and he needs to know our secret... *it's only fair*." She turned towards Hunter as my stomach turned into knots.

"What secret? What the fuck do you have over him to talk to him like that?" Hunter asked as he gestured to me, and I grimaced at the question. Well, it had been nice to know him for the few days I did. "He's the Shadow-"

"He isn't the Shadow, you dullard." Well that was a new one.

"What-"

There was a sharp edge to Caeli's tone as she cut off Hunter. That sharpness reflected in her silver eyes.

"Vincent Sinclair isn't the fucking Shadow, *I* am."

CHAPTER TEN

CURIOUS AND PERSISTENT BY NATURE

Caeli placed her hands onto the table, so she could sneer at Hunter, her head lowered and her eyes cold. God, was I glad she wasn't looking at me like that.

"You want to join our little team so badly? Well, that means you get to find out the truth about who I am. It also means that if you tell a single soul on this earth the information you're about to learn, I will fucking gut you. Do you understand?" This was getting out of hand. I had to get her to stand down, or she was going to scare Hunter off.

"Kid-"

"My name is Caeli Venatrix." Caeli cut me off, and an

icy heaviness expanded in my chest that prevented me from saying anything. "*I* am the Shadow. I'm the one trained to kill without a trace, not Vincent. I'm the one able to get in and out of where I need to be to take whatever I want without ever being caught, not Vincent. Everything you know about the Shadow is based on my achievements, not Vincent's." She stood up straight as that icy feeling coursed through my entire body. There was no going back now. "The worst part? What you think you know about me doesn't even scratch the surface. But you want to join us? Go ahead, you just need to remember that I'm the one in control here, *not Vincent.*"

I was surprised at the stoic expression on Hunter's face—or rather, the look of curiosity instead of fear.

"Okay, if you're trying to scare me off, why did you bother saving my ass back in Lima?" Hunter asked. It was a good question, one that I hadn't had the balls to ask yet.

"I was saving my ass-"

"If that's what you were doing, you should have shot me and left me for dead." Oh Jesus Christ, he did not just cut Caeli off. Every passing minute was just confirming the suspicion that Hunter didn't care whether he lived or died. "So why didn't you?"

"Because I was in a good mood, and could never have imagined that it would lead to this fuck-up of a situation," she replied as she crossed her arms over her chest.

"Am I supposed to believe that you didn't kill me because you were in a good mood?" Hunter asked. He tilted his head to the side as I realised now was probably a good time to cut into the conversation before it got out of hand. Again.

"Actually, relatively speaking, she was in a pretty good mood that night," I said. I ignored Caeli's glare as it shifted back to me. "But after meeting her in a similar situation where she also didn't kill me, I've learned not to question when she leaves someone alive." Silence followed my words, and I felt Caeli's glare soften.

Once I was sure that the conversation had ended, that there wouldn't be anymore questions on this subject, I pushed us back onto topic. "The question we should ask is whether you want to keep working with us, or if Caeli is going to be too much for you."

"Is she like this all the time?" Oh boy, this was not getting better. He really had to watch his damned tone.

"And what the fuck do you mean by that?" Caeli questioned. The softness that had entered her eyes before completely dissipated and left a cold silver wall instead. I honestly didn't know what else I could do, because Hunter hadn't taken any of the lifelines I'd thrown him.

"I mean, are you this protective and paranoid all the time? It can't be good for your health," Hunter said as he stood up and walked to stand directly in front of her. Maybe he could be of more use than I thought, if he could already sense how much her paranoia affected her. "I only just found out your name, and I'm both curious and persistent by nature. I'll find out exactly what's beneath that silver armour of yours, Caeli, even if it's the last thing I do."

Why did I feel like I shouldn't have heard that?

"I assume you two want to talk, so before I go, I'll give you some extra background information on me." Hunter didn't so much as look at me. He was too entirely focused on Caeli. Yeah, I really shouldn't be here for this, but it was far too late for me to leave.

"And why would you do that?" Caeli asked, and I watched the smirk that reached Hunter's face.

"To save you a little time," he answered. "I grew up in New Orleans, and I have a little sister who's being kept at a safe distance. My parents are long gone, and whether or not you believe it, Hunter is my real name. I swear it on my dad's soul." That seemed both believable and also not at the same time.

"And what about you having been in jail before?" Caeli asked, and, although it was difficult to do, I kept my mouth shut and waited for his answer.

"Got caught stealing... but I broke out easily, so I wasn't there for long," he answered. The sudden openness felt a little off to me, but I could work out what didn't sit right later. For now, we needed to use it to our advantage.

"So, are we supposed to trust you now?" Caeli asked, and I did not like being dragged back into this conversation. If I could have just left a few minutes ago, that would have been preferable, because I was just trying to pretend I wasn't here. "Is that what your little plan is?"

"I have a feeling it takes a lot more than a little honesty to break through your walls. I'm willing to put in the work, though," he said before he winked at Caeli. What the actual fuck was going on here? "I'll leave you two to talk. You know where to find me." He smiled before he walked out of the room.

"Why him?" Caeli asked, as I scratched my cheek. "What made you change your attitude all of a fucking sudden, Vince? You were against him when we first got into the car in Lima, and then, for some fucking reason, you switched up and started acting like you'd been friends for years."

"Back to calling me Vince, are we?" I asked with a smirk, and she shot me a warning look that I heeded. "Honestly? I see myself in him, back when I was your age, at least." All I could do was offer her that truth, and hope to God that it was enough for her to understand.

"God damn it, how stupid can you be, Vince?"

Immediately, a sour taste filled my mouth, and my stomach churned. My eyes squeezed shut and my father's voice echoed in my head. *How fucking stupid can you be?* I could hear skin hitting skin, but the sting of the familiar pain wasn't present. It was just the ghost of a memory, that's all it was.

"You didn't mean that," I whispered as I opened my eyes and looked up at her. Her eyes were wide and her mouth agape as she looked at me, her head shaking. "I know you didn't mean that, so it's okay." I continued to whisper as she looked at her hands.

It was hard to blame her for what she'd said. I'd trained her to strike people where it hurt. The unfortunate consequence of that was that she could strike me harder than anyone else could.

"You're one of the smartest people I know, Vince," she said instead of an apology. It was difficult for her to say sorry, and this tended to be the closest she ever got. It was fine, because there was no way she'd meant to hurt me in the first place.

"Let me guess, you're at the top of that list?" I asked. It was a broken attempt at lightening the mood, at moving on.

"Obviously," she replied with a forced smile. It was easy to read her, it always had been. Her eyes were far too expressive and gave her away. But it was best to move on, to not dwell on the past mistakes.

"Do you trust me?" I asked, and she nodded slowly as she sat down again. "Something in my gut tells me we can trust this kid. I might not be all knowing like you, little Demon, but I know how to read people." She tilted her head to the side.

"My faith in that knowledge is a little skewed," she pointed out, and I bit my lip.

"Still holding that against me, huh?" I asked, and all she did in response was stare at me. "Alright. Ashford was a mistake, a fucking huge one that cost me my daughter's trust. If you've lost faith in my ability to read people, then that's fine, but you should trust that I'll avoid repeating that mistake at all costs." The coldness in her eyes warmed, and she nodded.

"Okay..." she trailed off, and I hoped to God I hadn't read Hunter wrong. "But the second he fucks up or lets slip that he has an ulterior motive, he's gone, yes?" I nodded my agreement and so she let the topic rest. I couldn't have asked for more than a conditional agreement, because anything else would mean she'd lost her damned mind.

"Is Romania still your backup plan?" I asked to change the topic and prevent her from changing her mind. While I didn't like the backup plan, it might be less worrying for me if she took someone with her. She sighed and nodded. "You should take Hunter with you." It was a habit of mine to push her boundaries, and right now was no different.

"Don't push it, Vince. He can go with you, help you sell shit. I can deal with Romania by myself."

"And I can sell shit by myself. You're going into a drug lord's home so you can steal from him. Maybe just take the newbie as backup. He doesn't have to go in with you. He can wait outside for a distress signal, but it'll give me some peace of mind to know you have someone there with you." This wasn't me asking.

There were few times when I could demand something without having her arguing back, or having her tell me I was wrong and doing her own thing. Those times were always in regards to her safety, my concern with making sure she stayed alive. Caeli was my responsibility, my kid, and the times we were separated were the most anxiety-inducing hours of my life. What I was going to do wasn't dangerous, not when compared to what Caeli's task was.

And separating was best, because it meant I could do what I had to and she could do what she had to without either of us getting in the way. It also meant we could get this all done faster, we could have the funds to move forward and have our next heading at the same time. Impatience was a similar trait between us, just the same as stubbornness.

"Fine..." Caeli whispered before she ran a hand over her face. I let out a painful breath at her agreement. "He can come with me to Romania."

Chapter Eleven

WHAT IF I ENJOY MAKING YOU BLUSH?

Of all the things I'd done and said and promised to Vince, this would be the one I regretted the most. The plane ride from Egypt to Romania had been silent. There wasn't anything I really wanted to say to Hunter to bother breaking that silence. What could I say? Expressing my distaste for the situation we were in was as good as wasting breath.

Besides, aside from previous words we'd shared, I'm sure he could tell from the look that was stuck on my face.

"Are you going to say anything to me, or is this how it's going to go moving forward?" Hunter asked as we walked into the double room that Vincent had booked for us.

Booking a shared room was likely a not-so-subtle attempt at forcing me to spend time with Hunter. If I was honest, I wasn't sure just yet if being stuck within the same four dark walls with him would improve my attitude towards the American or just make it insufferably worse.

Well, actually I knew, but maybe the only way to convince Vince this was a bad idea would be to go through with it. That way I'd have a chance to gather evidence and prove that Hunter couldn't be trusted. All I had to do was pay attention to every minute detail. That way, I could notice the second he screwed up.

"That depends..." I trailed off as I watched him throw his bag onto the bed closest to the door. While there was no way in the nine hells that I'd trust him, my body still tensed at the thought of not being in that bed. It was always safest for everyone involved if I was the one closest to the door.

"On what?" He asked as he sat down on the edge of what should have been *my* mattress. My hands clenched at the sight of it. Fuck, I was really going to do this, wasn't I?

"On you," I replied. It took all of my focus to unfurl my hands and force them to grip the straps of my bag instead. "If we're going to work together, we need to make some ground rules." My focus shifted between him and the bed. As much as the fact he wanted to be the sacrificial lamb should have made me overjoyed, I knew I wouldn't be able to sleep tonight if I wasn't the one in that bed.

"Like what?" He asked as he tilted his head to the side, reminiscent of what he did yesterday when we talked with

Vince. Hunter obviously had no shame. Last night was enough evidence for me to believe that. "No more flirting?" Well, that would be a good start, but I had a feeling he wouldn't abide by that one.

"That would be preferable," I answered, which brought a pout to his lips.

"And what if I enjoy making you blush?" For the love of fuck. The patience I'd allocated for the next two days was already running out. Maybe it was best to just move on from here, maybe it was best to just leave that conversation there and change the topic.

"Rule one, I sleep closest to the door, no exceptions." It was also best to get that out of the way first. That way, my tense muscles could relax. My body wouldn't fully calm until I was in the same room as Vince again, but this would definitely help.

"Can I ask why?" I don't know why he even bothered asking that question, since he was already standing and had his hand on his bag strap.

"No, you can't. It leads into rule two," I replied. I threw my bag onto the bed before he could ask anymore questions. "Don't even think about asking me about my past. I won't tell you anything because I don't trust you, so it would just be a waste of our time."

"Kind of expected that one. I won't lie. However, I thought that would be rule one." His tone was light, as if he was making a joke. He settled onto his bed, a smile on his face and a piece of gum visible between his teeth.

What if I slit his throat right here and now? Who would stop me? Who would catch me? Any DNA I left behind would be worthless. I'm not in any system. There's no identity to tie me to, no fingerprints to connect me to what I touched.

The only issue would be the fact Vince would know it was me, because who else in Romania would want this American dead? That would be worse than any prison, because I could slip out of anywhere they tried to lock me up. Vince, though, could take away the only things that mattered to me. He could abandon me and that would be more of a punishment than anything else.

"Ground rule three..." I trailed off, deciding it was best not to give the reaction that Hunter was likely fishing for. Pure indifference. That was the only way to get him to stop. Hatred meant I had any kind of emotion attached to him, and I'm sure that's what he wanted. "You do exactly what I say *when* I say it. Any slip up could get us killed, especially if we're dealing with Templum. Understood?" That seemed like enough ground rules to start. They made a sturdy base to work with. I could always add more later if necessary.

"Understood." I let out a deep breath as a weight slightly lifted from my shoulders; even if I didn't believe for a second that he would actually follow them. "What happens if I break a rule?" Oh, he wanted to go there? Alright, I could give him a warning, but I'd keep it vague and leave it up to his imagination.

"Let's not get into the details yet, but if you break them, I will be fairly angry, and you haven't seen me completely and utterly infuriated yet," I replied.

"So last night…" He trailed off. Did he think last night was the peak of my rage? He had a lot to learn.

"Not even close," I answered the unasked question. His eyebrows furrowed and released within the space of a second, his eyes seeming to stare right into my soul like they had last night. Why did I get the sense he wasn't afraid of me? Maybe tonight would change that.

"Okay, no rule breaking then," he said before he took in a deep breath through his nose and kept chewing on that damned gum. "So, what exactly are we going to do here?"

"There is no 'we', there is an 'I'. The only role you have is to help ease Vince's conscience. You are of no use to me." I said as I pulled out the clothes I would wear tonight.

"So, am I meant to just stay here?" He asked as he stood up and walked over to me. "I'm pretty sure that's not what Vince had in mind, because that wouldn't ease his conscience. Since that's all I'm here for, I should probably take my role seriously." God damn it.

"No, what Vince had in mind was for you to be my backup, which I don't need," I replied as I crossed my arms over my chest. The movement caused me to grimace. A dull pain shot through my body as a reminder of the stab wound that was still healing on my stomach. It would be gone in a matter of days, but until then it would continue being an annoyance.

"Are you sure? Just yesterday, you had a dagger in your gut. It's probably a good idea to-"

"I've been through much worse than this, and past experience tells me you're only going to get in my way. My plan doesn't need a boy who's trying to prove himself to get involved and screw things up," I snapped. Even though he flinched at my comment, I didn't feel a damned bit of regret. Even though he rubbed his neck where the bruises were nothing more than yellow marks, I didn't feel any remorse.

"I don't need to be there. I just need to know what you're doing so I can help you if you get screwed over. I know you're capable of doing this yourself, that you can take on anyone you want and end up on top. But what if someone hits you in the stomach? What if you end up cornered and need backup, but you don't have any because you were too damn proud to let me be there?"

My head tilted back towards the grey ceiling, my eyes closed as I took a deep breath. The likelihood of me needing backup was so abysmally small that it wasn't even a slight concern of mine. But this was why Vince wanted Hunter here, because if something unexpected happened, then I would otherwise have to figure it out on my own. While I could still get out of any situation I ended up in, this was about efficiency. Having a person waiting on the side-lines would help with that.

"We're going to be stealing from Hansen." No matter how much I didn't want him to be here, he was. If Vince wanted me to let Hunter help me, then I would, and when he screwed up, it would give me the proof I needed to get Vince to give up on the idea of working with Hunter.

"Hansen?" Hunter asked, his eyes wide. "As in the internationally operating drug lord with billions of dollars to his name, *Richard Hansen*?"

"Yes."

"We're stealing from that guy?" His eyebrows drew together as he spoke, and I nodded.

"Yes," I repeated. While I could understand his concern, it would save us both plenty of time in future if he didn't question my plans from here on out. "Well, *I* am. You'll be waiting outside in case I need backup, which I won't." I uncrossed my arms and pulled out the rest of my clothing for the night.

"He has one of those statuettes?" He asked.

"Not for much longer," I replied. The options I had for weapons were limited. With what I'd have to wear, there wasn't much space to hide my daggers. If I wear my high-heeled ankle boots, then I should be able to carry two of my small blades, but aside from that, there wasn't much else I could take.

"What are you going to do, exactly?" Hunter asked as he looked down at my clothes, and I saw the realisation hit his eyes. "Jesus, really?"

"Not exactly what you're thinking, no." On the bed was a black skin-tight dress, a little shorter than what it should have been, with long sleeves and a high neck. I would have to wear tights with it, to make sure I didn't put Hansen off with my scars, but that wouldn't make a difference. "I have a contact who owes me a favour. They got me into the party

89

that Hansen is holding tonight in his mansion. So, I'll be acting as a server, and with some carefully chosen words and facial expressions, I'll come across as his perfect prey." Another flash of concern passed Hunter's eyes. "I can take this guy on, so I apologise in advance. This is going to be a very boring night for you."

"Are you going to kill him?" Hunter asked, and I smirked in response.

"Yes, violently," I said. Maybe he didn't know why I was targeting this man. "Do you know what he's done? How many people he's killed? And by people, I mean young women who couldn't survive the abuse he put them through as he raped them?"

"No..." he answered, and I was glad for the simple honesty.

"He's raped forty-six, and what he put them through killed thirty-two. Tonight isn't just about getting what I want, it's about teaching this man a lesson." I picked up my clothes so I could change, but stopped on my walk to the bathroom when he spoke again.

"Can I make some ground rules, too?" He asked. What made him think he could demand things from me? He was lucky I'd let him come along in the first place, and that I hadn't plotted his demise. "It's only fair if we can both set some boundaries. That's all I'm asking for." Fuck, I hated it when other people made valid points.

"Alright, I made three, so you can make three. That's it though," I replied as I did my best to stop a scowl from taking over my face.

"Okay, first I would like you to give me safety updates. I need to know you're okay." I just stared blankly at him. "For the sole purpose of filling my role, that is." Why did he feel the need to add that? I assumed that was the reason behind it. Was it not?

"I don't do safety updates. I have to focus completely on the task at hand so I can keep control of the situation. There's no time for me to confirm with other people that I'm fine. That should just be assumed." Judging from the look on his face, he didn't approve of my response. He had agreed to my three rules without argument, so maybe I could just negotiate a bit and make it seem like I cared. "I'll give a distress signal if I need you. Will that work?" And while his eyes told me he didn't agree, he nodded anyway.

"Second rule, if you ask me about my past, then I get to ask about yours. It doesn't make sense that you can ask about mine, but I can't ask about yours," he said. My hands tightened on the clothes I held.

"Okay, that makes it fair, I guess," I said through my teeth. It definitely ruined my plan to find out more about him, to find out whether or not he was trustworthy. But not being able to ask was a minor inconvenience in the grand scheme of things. I could pull information from people without saying a word, so I could likely trick him into talking without ever *asking* him to. "What's number three?"

"No more breaking promises with me. You say you're going to do something, you follow through." Clearly, he was still bitter about Lima, and me not giving him my name after we got out of the museum. His rule didn't make sense in that context though, because he had forgotten one extremely important detail.

"I haven't promised you a single thing," I replied. Before he could argue, I relayed the facts from that night. "I never said I would follow through, and we never agreed to a deal. You jumped ahead without getting my word for it, so don't blame me for your own failure at paying attention." He stayed silent for a few blissful moments, likely taking the time to replay the events from the other night over in his own head and coming to the realisation that I was right. And of course I was right, I'd never been wrong before.

"Okay, no manipulating me then." I sighed at the new rule, because it could technically count me out of the plan to get him to talk. But I guessed he didn't have to know what I was doing. He couldn't accuse me of manipulation if he didn't notice it.

"But it's so much fun tricking people into doing what I want," I complained. His golden eyes told me he didn't care about my enjoyment, which was a pity. "Fine, no manipulation tactics." It was a lie, but he wouldn't know that. Not until it was too late.

"Promise me," he said. "You said you never promised me anything, so I think when you promise something, you always follow through." I licked my lip and tilted my head to the side. Was I truly that easy to understand? Surely not. Surely this was just a lucky guess.

"I promise," I whispered, and he closed the distance

between us with his hand stuck out towards me. I sighed again before I shook his hand and ignored the way my fingers tingled at his touch. "Are you happy now?" I went to pull my hand away from him, but he used the grip to pull me closer to him, close enough that his chest was mere inches away from me and his face hovered over mine. How tall was he? How had I not noticed he stood a full head taller than me until right now?

I hated the way he smiled down at me, and I hated the way his gold eyes glinted in the dim light of the hotel room.

"I'm thrilled, *Princess.*"

Chapter Twelve

DAMN THAT FUCKING SOUTHERN DRAWL

I watched each person walk in and out of the kitchen, noted the time they were gone for and how often they returned. The servers were all young women, dressed similarly to me, although in looser dresses. Hansen's focus, and therefore everyone's focus, needed to be on me and the easiest way to do that was to show off my body.

"Does this make us even?" Michael asked. He was one of the people who owed Vince and me a favour, and getting into this event had been the perfect way to cash it in. While I usually preferred upfront payment, I was happy taking favours from those I'd worked with before and trusted.

Michael was one of those lucky few, and there was no chance he'd avoid paying up.

He was far too aware of what I was capable of.

"You won't be hearing from Vince and I again after this," I answered and spotted the look of disappointment that crossed his unremarkable brown eyes. His usefulness in this situation stemmed from his closeness to my target. They worked in the same circles and knew the same people, so when I asked for an in, he contacted the caterer Hansen used every event without fail. And here we were.

"That's kind of sad. You guys were never boring." I smiled at his words, because it was almost sad for me as well. Whenever we'd ended up working with Michael, we were always far too deep in shit we shouldn't have touched—but I thrived in chaos. "Do I want to know what's going to happen tonight?" He wasn't the biggest fan of Hansen, which was unsurprising, so when I'd told him who my target was, he helped without asking any further questions. Maybe that lack of knowledge was finally catching up to him.

"Hansen has something I need, and I figured it was best to come in under cover since it will probably be under lock and key." I cracked my knuckles as I spoke. He'd likely asked in regard to what it meant for him, since Hansen's death would benefit him as much as it would give me some catharsis. "And I thought I would take the opportunity to rid the world of one steaming pile of shit."

"Two birds, one stone?" Michael asked, as I tilted my head to the side. That was an apt way of putting it.

"Something like that," I said as I straightened the front of my dress. The small daggers in my boots annoyed me, but I couldn't let it show, lest Hansen notice something was off. "If you warn him about why I'm here..."

"There's really no need to threaten me, Riley." How many aliases had I used? I honestly couldn't remember. Was it seven? Seven felt right. "I've seen your work before, so the thought never once occurred to me." Good, maybe he would have an even better idea of my capabilities after tonight.

What I had planned for Hansen wouldn't be pretty.

———◦———

Playing the long game had always been my least favourite method of getting a job done, especially when the important bit would only take a minute or two. I'd planted the seeds early by locking eyes with Hansen within minutes of the party starting. It was relatively easy to pretend I was attracted to the man. All it took was a coy look as I tucked loose strands of hair behind my ears.

It was a patented method of mine, to look helpless and nervous to lure in my targets. Since I was shorter than most, there was the expectation I was easy to overpower. For him, I had to look fragile and naïve, so each time I looked in his direction, that was exactly how I acted. It was working, judging from the way his near-black eyes watched my every move.

God, I was going to enjoy what was to come. While I hated

the long game, it always had the most satisfying conclusion.

It wasn't until the night died down that I began the endgame for my plan. It started with me carrying a full tray of champagne flutes and *accidentally* bumping into him; the action spilled a bottle worth of sparkling wine all over his red silk dress shirt.

"I am so sorry sir, I wasn't watching where I was walking..." my eyes slowly lifted to meet his, false intimidation placed on my face as I took in his overly muscular build. He was more than a foot taller than me, but it wouldn't make a difference in the end.

"New to the job?" He asked, his tone strangely playful and light. I didn't enjoy it one bit, but I smiled none-the-less.

"Yes, sir," I replied as I knelt down to pick up the shards of glass on the ground. The placement of my body was particular; close enough to spark his imagination at what I could do on my knees and far enough that I didn't start killing him too early. Lacerating his Achilles' tendons was definitely a part of my plan; I couldn't have him running away.

"A word of advice, then. It helps if you look where you're going." No, I couldn't just turn around and stab him. While I was good at my job, I probably wouldn't get out of fighting everyone in here unscathed. Instead, I stacked the broken glass on the tray, stood up slowly, and let out a sigh.

"Yeah, I think I might have just figured that one out myself." I furrowed my brow as I spoke, my focus on the stain on his shirt. "I'm going to take this mess to the kitchen," I said as I gestured to the tray of broken glass. "Just wait right here and I'll come back with some serviettes for-" Hansen took hold of my arm and gestured for another server to come over to us. While I desperately wanted to take him out then, it wouldn't be beneficial.

He would learn his mistake soon enough.

"No need to bring me serviettes, instead you can help me choose a new suit," he said as another server reached us. Her eyebrows furrowed with concern as her fingers brushed mine under the tray. I winked at her to show I had control of the situation, and while it didn't seem like she believed me, she nodded and took the tray away.

"I wouldn't want to take you from your conversation," I said. I carefully curated my voice to be gentle, and pulled on my accent to soften my demeanour. There were a multitude of British accents, but the one I'd grown up around was the one that connoted wealth. It was useful, because it gave the idea that I'd never had to fight for anything in my life, which couldn't be further from the truth.

"They won't mind," Hansen replied. Michael stood in the small circle of men who'd been conversing with Hansen. While the others seemed to enjoy the fact that Hansen had found his target for the night, Michael's eyes were wide. While the others had their expectation of what would happen tonight, only he knew Hansen was the one in danger.

"In that case, I would love to help you pick a new suit, sir." Some men snickered as Hansen lead me up to the second floor. I already had their faces burned into my memory, added to the list of people who would die by my hands at some point or another. Not tonight though. Tonight my focus was solely on Hansen.

"So, what should I call you?" Hansen asked once we reached the grand hallway at the top of the stairs. We were no doubt heading for the primary bedroom, which I knew to be the last door on the left. Although I wanted him to think we would end up there—that we were going to do what he planned for the night—I had something else in mind.

"Riley, sir," I said as the first part of my plan fell into place. The room I was looking for was on my right; the entrance was just a large open archway, without so much as a door to hide the artefacts that were on display. "Is that a full set of samurai armour?" I asked as I stopped walking, my eyes locked entirely on the huge glass cabinet that drew you into the room.

Keeping him here would be easy. All I'd have to let him do was talk about his collection, and with some carefully directed questions, he would lead me to exactly what I wanted to see.

"A history buff, are we?" He asked as he moved to stand next to me, his eyes locked on the pristine armour.

Something stirred in my head, my forehead turned warm... but I didn't have the time to figure out why that was. That was a problem for later.

"Yes, sir, I'm working this job in order to pay for my history degree," I said. Instead of driving him forwards, instead of controlling the direction of the conversation, I

R. A. MAYES

would gently nudge him where I wanted. Instead of forcing him to do what I required, I would bring his guard down, allow him the illusion of control, and manipulate him into giving me the information I needed. "We should find you a new suit though, before that stain sets." I turned on my heel, ready to walk to his room, but he placed a strangely gentle hand on my arm.

"It can wait. I have plenty of suits that are just as expensive as this one," he said. I held back a disgusted shiver as his hand slipped along my body to sit on my lower back. With his new vantage point, he directed me into the room and walked me around to view all of his artefacts. "Is there anything you're particularly fond of? A culture or a figure?"

"I've always been interested in the Ottoman Empire and also Incan history," I answered, aware that the two things would spark continued conversation.

"That's two very different aspects of the past." Hansen's hand trailed up my back before he rubbed the back of my neck.

"Yes, the Ottoman Empire is because of my lineage. Incan is because I once travelled to Peru and found it absolutely fascinating. I've been drawn to learning about it ever since." I looked up at Hansen, the naïve façade stuck on my face as I worked out the nuances of how I would kill him.

"Well, I do actually have an Incan piece if you would like to see it." He fell right into the web I had spun for him, just as I knew he would.

"I would love to," I replied, and I didn't need to fake

100

my enthusiasm. The second I laid eyes on the statuette, I wouldn't have to keep up with the niceties, but I had to stay patient for a bit longer.

"It's not much, but I've been told that what's inside of it is worth killing for." How damned ironic. Hansen's hand drifted back down to my tailbone, and I felt my throat go bone dry.

Soon enough and I could spill his blood. I just had to wait a *little* longer and ignore the warmth in my forehead that started to burn.

"Have you ever opened it?" I asked. Although I knew the answer, it was a good idea to get confirmation.

"No, I don't need anyone coming after me for what's inside." If only he knew.

We reached the cabinet that I wanted to see and I investigated the golden statuette. It lacked a seam like the one I'd taken from the auction, which meant it was indeed unopened. My heart drummed in my chest as that icy feeling returned to my stomach.

"Do you think I could hold it?" I asked, as his fingers brushed the top of my ass. Immediately, that excited drum in my chest turned to a deafening roar in my ears.

"Hold it?" Hansen asked as I looked up at him. "I don't think so." Well, I guess my wait was almost over.

"Please? I'll do anything," I said as he leaned down to my neck, his lips on my ear. My blood turned to fire in my veins as he grabbed my ass, and since his eyes were no longer on my face, I dropped the exhausting, innocent façade. Fuck, it always felt like a weight lifted from my shoulders when I dropped my mask.

"I don't want compliance. The fun part is the struggle." My jaw popped as his breath fanned over my neck. So this was it. The act was over, and I no longer had to play nice. *Finally.*

"In that case..." I slowly picked up my left foot, reaching down my leg as I kept my balance without so much as leaning an inch. If I did, then it would give away the fact I was moving, and he needed to think I'd frozen in fear.

"What? Are you realising that you're in..." he trailed off as he likely noticed the nude coloured ear piece sitting in my ear. Maybe if he hadn't of been so focused on getting his dick wet, he might have had a chance to defend himself against me.

"I'm not the one in danger, Hansen. That would be you." My fingers reached for my boot and slipped out the dagger, no longer than the length of my hand.

"What the fuck are you-"

"Hands off what isn't yours, Hansen." Damn that fucking Southern drawl.

Chapter Thirteen

THE MISSING EXPERIMENT

My entire body froze as Hansen's hand left my ass. He turned away from me as we both realised there was someone else in the room with us. Someone who should most definitely *not* be.

When I looked beyond Hansen, I found the owner of the voice pointing a gun directly at the man on my right.

Hunter hadn't followed rule fucking three. Of the three I'd made, this was the second one I thought he'd break. For certain, I was sure he was going to ask about my past before he decided not to do as I had instructed—for *survival*, if nothing else.

I completely focused on Hunter's eyes. "What the fuck are you doing? I didn't tell you to come in."

"I asked for a check-in, and you didn't give one." A dark laugh echoed from my throat as I shook my head.

"I didn't fucking tell you to come in." I repeated. My concern wasn't with him thinking he could help me, or maybe that's where *some* of my concern was. My issue with him coming in without my asking was that he was about to see me at my most vile; Hansen deserved nothing less than the painful end I had planned for him.

Hunter being here wouldn't make me change my plan, not in the slightest. The only problem I had was that I hadn't planned on showing this side of myself yet, but maybe it would be a good thing. Hunter might actually leave Vince and me alone by his own accord, which would be more ideal than continuing to deal with him.

"What the fuck is going on here?" Hansen asked with a laugh. The man didn't know how deep he was in this. There's no way he'd realised he wouldn't get out of this alive.

"I wish I could tell you, but this wasn't part of the plan," I said as I took a step back from Hansen.

Because Hunter had thrown my beautiful plan out the window, the drug lord was now on edge. His body was tense, primed and ready to fight, which would make him slightly more irksome to take down.

"Did your plan account for my guards?" He asked. I tilted my head to the side as his focus stayed solely on Hunter. Maybe he felt more threatened by the young man with a gun than by me... what a stupid decision to make.

"It actually did, yes," I replied as I looked over at Hunter. He would be the fucking death of me. If he doesn't get me killed, then he'll give me a fucking aneurysm. "I swear, if you shoot that gun and alert said guards, I'll kill you with my bare hands." Maybe he didn't believe that threat because he hadn't seen me do it yet, but that would be remedied shortly.

"I'll only shoot if he tries anything." Great. Just fucking great. This was going absolutely perfectly.

"He won't try anything," I said, maybe a little too confidently, given the situation. "Will you, Hansen?" Finally, the brute of a man turned his eyes back towards me. A sparkle of entertainment graced his dark eyes, almost as if he thought there was a path out of this situation for him. "Instead, you're going to follow my exact instructions. You're going to get the keys that open this cabinet, and then you're going to hand me the statuette that's worth killing for. Cooperate, and it won't live up to it's reputation."

"And what makes you think I'll cooperate with you, little girl?" I took a slow breath to stop myself from prematurely losing control, and busied myself with my dagger. "Do you think I feel threatened by you holding a tiny knife? Or by your boyfriend pointing a gun at me? I've been in worse situations than this before. I survived, and my attackers didn't." Did he just try to threaten me? Was he serious?

"I'm not her boyfriend," Hunter said, as if it made a difference. I rolled my eyes and took another calming breath. Killing Hunter right now was a waste of time and energy, and it wouldn't benefit anyone.

"I'm not a little girl." I drew the attention back to myself—where it should be—and noted the way Hansen stood, so I knew exactly where to strike him. "And you haven't been in a worse situation before, because you've never been stuck in the same room as the Shadow until right now."

"The Shadow?" And here comes the denial of the situation he was in—the reasoning to save his sanity and his semblance of control. "I know Vincent Sinclair, and neither of you are him." Well, for once, my prey made a valid point... neither Hunter nor I were Vince.

"Vincent Sinclair isn't the Shadow, it's just a cover for me, so I'm a little more protected from the Order," I said as I readied myself for my imminent attack.

"And what 'Order' would that be?" Hansen asked, and I smiled in response.

"The Order of Shadows," I answered as I crept towards him. This was the fun part. "They've been looking for me since I slipped away from them eight years ago," I whispered, as if I wanted to keep the secret to myself.

I only gave away my closest secret when I was about to kill someone, because seeing the way terror filled their eyes always sparked some sick joy in me. The method worked once again. Hansen's eyes widened as his entire body went slack.

"The missing experiment..." he trailed off. Good, it was always best when they knew exactly who I was, and not just where I'd come from.

"That would be me."

I lunged and swiped at Hansen, who prevented my attack from hitting his chest by lifting his forearm. Instead of sinking into his heart, the blade ripped into his ulnar artery. Blood pooled on the floor, but it was just a fraction of what would be there when I was done with him.

"Do you know how exhausting it is to constantly have to prove who I am to people?" I asked as I spun the dagger through my fingers.

He jumped at me, and it was all too easy to avoid his punch. The attempted hit swung far too wide and far too slow to have ever had a chance of hitting me. Maybe this was when he'd finally realise who he'd entangled himself with.

"I'll assume that's you saying you don't know," I said before he swung at me again.

This time, I dropped to my knees to avoid the hit and slid in a circle to be positioned behind him. I'd moved too fast for him to even comprehend where I was, and that made the next part of my plan all too easy.

I didn't waste a breath before I sliced through both of his Achilles' tendons in one swipe. He still hadn't noticed where I was as he fell to the ground, which made the move even more satisfying.

"You fucking bitch!" He shouted as he forced himself onto his back.

I wasn't overly sure of what he was trying to do. In my experience, when a target is stuck on the ground with no ability to stand, they were undeniably fucked. Hansen was no different, almost looking like a turtle stuck on it's back.

"Yeah, I'm a bitch, but I'm also a problem. A fucking big one. And I currently have the rare opportunity to avenge an entire group of women who've been hurt and killed. Their killer never faced any kind of consequence. Tell me, how many have you raped and murdered over the last six years?" I asked as I stood up, making sure not to slip in his blood that now coated the marble floor. More would join it still. I wasn't even close to being finished yet.

In a last-ditch attempt at gaining control, he grabbed my ankle, but it was easy to kick him away since he'd grabbed me with his cut arm. And just for good measure, I stood on that hand and pushed until I felt the vibration of his bones as they cracked under the heel of my boot.

"I asked you a question, Hansen, and I want an answer," I said as I dropped my dagger just out of his reach. Fuck, I was going to enjoy this.

"I-I don't know," Hansen replied. It was entertaining to watch him still try to find a way out of the mess he'd put himself in. I'd stall the kill for a moment longer, because this was the part I enjoyed the most; when my prey realised there wasn't a way out alive.

"You raped forty-six women and murdered thirty-two of them. The survivors? They barely made it through what you did to them," I said as I dropped one knee onto his chest and let my entire weight fall onto him, which made it just a little harder for him to breathe. "Do you have any idea what those assaults felt like for them?" He shook his head. Well, at least he was honest.

"So you don't realise the pain you put them through when you punched them in the skull over and over again? That sounds like bullshit to me. It seems more likely that you knew, but didn't care." I fisted my hand as I spoke and slowly turned my focus to my curled fingers. "I'll tell you something, Hansen..."

I glanced up at Hunter to make sure he watched what I was about to do. He'd dropped his arms by his sides, and simply watched me with a slack jaw. Good. I turned back to Hansen.

"I just want you to know that I *do* understand the pain I'm going to put you through. The fact is that I also won't care, nor will I feel a damn shred of guilt about it, because unlike those women... you actually deserve this."

And there it finally was—the look I'd been waiting for. The last piece of hopeful light faded from his eyes, which meant it was time to begin his end.

My first punch landed on his temple, just to be sure he was disorientated and wouldn't do so much as think of fighting back. The second hit his nose, which broke on impact. The third cracked his jaw. And the fourth shattered his eye socket.

Each swing created a new gash. Each hit caused a shock to vibrate up my arms. Each blow fractured his face more and more. Satisfaction grew in me like a flower fed by his blood as it coated my hands and sprayed onto my face. His protests and pleads faded into groans of pain. Those pitiful sounds turned into even more pitiful whimpers.

This was what he deserved, and I would make it last just so he could suffer enough for all the women he'd hurt in his lifetime.

"Caeli, we're running out of time." Hunter's voice shocked me out of the meditative state I had lulled myself into.

I glanced over my shoulder at him and saw a completely blank expression staring back at me. Why couldn't I read him? Why couldn't I tell what he was thinking?

"I never get to have any fun these days," I whispered as I focused back on the slits that were left of Hansen's eyes. "This isn't over, Hansen. You're going to hell, and one day I'll be there too. I'll spend an eternity searching for you in the deepest and darkest circles, and when I find you, you're going to wish you were stuck with the devil instead of me."

So far, I'd pulled my punches. It was the only way to make him suffer for as long as possible, but I didn't need to hold back anymore. I threw one last punch, felt every one of my muscles as I launched it with all the strength I had left, and felt his skull shatter beneath my fist.

Hansen stopped breathing and he no longer shook from pain under my knee.

My plan had been to make it forty-six punches, one for each of the women he'd hurt. The plan had been to pulverise his face before I'd give the mercy of a final blow, to break some ribs and bruise some organs if I got bored. But of course, I wasn't permitted to do what I needed. Because of fucking *time*, I'd only made it to seventeen hits, but that was better than a swift and merciful death.

An icy feeling settled in my stomach. It was heavier than normal and flowed to fill my entire body. Proof again that what I was doing was the right thing, even if I didn't fulfil my ideal kill.

"Where are the keys?" Hunter asked as I slowly stood from my position over Hansen's chest. My knees protested with the movement, having been locked on the same angle for a few minutes too long as I did what had to be done.

"Left pant pocket," I answered.

From my new height I could admire Hansen's destruction in all it's glory. The visual of his battered face wormed it's way into my memory as I picked up my dagger and wiped the blood off it onto my dress. I'd cracked my knuckles open, and they would be bruised in less than an hour, but it was worth it.

"How did you shatter his skull like that?" Hunter asked as he fished the keys out of Hansen's pocket and retreated to a safe distance from me. It was a reasonable question to ask, considering the fact that Hansen looked like he'd been hit with a metal bat instead of a human fist.

"The Order." It was the only answer I had for him. Even if I knew more, I wouldn't tell him, but he didn't need to know that. All I knew was that they had a habit of experimenting on me—that they had attempted to make something out of me—but I had no clue whether the strength was because they'd succeeded or whether it was an addition to their plan.

My answer was enough to end the conversation, so Hunter opened the cabinet and took out the statue. He pushed the golden idol towards me, and I took it in my blood-soaked hand without hesitation. I didn't so much as wipe my hands. There wasn't any point in it.

"We should move," Hunter said. I looked up at him slowly as I nodded and handed the idol back to him. I'd need both of my hands free for what was to come, just in case we came across anyone else who would need to be dealt with.

We walked downstairs to find the mansion empty. Hansen had left with his target for the night, which meant the party was done and the guests had no reason to stay.

Even his guards had left, probably under the assumption that the small woman he'd taken upstairs wouldn't be a problem for him to deal with. They wouldn't discover Hansen until tomorrow morning when they returned to work, with the expectation there'd be a young woman's body to dispose of.

What a surprise they would receive instead.

Hunter and I walked into the kitchen, where Michael was in deep conversation with the owner of the catering company. They both froze when I walked in, most likely taking in the fact I was covered in blood and piecing together for themselves what I'd done.

My eyes settled on the caterer, who now seemed to feel a healthy dose of terror. He had threatened me during the night, told me that if I fell through on my promise and Hansen hurt one of his servers, that he'd send a hitman after me. Maybe he regretted that threat now.

"I hope you got paid before the event, because he won't be able to pay you now," I said as I tucked my dagger away and finally wiped my hands on the front of my dress.

"I always get prepaid." His voice shook as he spoke, and I smiled in response, which no doubt looked terrifying with the blood all over me.

"Smart."

"Did you get what you wanted?" Michael asked, so I shifted my eyes to him.

"Yes," I answered simply. The conversation felt like it was over to me, so I walked towards the door that lead outside and left.

Hunter followed me. I could hear his annoyingly familiar gait behind me as we walked back to the car. There was only silence as I jumped into the driver's seat, and the dried blood on my hands cracked as I took hold of the steering wheel.

"If you say a single word on our drive back, I'll abandon you here in Romania. I don't care what Vince says, or how he'll react. I will never work with you again," I said as I turned on the ignition.

My lips were dry, so I licked them and the metallic tang of blood reached my tongue. Of course, Hansen's blood was on my lips too. It seemed to be everywhere else, so it just made sense.

"What if I think we need to talk about what happened?" Hunter asked, and I looked over at him as he put his seatbelt on.

For some reason, he wasn't afraid of me. The usual tell-tale signs weren't there; the shaking and the avoidance of eye contact. Instead, he simply stared at me, and the weight of it fell right onto my chest. He ran his fingers over his forearm as his lips parted.

Alright, whatever was happening here had to stop. He was meant to be afraid of me, not whatever... not whatever this was.

"I've already had a taste of blood tonight, *Hunter*. I don't think you want me going for more." While I thought the threat might throw him off, or force him to look away from me, he instead licked his bottom lip and I saw a brief flash of his teeth and the piece of gum he was currently chewing on. I swear his canines were slightly longer than they should have been, but if I asked about it, then it would mean admitting that I was paying attention and I'd never do that.

So I turned my focus to the road and drove us back to the hotel. I ignored the fact that he stared at me the entire drive back...

And pretended my body didn't burn under his gaze.

CHAPTER FOURTEEN

HUMANISE ME A LITTLE

"Something's wrong..." I whispered as we walked into our hotel room. The drive had been silent just as I'd requested, but that silence made his fixation on me exceptionally worse. The warmth in my body had only grown during the drive, and at this point, I would do anything to force it to stop.

"What the fuck are you on about?" Hunter asked. He was likely tired, which was unsurprising given the fact it was in the early hours of the morning, or late hours of the night, depending on how you looked at it. The question he'd asked made me freeze, however, and not because of the snapped tone. Vince had never questioned me when I felt that something was wrong. The acidic feeling I got in my stomach had never been wrong before, and he knew to trust it.

"I get these feelings, ranging from ice to acid. They mean different things, but they're always right," I explained.

Our room was painted a forest green—likely meant to create a calming atmosphere—but it had been an overwhelming amount of colour for me. It overloaded my senses and that meant I couldn't check every nook and cranny of the room like I normally would. I was kicking myself for it now. The window was cracked open by two millimetres, as if someone had rushed to close it but ran out of time to make sure it clicked shut.

"Gun, *now.*" I ripped my dagger back out of my boot as I spoke and turned towards the bathroom as I felt the hairs on the back of my neck stand on end.

The acidic feeling in my stomach faded as I found the source of my problems standing in the open door of the bathroom—*fucking Malakai.*

He leaned against the door frame. His eyes took me in as I noted his clothes and weapons. Black shirt and black cargo pants, but no cloak. And also no gun. He wasn't here to take me down, or he'd have a pistol on him. No, he was here for something else. I just had to figure out what.

"I see you got another statue," he said with too much interest. His honey-coloured eyes flicked to Hunter—or to check that the statuette was intact. "And it seems you made a bit of a mess to procure it."

I tilted my head to the side as I took a step towards him.

While I wasn't sure exactly how unhinged I looked in that moment, I knew that the layer of Hansen's blood on me had to make me seem a little more threatening than usual.

"Where's your sister?" I asked as he walked out of the bathroom, completely alone. What an idiot. "Or your bodyguards?" My daily limit of patience had run out on the plane ride to Romania with Hunter. I was so past the point that even killing a rapist and a murderer hadn't been able to fix my sour mood. It was a pity, justified manslaughter normally worked.

"I'm alone," Malakai responded, like it wasn't obvious. If he was alone, then why was he risking a step towards Hunter and the statuette? Maybe because Hunter hadn't taken out that damned fucking gun when I told him to. Fuck, I hoped he realised his mistake.

"Only an absolute moron would come after me alone, Malakai, so I don't believe for a second that you don't have backup on the way." I walked to stand between him and Hunter... or rather between him and the *statuette*.

This was not what I wanted to do tonight. All I wanted was to have a shower and hop into bed, because punching someone seventeen times was more exhausting than it might sound—even if you enjoyed it.

"My Priest has begun my Pilgrimage, so I had to come alone to start with. You want to know what I've been tasked to do?" He asked, and I shook my head.

"I don't think I actually care," I answered honestly.

"I have to take down *Caeli Venatrix* once and for all."

Everything around me froze for a moment as my stomach turned to acid once more. He fucking knew. I schooled my face into a stony expression to cover how I truly felt. He couldn't get the upper hand on me. I wouldn't let him.

"You're making it sound like you would actually be capable of taking me down." It was easy to force my body into a calm state, because he didn't threaten me in the slightest.

I'd honestly expected that he would figure out my identity. He was a part of Templum Gratiae, and they were the organisation with the most resources following the Order. His knowing only turned my stomach because it meant that Templum themselves also knew, and their close relationship with the Order was a threat. It could pose a problem for Vince and me, a fucking big one—especially if Malakai and Templum *always* knew that my alias was bullshit.

"You against all of Templum's resources and men? You don't stand a chance." It was difficult to find a witty response from the deep recesses of my mind. He'd made a point I couldn't argue with, and that was the fact the odds definitely weren't in my favour. This wasn't similar to what I'd done with Hansen, where it was just one man much larger and stronger than me. This was an entire... *shit.*

"Can you count?" Hunter's voice made my body tense. "There's three of us against your precious Templum." *What?* I looked over my shoulder to see Hunter staring directly at me, and I couldn't hide the shock that ran through my veins. Was he really going to stand with me and Vince against fucking *Templum*?

I shouldn't have looked at him though—should never have taken my eyes off Malakai—because the idiot saw it as the perfect opportunity to attack.

There wasn't any time to drop out of the way or block the flying fist that cracked into my face. There was a pause in the room as the air stilled around us, and I gingerly touched my cheek.

While I might have also taken the opportunity if the situation was reversed, it wouldn't have been a mistake on my part. It definitely was for him. He had no weapons on him, which meant he wouldn't be able to beat my retaliation.

I swung my arm in anger, a bold move that he blocked extremely easily, but that's what I wanted him to do. It left his torso open for my actual attack, which was a swing from my left hand that held my dagger. The blade sunk into his stomach, pointed up towards his chest and coming to a stop dangerously close to his lung.

"You asshole," he whispered as if it would offend me.

"Well, at least I stabbed you in the *front*, Malakai." His face twitched in anger, so I ripped the dagger out of his body. With a wound that deep, he surely wouldn't try to attack me. He wasn't *that* stupid. His focus would need to be on doing whatever he came here to do as quickly as possible, or else risk bleeding out in front of me. Normally, I might have toyed with him a bit more, but I'd already had my fill of playing with my prey for tonight.

"The fuck are you talking about?" He asked before he

groaned and moved to hold the fresh wound in his stomach. "You're the one who left me for dead in Brazil, not the other way around." He threw his spare arm to the side for emphasis and I rolled my eyes.

He took a step back from me, but I stalked towards him to keep the same distance between us.

"I didn't leave you for dead, because you weren't alone. You had a plan to take me down back then, too. It was why there were at least five other assassins in our general vicinity at any given point in time. You were going to screw me over..." I trailed off as I tilted my head to the side. "Do you know what happened to the other guy who tried doing that?"

"I imagine he got that wonderful scar he sported at the auction," Malakai said. Of course, he knew Dallas. It made sense, and it made my life easier. His eyes shifted back to Hunter, which was a poor decision to make, but I'd let it slide. I was interested to see where this would go. "Do you see what she's like? She's covered in blood right now, so how did she kill Hansen tonight?" What was the play here? Why speak to Hunter like this? It was exactly how Dallas spoke to him only two nights ago.

"I used my bare hands, like a big girl." My voice was hollow as I narrowed my eyes at Malakai.

Something was going on—something I couldn't put my finger on. The words that Malakai had asked had been purposeful. They had a point. It almost sounded like Malakai was attempting to deter Hunter from working with me, just as Dallas had. Why did either of them care?

"You caved in his skull with a punch," Hunter said, but his voice didn't sound concerned or fearful.

I backed away from my protective stance in front of him to view his body language. It reflected his voice, showing no signs of fear, just as he'd looked at me when I'd killed Hansen in front of him—exactly like when we got in the car and something took a hold over him rather than self-preservation.

Whatever it was... it wasn't what I wanted.

"And you'd risk working with a loose cannon like that? You don't know when she's going to snap. Best-case scenario is if you fuck up, she'll carve into your face and smile while doing it. Worst case? She smashes your skull in," Malakai said. Seriously, what the fuck was going on?

"I think the moral of the story is not to fuck her over, and like I told Dallas at the auction, I don't plan on doing that."

This conversation was purpose built to prevent Hunter from working with me by pulling on his non-existent sense of self-preservation. This visit from Malakai wasn't about taking me down, not yet. His purpose today was to weaken my group, to take away one of my team and attempt to make it easier to destroy me. This was part of a long-term plan, one that was attempting to protect Templum.

"What threat do I pose to Templum?" I asked as I turned my eyes towards Malakai. This would be my focus for now; getting all the information I could from Malakai while he was in my vicinity and severely wounded. I'd figure out the Hunter part of this equation afterwards.

"Do you really think you pose a threat to Templum?" Alright, two could play at this game.

"You said your Pilgrimage is to take me down, but instead of turning up with a gun to kill me, you're trying to dissuade my newest partner from working with me. You're trying to remove me as an obstacle, and Ryne wouldn't waste his time if he didn't feel jeopardised by me." I took the statuette from Hunter's hand and lifted it slightly, just enough to prove that his focus wasn't on me, but on it. "It's because of this, isn't it?"

"You don't know what you're talking about," Malakai replied. He retreated another step from me, his eyes darted around the room. He was uncomfortable, *defensive* even.

"It *is* this. You've barely looked at anything else since we came back, and Hansen said this was worth killing for." I pointed out the evidence that ruled in favour of my theory. "But surely, with all your *resources and men*, Ryne already has one. Surely he's opened it and knows exactly where it leads." I tapped the bloodied idol on my chin and smirked at his slightly widened eyes. "He's trying to remove me as competition because he thinks I have a chance at winning this race. So tell me, what does this lead to that makes it so damned important?"

"It leads to a place of power, *Caeli*." Right, the light threat of him knowing my name. If only that overruled the bullshit that had spilled from his mouth just before it.

"Try again," I said as I threw the statuette back to Hunter. The action was for no other purpose than tricking Malakai into thinking I trusted my new partner.

"I'm serious." Oh, he didn't think I believed that, did he?

I laughed, the sound echoed off the green walls. It was melodic but hollow, and it gained no spark of life as it rebounded back to me. "You've got to be kidding me, Mal. Don't tell me you believe in that conduit bullshit."

"Of course I believe it. My Priest has conduits in Templum, some of them have gone through their incitements." Malakai's eyes flicked towards Hunter before they settled on me again. "I've seen them use their powers. It's all real."

"Hell, I knew they brainwashed you in Templum. I didn't realise they put you through a round of hallucinogenic drugs as well." I rolled my eyes as I spoke.

This was taking too long. I needed to get this dress off and shower. The sensation of dried blood on my skin was affecting my ability to think clearly.

"I know you're sceptical, but the only reason you don't want to believe that conduits exist is because if they do..." he trailed off. This was the moment he'd reveal *exactly* how much he knew. If he did, then I could work out how much danger I was in, how close the Order was working with Templum to find me. "If they are, then you're one as well. That's what they made you for. We got a copy of your file from the Order, and it's why he doesn't want you to follow the clues. If you find this place and go through with your incitement..."

They had my file. They knew *everything*. God, what if this

was a ploy to get me back to the Order? What if they were working with each other? No, surely not. Ryne wouldn't want me to go back to the Order, it would make me a threat to his organisation, because if I was forced back then I would have to go through with an incitement. If it worked...

Malakai had probably said too much, but it was too late for him to take it back. And it wouldn't break me out of my denial. The only way I'd kept myself sane these past eight years was believing that conduits couldn't be real. It was the only option that ended well for me, so I would hold on to it. Until I saw magic with my own two eyes, then it didn't exist. It *couldn't*.

"There has to be something else this leads to, otherwise it wouldn't be so infamous." I tapped my dagger against the side of my leg as I spoke. Maybe it would be best if I just killed him now. It would save me time and energy in the future.

"There's gold, lots of it," Malakai answered. It was a response I liked, so I tucked the dagger back into my boot.

"Excellent, consider me competition then," I replied. I then gestured towards the door. Killing him would create a problem I didn't want to deal with right now. Disposing of a body wasn't how I wanted to finish my night. "Now fuck off, and tell Ryne that if he wants me dead, he's going to have to do better than sending an immature brat after me."

"Coming from you?" He asked as he crept towards the door, wary of Hunter and myself. The colour had slowly leeched from his golden face, and I honestly hoped he'd bleed out before he could get any help.

"Malakai, I'm not an immature brat. I'm just a greedy bitch." I corrected him before I pointed to the door again. "Now get the hell out before I decide to kill you." He did as he was told, and the second he stepped out of the room, I slammed the door behind him.

There wouldn't be much time now, because Malakai wouldn't leave me alone. Not after that fun conversation. No, we had to move.

"Pack your shit. Our location's compromised," I said as I snatched the statuette back from Hunter and shoved it into my duffle bag.

"That was unnecessary," he said, and all I did was glare at him. Maybe I'd acted so well in front of Malakai that Hunter thought I trusted him.

"Just because I wanted Mal to think I trust you doesn't mean I do. It's called acting, American." I broke eye contact because there were more important things that needed my attention than an offended boy. My bag needed to be packed, and I had to find us a new hotel. Although, Hunter was the one who'd have to go into the reception so I could slip through the back. I was still covered in gore and shouldn't be seen by civilians.

"Really? You're going back to calling me that, *Princess*?"

I froze, and when I turned to him, I finally saw what I'd wanted to creep into his eyes from the moment we met. Fear. For a few seconds all I did was stare at him and allow him to feel the heavy weight of my undivided attention.

"This is the second time Malakai has shown up while you've been with me," I pointed out the obvious. It was something that unsettled me, just like the second conversation that had taken place in front of me regarding his allegiance with me. "I don't believe in coincidences, and there is no way he should have known where we were."

"Are you accusing me of something?" He asked, and I just continued to stare at him.

His body went rigid as he realised I was, that I was questioning where his loyalty truly lay. He might have said before that he was on my side, but I knew better than to trust words. All I could trust were actions, because it was harder to lie through them than by simply speaking.

"You know there's another common factor here, right? Two actually." He *surely* wasn't about to do what I thought he would. "You and Vince. He may not be here right now, but he knows where we are. What makes you think it wasn't him?" I laughed again, and the sound was just as hollow as before.

"The fact you just insinuated..." I took a slow breath to calm myself and ran a hand over my ponytail. I had to let the accusation slide, only because he didn't understand how Vince and I worked yet. "You know, when we met, I thought you were one of the intelligent ones. Maybe that assessment was wrong." I zipped up my duffel back and looked at him once more. He should have taken the compliment and apologised, but he didn't.

"Look, you can think whatever you want of me. You

could think I'm the dumbest person on the planet and I wouldn't care. Just use my name and humanise me a little. If you did, you might realise I don't want to get fucked over here, just like you. You don't have to trust me, but you *can* trust that maybe I don't want to die while we look for whatever the fuck it is that we're chasing after." His gold eyes seemed desperate, like they were searching for any kind of empathetic reaction from me. He wouldn't find one.

"You want me to humanise you a little? You want me to use your name?" I asked, and he nodded. Sure, I could indulge his wish, but it wouldn't go the way he wanted. "You want me to use the name you gave me? The one you initially wanted to keep secret for your safety, and then blurted out to Vince? That name? The one I know for a fact is fake? You want me to use *that name*?"

I picked up the duffle bag and threw it over my shoulder. It was safest I did so, because it meant I had an obstacle between me and enacting even more bloody violence for the night.

"Sure, I'll give it a shot. Tell me what you think of this..." I trailed off before I ran my tongue over my bottom lip. "I don't trust you, *Hunter.* Nor do I believe your stories, *Hunter.*"

I crept towards him, my head lowered as I looked at him through my eyelashes. "And if you fuck me over, or if you hurt Vince, *Hunter*, you will end up dead at my feet with a shattered skull, just like Hansen."

His warm eyes turned cold. Good, he finally realised that this wasn't just some fun field trip for us. This was business, and my business was doing whatever it took to get whatever I wanted, and I had yet to fail at it.

"Do you understand me, *Hunter*?"

"You need to learn to trust people, Caeli." Even though his eyes were colder than before, they never strayed from mine.

For a brief second, I looked to his lips *again*, and saw them parted like they'd been in the car. Why did I keep doing that? Especially when we were closer than we should be?

"I do trust people," I told him as I levelled my head once more and noticed his hand move to run along his forearm *again*. "That trust is just reserved for the people who don't fucking lie to me."

Chapter Fifteen

IF YOU SAY SO, BROOKLYN

I was bored, to say the very least. The deal wasn't going as smoothly as I'd planned, and that was probably why I was distracted.

My eyes drifted away from the man across the booth from me in this questionable bar. Instead I turned my attention to the news playing above the wall of bottled alcohol. The current report was on a brutal murder in Romania, where the only way they'd been able to identify the victim was through the tattoos on his body.

They weren't sure what the motive was behind the murder of Richard Hansen, since the only thing missing from his mansion was a small statuette. The police had no leads, and judging by their expressions and carefully chosen words, they wouldn't be working too hard to find any.

Hansen got away with too much because of his wealth, and *whoever* had killed him was more likely to get a pat on the back from law enforcement than be arrested.

"American, your attention seems a little divided," Dmitri said, probably noticing the smirk on my face. I dragged my eyes back to the man sitting across from me. Maybe I should have felt a little more threatened by the fact we were in the Russian mobster's favourite bar. Instead, I felt rather comfortable, like I had control of the situation. It was probably because Caeli's dominating confidence had finally rubbed off on me. It was about damn time.

"I'm getting tired of your games, Dmitri, and your empty threats..."

I shuffled in my seat so I could pick my feet up and rest them on the corner of the table. It felt like something Caeli would do, as a bit of a power move, so it should work for me as long as I kept channelling this false bravado. I then pointed to the screen and ignored the look of disgust on Dmitri's face.

"Do you know who did that?" I asked, and he looked over his shoulder to see the report that was finishing up on Hansen's murder. When he looked back at me, he had a furrowed brow, like he didn't know what significance the murder had to him. Well, he was about to find out.

"Hansen was competition, so why the fuck would I care?"

"Because I know who it was." I crossed my arms over my chest and decided to continue pushing the situation. There was a timeline I had to stick to, so we had to speed this up, and I had to pull my best work out of my ass to close this deal. "Do you know why they call me the Shadow?"

"What is this? A fucking pop quiz?" Okay, I'll ignore that simply because I didn't have the time to deal with it. Caeli was expecting me in Romania by nightfall, and I was cutting it close to make it on time.

"They call me that because death follows me, as close as my own shadow. Very few people know this, but it's not luck. I have someone who watches over me and cleans up my messes," I said as I took my feet off the table and leaned my elbows onto the sticky surface.

It was a move I'd hoped to avoid because of the questionable tabletop, but I had to do everything I could and this was all I had left in my arsenal. Well, that and the ability to stare into people's souls with my *unnervingly blue eyes*. So I did both, it was the best option I had.

"That person murdered Hansen, and she did it because he hurt and killed tens of women she'd never even met before. What she did, it wasn't personal, but she still caved his head in. What do you think will happen to the people who kill her father?" I asked, my eyebrows pinched at the hypothetical I'd posed.

It was something I'd often wondered; how she might avenge me if I died. The thoughts usually made me nauseous, but I needed that right now. Dmitri had threatened to kill me if I didn't take his lowball offer, so it was time to pull out the Caeli card.

131

"You're bluffing, old man." *Old man*? I was only three years older than this asshole, and I had far less grey hairs.

"Am I?" Once again, I didn't have time to say what I wanted to. I had to get straight to the point so I could get out of Russia. "I think she'd take a few days with whoever kills me, just so she could inflict as much pain as possible. She once told me that she's never skinned anyone alive before. I think she might give it a try... if she can't come up with a new way to kill someone that's slower and even more painful."

I picked up the photos of the artefacts I'd been trying to sell to Dmitri; I had to put more pressure on him to get him to fold.

"I do not take lightly to threats," he said, and I nodded my head.

"Neither do I, so I'm going to leave." I folded the pictures into my folder. "You clearly don't want to take this deal. So, what I'm going to do is walk out that door, and you won't come after me or try killing me or anything along those lines. We both know you'll let me go because you've heard the stories of what's happened to the people who've hurt me in the past. You don't want to end up like them, or possibly worse." I stood up from the booth and took two steps.

"Wait." Dmitri's voice echoed around me, and it confirmed that Caeli's confidence had indeed rubbed off on me since I didn't feel the least bit intimidated.

"Yes?" I asked in a bored tone as I slowly looked towards him.

"One million." That was hardly better than the original

offer he made me.

"We're talking about a cache of items that belonged to the Romanov family. These things should be in a damned museum like the one we took them from, and you want to pay one million for them? No. It's one and a half or there's no deal," I said like there was a choice in the matter for Dmitri.

"Fine, one and a half million US dollars."

I smirked as I shook my buyer's hand. "Once you make the wire transfer, then I'll get the items dropped on your doorstep." I let go of his hand and walked out of the bar. My smirk grew into a smile as I moved.

I still had it.

After I made the drop of the Romanov items. I made my way to Romania, reaching the hotel address Caeli had sent to me. Apparently, they'd had to move after a surprise visit from Malakai... I'd never really liked that kid.

"Please tell me everything's okay," I said as I walked into the overly sterile hotel room. The awfully *quiet* hotel room. Well, the lack of arguing meant one thing and one thing only.

"She's gone for a walk," Hunter said. Yep, that's what I thought.

"I'll take it things went well last night then," I said sarcastically as I dropped my bag on the ground. It was best to wait for Caeli to come back. I could be patient, and knowing her, she could be gone for a few minutes or a few hours. She'd take as much time as she needed to calm down, and the duration would depend on how badly Hunter had screwed up.

"If by 'well' you mean it went to shit, then yeah." Hunter was seated at the small table in the room, his eyes locked on his phone screen. "Does she do this often?" He asked as he looked up at me.

"Well, I do have a habit of pissing her off without intending to..." I said as I sat across from the kid. "So, the answer to your question would be *yes*. She definitely does this often."

"Great," Hunter replied. His voice was a little quieter than usual, his back a little more slouched.

"It's a good sign. It means she doesn't want to kill you. Instead of launching into violence, she's giving herself time to breathe, to calm her body down and cool her anger," I explained, but Hunter lifted an eyebrow and tilted his head to the side. "It also means that she cares about whatever happened. If she didn't then she wouldn't be angry."

"So I should be happy because she's angry at me but isn't actively trying to kill me?" Hunter asked. I narrowed my eyes and crossed my arms in front of my chest.

"Trust me, they're both good signs," I confirmed his assumption. There were a few moments of silence as Hunter nodded before he looked back at his phone screen. "What happened last night?"

"She killed Hansen-"

"Yeah, I know that. I saw a news report while doing business today," I cut the kid off, and Hunter nodded again. Whatever happened last night had to be severe for her to still be walking it off, but it couldn't have been unforgivable, or Hunter wouldn't be breathing right now. Very few options toed that line, but I knew the border well.

"She punched him sixteen times before she caved in his skull. I just don't understand how she's that strong. She said it was to do with the Order, but..." Hunter trailed off before he let out a sigh and put his phone down.

So Caeli had told him about the Order. That was either a good thing for us, or it was a sign she'd kill him. There was absolutely no in between for that.

"Look, Caeli is... she's an enigma. Even she doesn't know everything about who she is or what she's capable of, and she especially doesn't know the *why*," I told him and Hunter just stared at me, clearly waiting for me to continue. "They kept information from her and never explained what they were doing, they just did it. It's not my place to say what she's gone through, just know that they ingrained violence in her from a young age. Did she tell you how old she was when they made her go through with her first kill?" I asked as I placed my crossed arms on the table in front of me. I kept my eyes on Hunter, who shook his head.

"She didn't tell *me* anything. I was just there when she told Hansen that she's their missing experiment or something." Right, that made more sense than her willingly handing information over.

135

"She was nine when they first told her to fight to the death against another kid they had. There was a small group of them, and they were labelled by a hierarchy of numbers instead of named. Whoever they thought had the most promise was called One, and so on. It changed weekly." I wasn't sure which part of her history was most horrific, but that was definitely near the top. "By the time she turned fourteen, she'd killed the other seven kids in her group because it was them or her. It was all a test, because she was the only one that they had *made*. The others were just orphans, and they were used specifically to fuck with her head when she had to kill them." God, I did not mean to say that much, but it was too late to take it back now.

"Am I supposed to believe that?" Ah, *denial*. I've already gone through that stage. "How do you know she wasn't lying when she told you that? That she wasn't trying to get your sympathy?" Hunter asked, to which I smiled a sad smile. That had been my immediate thought when she finally told me what she remembered of the Order a few years back, but I also immediately realised she was telling the truth.

"Two reasons. The first... if you've looked into her eyes, then you've seen the darkness there, similar to yours," I said. He seemed a little shocked that I had picked up on it, on the torment he kept hidden behind his bright exterior. "They did a number on her, so whatever she tells me, I'm going to believe because I doubt anyone would make that shit up." And was I really going to tell him reason number two? Caeli might actually kill me if I did, but that could only happen if she ever found out. "Reason number two is something you can never tell her about."

"Okay..." Hunter sat up straighter in his seat, seemingly very intent on listening to what I was about to say.

Well, here goes nothing.

"Caeli has a tell when she lies. It's how I know when she's trying to cover something up." Yeah, I really was about to tell him. God, I hoped I was right about trusting this kid. "The tell is similar to when she gets anxious, but there's a difference between the two. You might have already noticed if you've been paying attention to her," I said as I looked at my hands.

"When she's anxious or panicking, her hands run over these same movements." I showed the memorised movements as I spoke. "They're understated, but they're the same each time. It's the result of some kind of training from the Order. She's never told me what it's for." I'd seen her perform the same circles and shapes countless times in the eight years we'd been by each other's sides.

"And lying?" Right.

"It's a little more understated, but it's still her hands. Instead of the circles, she hits her pressure points. It can be pressing her fingertips together, clenching her fist..." The kid leaned back in his seat, his jaw slack. So, he could recall a point in time when she did that. "When did she do it?"

"Lima..." Hunter looked at his own hands. "She curled her fingers before she implied we had a deal." That made sense.

"She likes to think she has the upper hand on everyone,

137

and for the most part, she's right. But once you know her, she's extremely easy to read and understand. Give it some time. It took six months before she gave me a name to call her," I explained. Hunter nodded as he relaxed in the chair. Good.

"What did you call her for six months?" The kid asked with a smile. God, what did I call her? Pretty much all the things I still called her.

"Kid, kiddo..." I trailed off as I tried to compile the others. "Little Demon, little *Heathen* and after a couple months, I started calling her little Shadow. She was always a step behind me, just like my shadow."

"So that's where that name comes from," Hunter said, to which I nodded. "I thought it was because she disappeared into the shadows, not as a result of some..."

"Childhood nickname?" I asked with a smile.

The mystery behind the name was part of the reason that Caeli liked it. No one aside from us, and now Hunter, knew that it was because of how she used to follow me around, almost attached to my side.

God damn it, I was going to regret spilling all of this information if Hunter turned out to be exactly what Caeli thought he was. Something in my gut told me that we could trust him, though.

"This is what I'm saying. You don't know her yet, but her constant paranoia is warranted." I said. "I understand that there's a lot to take in, but if she's gone on a walk to cool off, then is warming up to you. She's violent, but that's how they made her. And not that she would want you to know, but she deeply cares about her people and is extremely protective of them. Give her some time. Maybe she'll become protective of you, too."

"If you say so, Brooklyn." Hunter replied, which made me smile. So not only had I closed what should have been a failed deal, I'd also succeeded with getting this kid to trust me a little more... today was turning out to be a damned good day.

"I do say so, Rookie."

Chapter Sixteen

WOULD YOU LIKE TO DO THE HONOURS?

Maybe I should have expected that Hunter and Vince would have a heart to heart while I was out for a walk; but it was still a shock to see them sitting across the table from one another when I came back. Instead of making a scene or being dramatic, I stalked over to the table and sat with them. There wasn't much point in expressing how much I distrusted Hunter. Or that last night had only made that feeling worse. Both of them already knew the extent of my feelings.

For the moment, it was best to just go with the flow of whatever Vince threw at me and deal with the issues when

140

they arose.

"So what do you think is inside this thing?" Vince asked as I placed the statuette on the tabletop. I'd taken the damn thing with me on my walk, because there was no way I would leave it alone with *Hunter*.

"Hansen said it's got a reputation—that it's worth killing for," Hunter said.

"Malakai said it leads to a place of power and a lot of gold," I added. I looked away from the statuette and turned to Vince, who nodded his understanding.

"So we're thinking it's important then," he said. I rubbed a hand over my face and nodded. *Important* was an understatement, considering the fact this was the third time I'd stolen one of these fucking things, and it would be the first time we'd see the contents of it.

I was getting tired though, and maybe that was the reason I'd stopped caring about what happens.

I didn't get enough sleep the night before. After we arrived at the new hotel and Hunter got us a double room, I snuck in without being spotted and immediately jumped into the shower fully clothed. It was easier, by that point, because the dress was stuck directly to my skin on account of all the dried blood.

I'd spent an hour under the cold water, peeled the dress from my skin and scrubbed myself raw. It was a pitiful attempt at scouring the sensation of Hansen's hands on my body out of my memory, and so far, it hadn't worked.

It was why—after that failed shower—I'd stared at the

141

ceiling with my damp hair in a braid under my head. I'd laid there for hours, with my comfiest jumper and sweatpants on, and my headphones playing music on full blast so I could pretend Hunter wasn't in the room with me.

But even as I sat at the table, I still felt the ghost of Hansen's fingers run down my back, rub my neck and grope me. I could feel his lips on my ear and hear his voice echo in my head. Maybe he'd decided to haunt me for killing him—to torment me for the rest of my days. I doubted that one, but it sounded better than the other option I was left with.

"Would you like to do the honours?" Vincent asked. His voice shook me from my thoughts and drew me back to the present.

Apparently, while I'd been lost in my own thoughts, I'd pulled my knees onto the chair and had hugged them against my chest. Even wearing leggings and a sweater wasn't enough to help me feel comfortable...

"Sure," I whispered as I corrected my sitting position and took the statuette back in my hands. I held it just like the first one, with the top in one hand and the bottom in the other, before I smashed it onto the edge of the table. It fell perfectly in half like the other one had, but this time, an object fell in my lap.

"What is that?" Hunter asked as I picked it up.

"A wax seal press," I answered as I inspected it. What the fuck did this have to do with anything? I looked at the detailed end, but even my eyes couldn't tell exactly what was going on with it.

"Is there a candle in the bathroom?" Vince asked, and I thought about it for a second before I nodded. There was a small scented candle, one that I had stared at while standing under the cold water of the shower. It was the only colour in the room, a bright pink compared to the white of the tiles and towels.

Vince retrieved it before he lit the wick, and Hunter went to find some paper. I stayed still, staring blankly at the broken statue and the wax seal press.

I ached all over. My stomach was almost healed from the self-inflicted wound I'd made a few days ago, my cheek throbbed from Malakai punching me last night, my knuckles were bruised and cracked open from the punches I'd dealt Hansen and then there was the constant chill from the memory of his touch.

"Alright, let's see what this seal press is going to show us," Vince said once there was enough melted wax in the candle jar to pour.

He tipped it onto the paper that Hunter had already placed on the table and I pressed the seal down. We let it sit for a few seconds before I lifted it and took in what was left behind.

"Shit," I whispered as I observed the image in front of me. Hunter jumped up to look at it over my shoulder, and I felt his warm exhale over my neck.

"It's the seal for the Vatican Archives," Hunter said and I looked up at Vince, who had furrowed his brow.

"I'm sorry, what?" He asked before he ripped the piece of paper off the table so he could inspect it closer. "Holy shit."

"What would the Vatican have to do with this?" Hunter asked, but I didn't have an answer for him. How could I?

"Do you know what information is in the Archives?" I asked. My eyes flicked to Hunter before I gently took the piece of paper back from Vince. I needed to investigate the other little symbols involved in the seal's design, because something didn't feel right.

"I think the real question is what's *not* in the Archives." Well, that didn't even begin to answer my question. "There's over fifty miles of shelves there. Just knowing that's our heading is nowhere near enough to know what to look for."

"There's the initials A.L. in the details here and the year 1600 here." I pointed to it as Hunter leaned over my shoulder once more, just to check I was telling the truth.

"Well, that could mean anything. It could be an entire century-"

"It couldn't," I cut him off as I looked up at him. He waited patiently for me to continue, which was odd. What had Vincent said to him while I was gone? "You go to all of this effort to make these statuettes with seal presses inside of them, with details of a year obscured within the notches in it... the people who made these knew that the Archives have *fifty miles* of shelves."

"Fifty-three if you want a specific amount." Damn, that's a lot of shelves.

"Well, my point still stands. You don't bother making

something like this if you don't want people to find what you're directing them towards. Whatever we're looking for has to be specifically from the year 1600, otherwise there was no point including the information. It has to be specific because it would be a miracle to find the right thing in fifty miles of shelves in the first place," I explained my theory. Hunter nodded in response.

"Okay, but that might not help us too much, either. That point in time was during the Spanish Conquests, the amount of information and letters and reports from that year alone..."

Why could these things never be easy? "How hard is it to get into the Archives *legally*?" I asked, since apparently Hunter knew everything about the damned place.

"It takes years of interest and specific documentation and other shit we don't have time for. It'll be easiest to just break in."

I didn't believe in a god, but if one existed, then whatever I was about to do would likely piss that god off. "Okay, I guess we're heading to Vatican City then," I said as I looked over at Vince, who nodded slowly.

Well, having a vague heading was better than nothing. Even if we had no idea what the fuck we'd be looking for once we arrived.

The hairs on the back of my neck stood up, and while I'd brushed the feeling off before as a part of Hansen's ghost, something told me it wasn't. This was for something else entirely. I looked over my shoulder at the wall opposite us, and was immediately drawn to the framed artwork on the wall.

"That fucking *brat*," I said as I stood up and walked over to it. There was a small dot on the frame, one that shouldn't have been there.

"Caeli, what are you-" Vince was cut off by the sound of my fist hitting the frame, right over the reflective dot. "Jesus, kid, what the fuck?" I didn't even need to look at him to know he was likely rubbing his forehead, but his disappointment didn't matter. Not when the frame fell to the ground in pieces and I could pick up the remnants of a camera the size of my thumbnail that had been imbedded in it.

"He's been watching us," I breathed.

How had I not noticed it before? Was it there last night while I was still reeling from the events that had preceded our arrival here? Or had it been placed during the day when I was walking and Hunter had clearly left the room unattended?

"Malakai?" Hunter asked, and I nodded my head. "We should find a new hotel-"

"No." I cut him off, and he immediately froze midway between the table and his bag. My response had clearly shocked him, as well as Vince who looked at me with a furrowed brow. "If they've been watching us, then they've had plenty of time to attack. This wasn't about getting us here for an ambush. This was to make sure we got the clue and would push ahead. They'll be waiting for us at the Archives."

This entire situation was getting more and more confusing by the day.

"So what do we do?" Hunter asked. *We*? Had I mislead him?

"*I* tread carefully, and quietly. *I* get in and out without leaving a trace. *I* find whatever it is we're searching for and get out again before they even know I'm there," I replied. Vince shook his head, so I prepared myself for the argument he was about to give.

"You're not going in alone, kid." I took a deep breath and looked up at the ceiling. Hunter hadn't told him everything about last night. That was the only reason he was fighting this. It had to be. "If there's that many shelves, then you'll need another set of eyes."

"Hunter's going to get in my way. The chances of being spotted are going to climb astronomically if I have someone following my every step." I fought back as I crushed what was left of the camera in my hand.

"But they know you're coming," Hunter interjected, like I wanted to hear his voice. "They'll be working specifically to catch you, so it might be best to have a second set of hands." Fucking hell, there was no way in hell I'd actually be able to keep working with this idiot.

"And you want me to bring you along? So you can ignore me and fuck us over like you did last night?" I asked, as I stalked towards him.

"Ground rules..." I whispered, and he looked down at me with a tired look in his eyes. Maybe he got as little sleep as

I did last night. Good. "I made three fucking ground rules, and you agreed to them. The bar was so god-damned low I thought three would be reasonable for you to keep track of, but you broke one less than five hours after you agreed to them!"

He didn't say anything, but I desperately wanted him to. I wanted someone I could shout at and not feel guilty about it. If I could take out everything I felt on him, then maybe I could move forwards. Maybe it could help ease the acid in my stomach. Maybe it could help stop the phantom touches I felt all over my body. But I couldn't be guilt-free if he just sat there and took it. I needed him to give it back... why wasn't he giving it back?

"You made your three rules, and I didn't break one of them. You... you fucking broke rule three; *do what I say when I say it.* I told you I would give you an emergency signal if I needed you, but I didn't give one. I didn't want or need your god-damned 'help'. What I needed you to do was stay out of my way, and you still came in with a fucking gun pointed at Hansen like that would help anything!" Something sat in his eyes that I couldn't understand, something that I couldn't explain, and didn't have the energy to work out.

"I get that you're angry, but-"

"Angry? I'm fucking *livid.* There is no excuse for what you did!" I cut him off again. Fuck, I needed someone to fight against, and he was not helping. *This* wasn't helping. "You wanted me to never break a promise. You wanted me to be honest and never manipulate you again. And yet somehow you think it's okay for you to go against your word? You absolute fucking hypocrite." I hissed.

The air around me became too heavy to breathe, but he didn't need to know the struggle was because I was overwhelmed. He didn't need to know that shouting at him wasn't helping a god-damned thing and that there was a blossoming pain in my chest.

"I never would have done that to you," I told him, not caring about the way his eyes were turning red in front of me. "If you say you can handle something, then I expect you can handle it. I would never risk going in and screwing up an entire plan that could've ended with you or me dead. I never would have kept my gun in it's holster and given our enemy the chance to punch you in the fucking face!"

Why couldn't I fucking breathe?

"You're the one who can't fucking fight to save their life, and you thought you could fucking help-" I choked on my words as that pain in my chest stole the last of the air from my lungs.

"You could have *killed* us, and yet you want to face *Templum* with me? You want to help me fight fucking assassins who would be so much worse than Hansen, like you would be of any benefit to me? All you'll do is weigh me down and get us shot!"

I coughed as my body tried everything it could to suck in some air, and I clenched a hand over my sternum. The world around me spun.

Shit, I was going to pass out.

Chapter Seventeen

WELL-DIRECTED ANGER

"Okay, Hunter, I got another room when I came here. You can stay in that for the night." I heard Vince say as I ripped my focus from Hunter. Why were there tears sitting in his eyes? Why did none of this make fucking sense?

"I didn't..." Hunter trailed off as I turned towards the wall, my hand over my mouth to stop any desperate sounds that would leave my lips as I struggled to stay upright.

"Just go. We'll talk in the morning."

I wrapped my arms around my chest, squeezing myself as I heard the door open and shut behind me.

"Caeli, we're okay." Vince's calm voice reached my ears through the haze, but it didn't help to ease the pains in my body. "We're okay, kid. We're safe, we're okay." I barely felt his hands touch my shoulders, was hardly aware of him directing me to sit on the edge of my bed. "We're going to be okay. Everything is going to be okay."

The air continued to become thicker around me, and I felt like I would throw up.

"Vince," I whispered out his name.

"Hands on the back of your head, head between your knees." He said as he helped me into the position. "Now just think about your breathing, okay? In and out."

He knelt on the ground next to me and rubbed my back in perfectly timed circles, circles that told me how long to inhale, hold my breath, and exhale for. "We're going to be okay. You've just had a lot happen at once. It's okay to feel overwhelmed, but the feeling will pass. We'll be okay."

It took close to eight minutes to feel like I wouldn't pass out, to get my breathing back under my control.

By that point, I was upright again, tucked against Vince's side and under his protective arm. This had only happened because I was close to him again, because I felt secure enough with him in the room that my body finally let go of the bottled emotions from last night.

"What happened?" He asked, and I was far too exhausted to even think up a jab about Hunter and why he hadn't filled Vince in himself.

"The plan... and then *not* the plan," I whispered as I rubbed a hand over my aching chest. "I knew what would happen when I targeted Hansen. The best way to get close without killing him immediately was to pretend I was his ideal prey, so that's what I did. He started touching me, and just like normal, all my negative emotions instantly became anger and I didn't understand what I actually felt until after the fact. The plan worked, though, and I was drawing my dagger when Hunter turned up."

"Okay, but this isn't just because he turned up." Of course, Vince could tell this was more than just anger at being disrespected by Hunter.

"I didn't want him to see what I had to do to get Hansen with his guard down. Not only was I absolutely disgusted with Hansen, I was... I was embarrassed because he walked in while Hansen had a hand on my ass and his lips on my ear." My body shivered at the thought, and all Vince did was squeeze me against him even more.

"And Hunter watched as I killed Hansen, and *you* haven't seen me lose my shit like I did last night. But he didn't react like he should have. He should have yelled at me to stop, or acted like I was doing something wrong. Instead he kept calm and made sure I didn't take too long." I still didn't understand what that meant, why he'd been so *okay* with what I'd done.

"Right, and what happened after that?"

"We took the idol, came back to the hotel and fucking Malakai..." I trailed off before I forced myself to take another breath. "I told Hunter to take out his gun because I had a gut feeling, but he didn't listen. So I put myself between him and Malakai since he's fucking useless and he had the statuette. Then Malakai fucking punched me after Hunter said he was one of us. Malakai hit me because I was distracted by Hunter, and that happened because he hadn't taken out his gun when I told him to."

"And then you found the camera, and I implied you should let Hunter help you." Vincent summarised my tipping point. I looked up at him and saw the clear regret on his face, but this wasn't his fault.

It was all on fucking Hunter.

"What if Malakai had drawn a knife? And what if he'd gone for my neck? What if Hansen had a fucking gun while he was that close to me and Hunter spooked him? He promised he'd listen and do as I told him. He didn't and I could have died *twice* last night because of it."

I wouldn't ever say it out loud, but in those moments I'd felt pure terror and masked it perfectly with well-directed anger.

"Then he's done." I tensed at his words. "We agreed that the moment he fucked up that he was gone, I would say that's a couple of huge fuck-ups."

"I thought you liked him as an option to expand our little operation with..." I whispered. For some reason, my gut twisted, almost in protest of where the conversation was going.

"Yes, and then I talked to him before you came back from your walk. I told him about your history and he didn't so much as give me the courtesy of telling me what actually happened last night." Vince told Hunter about my past? Why was I not angry about that? I should have been, because it wasn't his place to tell people about what happened to me. Was I not upset because Hunter hadn't looked at me any differently? "He risked everything I have left, so he's done."

I couldn't stop the hot tears that rolled down my face. This was what I wanted, the opportunity to show that Hunter wasn't suited to work with us and that we couldn't trust him. I'd wanted him gone. But if what I wanted was going to happen, why did my stomach feel like acid instead of ice?

"Vince..." I sat upright and looked at the man who had become my father over the last eight years. He was my only family, the only person in the world that I actually trusted...

"You need to learn to trust people, Caeli."

I could not believe that I was about to do this.

"He never looked at me with fear," I whispered, which likely made it obvious how unsure I was about my decision.

"That's great, but he almost got you killed," Vince replied. Fuck, I could *not* believe that I was about to argue in the American's favour.

"You've done that before." Holy shit. This felt beyond wrong, but the acidic feeling in my stomach was fading, so it had to be right. Some part of me wanted to be wrong about Hunter, wanted him to *not* be the person I thought he was. "You got me shot in the shoulder two years into our partnership. If it had been a two inches to the right..." he let out a slow breath.

"I was stupid back then, and I've learned from my mistakes," he replied as he rubbed his eyebrow.

"Look, I can't believe I'm about to say this just as much as you can't believe you're about to hear it but... if he apologises, then maybe he could keep working with us." I kept my eyes trained on him, just to prove I wasn't bluffing.

There was silence in the room for a few moments, and my hands twisted through their familiar motions. Vince's hand fell from his eyebrow to rub his entire face. Maybe I needed an extra push.

"Two strikes, he has two strikes. If he swings and misses again..." Baseball. All I had to do was involve baseball, the one sport he'd tricked me into caring about.

"Three strikes and he's out?" He asked, and I nodded. "Well, you're the one who could have died, so I guess it's up to you. But from here on out, I'll be treading even more carefully around him."

The acidic feeling in my stomach finally cooled, and I gave a quiet smile in response. Fuck, I hoped this wasn't going to end badly for us.

CHAPTER EIGHTEEN

SUDDEN COMRADERY

"Okay, I'm thinking this time we definitely need code words." Hunter's voice forced me to roll my eyes.

That morning, after the events of the night before, Hunter had come to mine and Vince's room unprompted. He'd apologised, admitted that he'd screwed up and said he assumed our partnership was over.

When I'd told him he would get one last chance, he'd seemed far too relieved to be normal, and bought Vince and me coffee as a gesture of his gratitude. It was something I appreciated, because even though I had slept like a baby after my exhausting events the night before, I was still beyond exhausted.

I was too drained to actually want to deal with his bullshit, but I couldn't blame Vince for being stuck with Hunter anymore. This was completely my decision, and I would have to live with that moving forwards.

"You and your fucking code words," I whispered. My eyes flicked around, on watch for any kind of movement and any evidence that we were being followed.

We'd spent the day flying to Italy, making a plan for the night, getting into Vatican City, and—specifically for me—staying as far away from Hunter as possible. While I appreciated his apology, I was still working out exactly how to feel about him, and until now, just pretending he wasn't around me had worked.

But now we were stuck by ourselves, and I was no longer capable of blissful ignorance.

We walked through the Vatican gardens, where we'd stayed hidden during the day so they could lock us in with the residents of the city. I had no doubt this place was beautiful to see during the day, but the visit had consisted of finding a place to hide rather than taking time to admire the sights.

"Hey, if we'd actually set a code word for danger, I might not have stormed in on you and Hansen." His tone seemed slightly playful, but I didn't care. "Too soon?" He asked, and I looked over at him.

Fuck, was that really his attempt at a joke? It was pitiful.

"No, it's just... *stormed* might be too strong of a word for what you did." I told him, and his eyes widened for a second.

"Are you joking around with me?" He asked. I didn't give

anything away on my face to impart any form of comfort to him. "Okay, well, if you won't answer that question, tell me what's the worst that'll happen if we set some code words." I didn't answer that question either. I had to reserve some of my energy for stupid questions for the rest of the night, which was far from over. "Maybe we could use eye colours."

Since when was a lack of an answer a form of agreement? I ran a hand over my face and sighed. The 'ignoring' tactic wasn't working, so maybe it was best to just fall to this whim and get the conversation over with as soon as possible.

"So what would the actual code words be, then?" I asked, and he nearly vibrated with excitement next to me.

"Well, if I was talking to you, then I would use your eye colour. So if I was safe then I would work *silver* into my sentence, but if I was in danger, then I would say *grey*," he explained.

"You realise they're the same colour, right?" I asked as I looked briefly at the Eagle Fountain before I checked the roofs of the buildings in front of us. Empty. If Templum were supposed to be waiting for us here, where were they all?

"No, they're not. Silver has a depth to it, a brightness. Grey is just grey." Yeah, that totally made sense.

"What would I use for talking to you, then?" I asked.

This conversation had already taken longer than I thought it would. It should have been easy enough to pick a single word and be done with it, but of course, it had to be convoluted. From what little I knew of Hunter, overcomplicating things seemed on brand for him.

"Well, I like to think my eyes are golden brown, so maybe *gold* for safety. *Hazel* could be for danger." The self-compliments also seemed on brand, so I'd let them slide without comment. My primary concern was how he thought the word *hazel* could be easily slipped into a sentence.

He then grabbed my shoulder for a moment out of excitement, but immediately let go again once my focus landed on his hand. "And Vince could be like *azure* for safety and *sapphire* for danger." Seriously, how did he think we'd be able to slip these words into casual conversation?

"Once again, you do realise that they're the same colour?" I asked, and I swear I felt the patience I'd rationed for the night slip out of my grasp.

"No, sapphire is darker and Vincent doesn't have dark eyes. They're quite bright, actually." Oh, for fuck's sake, did he never shut up? "Azure is the perfect shade for his eyes."

"Great, now that we got the important stuff out of the way, could we focus on the minor issue of how quiet it is?" I asked as I looked at our surroundings once more.

There wasn't a single soul outside, and it felt so extremely *wrong* to me, but my stomach filled with familiar ice. We were on the right path.

"It's Vatican City. It's going to be quiet," Hunter pointed out, but I shook my head. Sure, it should be quiet, but not like this. And sure, Templum knew how to obscure themselves in the shadows just like I did, but they couldn't hide from *me*. That much I knew from experience.

"There's no security, and we haven't seen any Templum

assassins yet," I said, which prevented him from saying another word. I had a point, and he couldn't argue against it.

We crept towards the library, but even inside, there wasn't a damned soul to be seen—or maybe that should have been a *holy* soul.

"Why's there no security?"

"They have their faith in God, I guess..." Hunter said, and the patience I'd already run out of gave a shuddered breath of ultimate death.

"Everything in the archives would be worth too much to just leave it up to God. Not having any security implies that Templum is definitely here, but..." *oh.* They were here. They were just all where I wanted to be. "Shit."

"What?"

"They're all down in the archives, and likely focused around whatever we need to find. It's exactly what I would do to keep something out of someone else's hands." I pulled out my daggers as I spoke, and immediately ran down the stairs we needed to take to get into the tunnels.

"Are you serious?" Hunter asked. I shook my head and dusted off the front of my black long-sleeved shirt.

"Oh, *no*, I'm kidding around." The blunt sarcasm wasn't lost on Hunter, which was helpful. Sometimes I wasn't obvious enough, and it slipped over Vincent's head.

"You know, I do like this comradery you've suddenly whipped out for me," he said. He was less than two steps behind me, but his weren't the only ones I could hear. "It's almost as if-"

"Shut up," I hissed as I pointed a dagger at him.

With us frozen at the bottom of the stairs, I could clearly hear the other footsteps getting closer to us. Shit. We had two options, and they were to hide or to kill whoever was coming towards us.

It felt a little early in the night for murder, so I looked for a decent hiding place, but there weren't many options. We'd either have to book it up the stairs again and do so quietly so we weren't caught, or risk the door a couple of steps down the hallway. It was likely a cleaner's closet, and that meant having to be in close proximity to Hunter.

So my choice was being stuck far too close to him or risk being found early and killed. This was a tough choice.

Those damned footsteps sped up.

"Damn it," I whispered.

I tucked one dagger away and grabbed the front of Hunter's shirt to pull him behind that door with me. My guess had been right, it was a fucking cleaner's closet, but there wasn't a damned thing I could do about it now. I'd made my choice, now I'd have to live with it.

Before he had the chance to say a fucking word, I slammed my empty hand over his mouth, and quietly pulled the door closed behind me with my armed hand. Once I was sure it had clicked shut, I rested my back against the door and took in my surroundings.

Fuck, this closet was smaller than I thought it would be. I closed my eyes in a pitiful attempt at pretending I wasn't stuck in a tiny dark room, with Hunter standing *far* too close to be comfortable. I only opened my eyes again when I realised Hunter had placed his hands on either side of my head, and when I did all I saw was his gold irises.

Oh *shit*, I was in trouble.

CHAPTER NINETEEN

CHAI AND A WINTER FOREST

It had been just over a year since I'd been this close to someone. With the proximity and the way he kept looking at me, I had to somehow distance myself. Hell, I had to stop touching his fucking *lips.*

I ripped my burning hand away from his mouth and tightened my grip on my dagger to divert some energy.

I should have gone with the stairs. The risk of death was preferable to whatever *this* was.

"If you wanted me all over you, you could have just asked," he whispered. I tilted my head back to get a better view of his eyes, but inadvertently brought my face closer to his.

Fuck.

The way my body warmed had to be because of how touch-deprived I was. It *had* to be. Thankfully, in the dark of the room, he surely couldn't see me blush. He'd use the bodily reaction against me if given the chance, and he hadn't mentioned it yet.

"I'd rather skin myself alive than have you all over me," I replied, also in an extremely quiet whisper. Maybe the best way to deal with the danger I'd trapped myself beside was to vehemently deny it. There was really only one way to find out if the method would work, but what other choice did I have?

"That was a tad harsh..."

The footsteps outside reached the hallway, which confirmed the decision I'd made had been the right one, but at what cost?

"Can you please just *shut up*?" I asked.

I tried to listen to the voices in the hallway. There were three of them, I was sure of it, but it was hard to focus when all I could feel was Hunter's distracting body heat.

"I think we both know that's not going to happen." He leaned closer to me, dropped his forearm against the door and tucked his head to the side of mine.

For fuck's sake, he was getting far too close for me to be comfortable. His hair brushed my cheek, which meant he was no doubt close enough to hear my heart as it hammered in my chest so hard that it could shatter my ribs.

"Get away from me," I hissed as I shuffled my position

against the door.

Why was it so hard to stay still? And why had my throat gone completely dry? And why was I so fucking warm?

"There is shit all over the floor. I'm on the balls of my feet because if I put my heels down, I'm going to step on something. Just let me lean against the door." I let out a shaky exhale and nodded. As long as it stopped us from being caught, then I would just have to pretend my fingers weren't aching with the need to touch *him*. "It's not like I want to fuck you in this broom closet." My body involuntarily shivered at the insinuation.

Fuck, this was not going as planned.

I didn't argue back. Instead, I stayed perfectly still while the three Templum assassins stopped in the hallway for an in-depth discussion about the damned weather. My head fell against the door, my eyes locked on the ceiling as I felt his warm breath fan over my neck.

If I had just killed him back in Lima, then we wouldn't be stuck in a broom closet together. In fact, so much would have gone differently. For example, I wouldn't have almost been killed twice in the last seventy-two hours. But alas, I had to be in a generous mood for the second time in my life.

What a good lesson this had been.

"God, you smell good, Caeli." His words caressed my neck, and I couldn't stop the shiver that ran down my spine *again*. Who the fuck gave him permission to illicit a physical response from me? Because I sure hadn't... *had I?*

"Shut the fuck up, Hunt." Right. That empty threat should

be more than enough to stop him from pushing my buttons any further.

"That's the first time you've called me by a nickname." Fucking damn it.

So not only was I incapable of hiding the physical response, I'd also forgotten about covering up the mental one. Someone kill me.

"I *will* cut you." Okay, that surely didn't make it seem like I was in denial. No, that was a perfectly normal response from a person who was completely unaffected by the other person who was breathing on their neck and putting questionable thoughts in their head.

"I might like it." *Fucking hell.*

My body tensed. My lungs forgot how to breathe air. My brain threatened to shut down.

No. There was no possible way I was attracted to Hunter. This was just a response because he was the first person in a while to show any interest in me. Shit like this happens to the best of us, *evidently.*

"I'm sorry, I'm just freaking out. I hate small spaces and I think we both know by now that I cover up negative feelings with humour, so…" and the interest was fake. Of course it was. It could only ever have been a way to help him dissociate from reality because he wasn't attracted to me and I wasn't attracted to him.

I remembered how to breathe after the admission, but it was too late to stop the warmth that had flooded my veins.

Then would have been an ideal time to run out of the

closet and head into the archives, but no. Those three fucking assassins were still in the hallway, where the conversation had moved from the weather to books they'd read. It made sense; it was the only form of entertainment they were allowed to consume.

They disallowed television and modern music in Templum; they thought it to be a distraction from their training. If I ever had to go without music, I think I'd rather just *die.*

My jaw popped.

I'd be stuck with Hunter for a little longer, which meant I had to pull some patience out of my ass and figure out a way to prevent him from flirting with me.

"What do I smell like?" I asked.

Wow, what an ideal way to get him to stop flirting with me; give him a wide fucking opening to do so. I'd forgive myself for the mistake. This was not my specialty and it was the best idea I could come up with to keep him distracted from the fact we were stuck in a small space together.

He smirked as his eyes locked on mine, and I could have sworn the gold of his irises had a slight glow to them in the inky room.

"You smell sugary, but not at the same time. Kind of similar to honey mixed with spices like cinnamon and cloves." The warmth from him grazed my skin. "Oh shit, you smell like chai."

"Do I now?" The question was rhetorical, since I needed this conversation to be over, but he didn't seem to pick up on that fact. Or he didn't care.

Fuck, this was killing me.

"Yeah, I noticed back in Lima how nice you smelled, when I had you pinned to that wall kind of similar to how we are right now." Damn it, why had my stomach twisted itself in knots? "Now... what do I smell like?" My nose immediately scrunched at the question.

"Like the deodorant you use every day." I couldn't allow myself to go into more detail, because more detail meant more attention. The one thing I did *not* need to do was pay him anymore more attention, especially since we hadn't broken eye contact yet.

"Come on, what do I actually smell like to you?" The depth of his voice swept over my body, and my lips parted as the air left my lungs again. For some reason I wasn't averse to it, or the smirk that had made it's way to his incredibly soft looking lips.

"Like your deodorant, and that peppermint gum you're always chewing on for some fucking reason." I had to distance myself, had to bring myself back to reality. It wasn't an option to think any other way, because I was stuck in here with *Hunter*, the person I didn't trust, and knew to be hiding his identity from me.

"Caeli." The way he said my name, the way he whispered it like a carefully laid out prayer, made me wonder what I might do if he brushed my neck with a gentle finger. Would I pull away or would I lean into that touch? "Surely, you could do better than that."

"Fine, you smell like mint and pine, is that what you want to hear?"

What would I do if his nose brushed that sweet spot just below my ear? Would I push him away or run my hands up his muscular arms?

"Surely that reminds you of something a little more poetic than an herb and a type of tree."

If his lips were to graze my collarbone, would I break his nose or fall into the sensation?

"A winter forest."

I forced myself to look away from his damned eyes, because my breath was shaking far too much. Maybe he hadn't noticed it, or the warmth that no doubt flushed my cheeks. Maybe I could change the topic so he *wouldn't* realise.

"What's your problem with small spaces, anyway?" I asked in a last-ditch attempt to change the topic and force the warmth to leave my body. In that moment I didn't care for the I'd potential consequences of breaking his second rule, I just needed the focus to shift.

And my plan worked, maybe a little too well.

"I used to be punished by being locked in a chest not much bigger than I was." Oh *shit*.

I looked back at him and saw he was no longer watching me. The pain of the admission seemed to be too much for him to do so.

"I'm sorry." My response was genuine, and there was no doubt in my mind that he had just told me the truth. I could see the torment in his eyes that was similar to my own. *Like recognises like.*

"Don't be. It happened years ago. The fear has just stuck with me. It might be a little stupid but-"

"Well, I have a complicated relationship with water. I'm scared of bodies of it and *hot* water." I cut him off as I looked at him from the corner of my eye. It gave me the perfect view of his bright irises as they turned back to me again. "Having a fear because of something that happened in your past isn't stupid. It's trauma. It's normal."

"I'd say it sounds like you're working through your emotions healthily... if I hadn't watched you brutally murder someone who reminded you of your past." Shit. It hadn't been that obvious, had it?

"I don't know what you're talking about." More denial on my part, perfect.

While I liked to say that Hunter was useless or stupid, I knew better. He was detail-oriented and liked to pay attention to the people around him. Of course he knew the way I'd attacked Hansen wasn't just to avenge the women he'd raped and killed.

"I don't think what Hansen did to his victims is exactly what happened to you, but you mentioned you knew the pain he'd put them through. It was similar enough to your experience that it all struck a chord. You don't punch someone seventeen times because of justice; it has to be personal."

I licked my bottom lip. Maybe giving him a second chance

had been a bad idea. He knew too much about me, and I hadn't told him a damned thing. And now I knew something about him, which was what I originally wanted, but there was an unforeseen issue with it. It made me feel some kind of empathy towards him—some *sympathy* even. That wasn't okay.

That type of understanding wouldn't help the weird thing my body was doing. None of it would help slow my racing thoughts, not when his breath warmed my neck with every exhale.

"I think they're gone. We should move before they come back." I whispered after a few seconds of silent agony.

The footsteps had echoed away from the door a few exchanges ago, the voices with them, but it had been safest to stay for a little while longer, just to be sure. It had nothing to do with the fact that I was becoming more comfortable with our closeness with every passing breath.

"That's probably for the best, because I'm pretty sure everything I'm thinking right now is sacrilegious," he replied as he slowly stood up straight and put his heels down. His arms finally left their stance next to my head, and his face moved away from mine.

I noted the fact that I'd heard nothing crinkle under his weight, which meant he'd lied about why he was propped against the door and over me. I could ignore that for now. It was more important to find out exactly what he'd been thinking.

"How so?" I asked. Maybe this was a bad idea, to figure

out what he'd been thinking, but it was too late to take it back.

"I know I said before that I don't want to fuck you in here, but..."

Wait. Did that mean everything he said *hadn't* been to distract himself? Had he *not* been screwing with me?

"Yeah, it's definitely sacrilegious," he breathed.

Well, if that was the case, then maybe I could screw with him a little too—for the sake of fun.

"We're not in a church, so maybe not," I said. I turned away from him and opened the door before I could regret saying anything. And before I could think too much over what he'd been imagining in his head.

What if it was similar to what I'd seen? What if the questions he'd asked himself were similar to the ones I'd thought of?

I took a deep breath once I walked into the hallway. Flirting with him would be a stupid idea, because that would mean I was forming an attachment. Attachments were dangerous in this line of work.

Flirting was a bad idea.

Whatever had just transpired in the closet had to stay there.

"You really don't know what I was thinking if you assume location would make a difference." So much for leaving what had happened in the closet there.

Maybe I should start walking. That way I could act like my shortness of breath was because of the movement and not my thoughts.

"It can't be that bad," I said as I looked over my shoulder at him. It was an attempt to calm whatever burned between us. He either didn't realise what I was doing or wanted to stoke the flames.

He caught his bottom lip under what was definitely a sharper canine than normal. His eyes locked on mine and the gold irises were darker than when we'd first been in the hallway.

"Princess, just assume that whenever I think about you, it's definitely something I should be burned at the stake for."

Why the fuck did those words make warmth pool between my legs? Even if his voice had lost its playfulness and had turned to something cold and dark, the words *still* affected me.

"Now, we should get a move on. We have far too many shelves to scavenge through, and we still don't know what we're looking for." And suddenly he was back to normal.

There was a smirk on his face as he walked past me down the hallway, and all I could do was stand as still as a statue for a few moments.

Just when I thought I had him figured out he liked to throw me a curveball...

Ice sat in my stomach as I watched him walk into the dark hallways of the archives. Whatever happened between us was illogically *right*. It had to be for me to get that sensation.

So I followed him into the darkness.

CHAPTER TWENTY

LOOKING LIKE AN IDIOT

"Any luck?" I asked as I looked at Hunter through the shelves.

We'd searched the Archives for a good twenty minutes to no avail, avoided all signs of Templum and found absolutely nothing to do with the clue. It proved my assumption was right, that Templum were concentrated around what we needed to find. And with my assumption being right, it also explained why we'd made it down so easily—not including being stuck in that closet together for what felt like an eternity.

"Not yet," Hunter replied as he caught my eyes through the old books and records.

"If it was here, then there would be Templum assassins

everywhere. The clue was a wax seal press for a reason. We have to be looking for a letter." I told him what I'd been thinking for a while now. He nodded his agreement.

"There's climatised rooms for fragile documents. A letter from the 1600s might fill that classification." A reasonable assumption to make, but it left me with another question, one that shouldn't break his second rule and hit me with the consequences of it.

"How do you know so much about this place?" I asked as I skimmed the rest of my shelf and walked over to him. A sadness filled his golden eyes, and I didn't enjoy the way it made my breath catch.

"My mother had the privilege of coming here to complete research using these documents. So, my sister and I agreed to come here ourselves at some point. Instead, I'm here with you and she is going to kill me," he said with a quiet laugh. I knew that laugh all too well. It was the same one I'd heard Vince use when he tried to cover his feelings.

"You should have brought her if it meant that much to you both. You said she was at a safe distance, we could have-"

"It's not that simple." He cut me off, which helped prevent me from looking like an idiot.

Had the closet situation really changed my perspective on him that much? Surely not. I was just figuring out his past without asking a question. All I was doing was fishing for information he'd give me without thinking.

And to keep fishing, I had to continue *not* asking questions.

"So, she doesn't approve of your line of work then," I said, and I leaned against the bookshelf to feign disinterest in his response.

"No, it's not that. The nature of the distance is what makes it complicated," he said as I walked down the hall towards what looked to be other rooms.

It took everything in me to hide my smile, to keep my calm façade and not get excited over the fact he was falling right into my trap. He was a handful of steps behind me, close enough to follow but not close enough to distract me.

"What's the nature?" I asked, and I realised far too late that it was a question. But instead of the smart comment I assumed I would receive, all he gave me was silence.

Why couldn't I hear his footsteps? Or his breathing?

"Hunter?" I looked over my shoulder and saw an empty hallway behind me. "*Hunt*?" I crept back the way I'd come, my dagger in hand as I spotted a door sitting slightly ajar.

My fingers brushed the cool metal of the door handle, and I heard whispers inside of the room. Before I could make a jump attack, the door ripped open, and a nimble hand jerked me inside.

The door slammed shut behind me, and without a second thought, I swung at my attacker. My blade missed their head by less than half an inch, which meant they'd just succeeded at a very lucky dodge.

"I'm not here to hurt you!" The assailant shouted, throwing their hands in the air. I stopped for a moment to breathe. What the fuck was going on here?

It was the girl, the one from the auction with topaz eyes. What the fuck was this kid playing at? I could have killed her.

"What are you here for, then?" I couldn't risk letting my guard down. While the icy feeling in my stomach told me I could trust her, I liked to have confirmation in this kind of situation.

There was only one thing that made me want to hear her out, aside from the ice, and that was Hunter. He stood behind the girl, his eyes calm and his body relaxed. He felt safe around the girl, which was even stranger.

"I'm here to help you," Nylah spoke with enough conviction that it made me tilt my head to the side.

"And why would you do that?" I asked, taking in Nylah's body language. Her hands shook as she dropped them to her sides. She was nervous or terrified, or maybe a bit of both.

"Because I need *your* help, and I was hoping we could work something out," she said as she pulled a folded piece of paper out of her pocket and passed it to me. Judging from the colour and texture, it was quite old, so I took care while I opened it. "I can guarantee that's what you're looking for."

"How do you know what I'm looking for?" I asked, as I began skimming the page.

Even though the entire letter was written in Latin, I could see enough information to know that Nylah's assumption was correct. The letter was dated 1600, and written by one Andres Lopez, *A.L.*

"I know because I'm the one who found it for Ryne four

years ago. He found a statuette like yours, and we followed the clues like you did." There were two things to consider with that information. The fact she had called Ryne by his name instead of his title, and that she implied she'd been in the archives before.

"How did you find it?" I asked, watching as Hunter edged his way to my side again.

"I'm a Templum researcher, so I've had full access to the archives since Ryne forced me into my position." *Forced.* Nylah had specifically chosen that word to communicate her situation with me, I was sure of it.

"The Vatican likely owes Templum for some deed done in the past, so that makes sense." I skimmed over the page once more.

Of all the languages I knew, Latin wasn't one of them. The Order had been more focused on force-feeding me languages that would help me get closer to *living* targets. But a language barrier was a simple thing to work around, and it sure as hell wouldn't stop me.

"Why give this to me?"

"It leads to a place of power, and I need you to get there first so you can destroy it." Nylah's body went rigid as she spoke, and all I did was stare at the girl.

I needed more information before I agreed to help her, and she surely knew that.

"Ryne has only kept me around because of my blood. My mother was a custos, so the working theory is that I'm one too. They want to put me through my incitement but the chances of death..."

If I remembered correctly, a custos was a guardian, a conduit that was fuelled by protective magic. Or they would be, if they existed.

"You don't actually believe in that bullshit, do you?" I asked as Hunter finally reached my side again.

"I do." Nylah's voice shook, her hands moved without purpose. "My brother is a lamia, and he's already been through his incitement. I watched it happen." A lamia was a vampire, or a vampire-*like* being. But Nylah wasn't talking about Malakai, she was talking about Samael. "And I watched my mother use her power to protect Sam and I when Templum came for us." Her eyes flicked towards Hunter.

"But a custos' downfall..." he trailed off. It forced me to look at him, because I wasn't aware he had any knowledge of conduits in the first place.

It was once common knowledge, yes, but in the modern world it had been forgotten. Risky magic was unnecessary when you could buy a gun without repercussions instead. The risk of death wasn't worth the chance of power anymore.

"The bad karma for loved ones? It hit immediately," Nylah explained. Her eyes flicked to Hunter again before they settled on me. "She died the second after she used her power. A sniper shot her. And then we were taken into Templum despite her efforts. I don't want that power. My brother is all I have left." It seemed almost believable, like the girl wasn't actually lying. "You need to get there before Ryne does."

"And what do I get in return for helping you?" I asked before I folded the piece of paper back in half and crossed my arms over my chest.

"Malakai told you about the gold, and whatever he said was an understatement. You'll understand once you get the letter translated, but you can take as much of it as you want." Nylah replied as she checked the small watch on her left wrist and became even more nervous.

"Why don't you tell me right now and save me the trouble?" I asked, letting my impatience get the better of me.

"Because Templum would have just realised that I'm missing from my post. I have to go. They're going to swarm the room I took that from, which will give you plenty of space but a limited amount of time to get out of here."

This entire situation felt off to me, but I couldn't put my finger on why. I would look past it for now though, because the girl was coming to me for help and people only did that out of pure desperation.

"What language is it in?" Hunter asked, looking at me as I tucked the letter into the buttoned pocket of my cargo pants.

"Latin," I answered. His golden eyes flashed with something I couldn't quite describe.

"I can do Latin." Wow, it seemed he was full of surprises now he was attempting to get on my good side. "We need to use the window she's giving us to get out of here. I don't want to get caught by Templum." I thought about it for a second and looked between him and Nylah before I settled on the girl.

"If this is a trap-"

"You'll kill me, I know." Nylah cut me off as she pushed past me to get to the door. "The threat of death doesn't scare me like you think it does, Shadow. You need to consider the fact that I'm being held in Templum against my will, and that I hate Ryne even more than you do. After everything he did to my brother... just get there first, *please*."

There wasn't any time for me to respond to the plea before Nylah slipped out of the room and gently clicked the door shut behind her. I looked over at Hunter as the girl's footsteps faded into silence down the hallway. He drew together his eyebrows as he stared at the wall, in the direction that Nylah run, almost like he could still hear her.

"Do you trust her?" Hunter asked as we stayed put for a few extra seconds—just to be sure that the coast was actually clear. His gold eyes landed on me, and I felt their weight fall on my soul.

"I don't know. There was genuine fear in her eyes, but she's from Templum and they're all outstanding actors," I answered.

His eyes shifted away from me as he took a step back.

Maybe he'd realised how screwed our situation was, especially if that girl's mother had been a guardian. While their power was based on protection, it was strong enough to level armies with one swipe of their hand. And if Samael was a vampire, and he'd already gone through his incitement...

"Do *you* trust her?" I asked, and he hesitated.

"I think so. She pulled me in here and instead of threatening me, she asked if we were both okay." That didn't surprise me. The girl seemed relatively quiet and reserved, caring, and there wasn't a chance in hell that she'd been trained for the field. She'd done this specifically to ask for my help, and I'd be damned if I didn't do my best. "She said the only reason she's here is because of her familiarity with the archives. I'm inclined to believe that because she didn't even have a weapon on her." That was true. I hadn't spotted a knife or gun on the girl, which was unusual for a trained Templum assassin.

I furrowed my brow and nodded. While I didn't have to believe the entire story like he seemed to, I agreed regardless. There wasn't any time for me to argue otherwise.

"Let's get out of here before something else goes wrong," I said before I slipped out of the room and gave Hunter the all clear. We ran back the way we'd come in. Just like the girl had said, the halls were quiet, with the assassins assumedly swarming the area that Nylah had gone missing from.

We made it to the stairs, and I sprinted up them two at a time. We didn't stop until we were in a black hatchback with Vince in the driver's seat. The car took off the second we closed the doors.

"Did you find what you were looking for?" Vince asked, and in response I pulled the folded letter from my pant pocket. I had to make sure I hadn't just imagined stowing it away.

"You could say that," I answered as I handed the letter to Hunter. "Can you read any of it now?" I turned my focus to Hunter in the backseat, who turned on his flashlight to look at the cursive handwriting.

"Some of it, but it's not making sense," he replied. I furrowed my brow at the response.

"Did you lie when you told me you could read it?" I immediately spat the question out, but he shook his head in response.

"No." His eyes lifted to meet mine, a glint of excitement glossed over the gold. "I can read it, it's just... I don't believe what it says." Surely he wasn't going to leave me hanging like that.

"What does it say?" I asked, and he smiled.

His next words made my lungs tighten, and my fingers tap my leg. If what he said was true, and this was what we were on the path of, I would be fucking happy to continue working with Hunter for the rest of my damned life. This would outweigh any of the distrust I felt.

"That there's a city of gold, and this letter has the location of the last clue we need to find it."

Chapter Twenty-One

A LOST CITY OF GOLD

"Did you just say a *city* of gold?" I asked, unsure of whether to believe the kid in the back seat or not. Of all the things that Caeli and I had chased after, an entire city made out of gold was not on the list.

"Yeah, in Peru," Hunter answered as I drove us back to the hotel. So we'd come all the way to Europe... to need to head back to Peru? *Spectacular.*

"You're not... you're not talking about Paititi, are you?" Caeli asked, and her silver eyes sparkled as her words tumbled from her mouth in an unusual rush. Paititi was that place Caeli mentioned after she researched the statuette the first time around.

"I don't know. It doesn't really specify what the place is

called." Well, how was that supposed to be of any help then?

"What does it say?" I asked as I looked in the rear-view mirror at Hunter.

"It's a detailed account from the Conquests in South America written by Andres Lopez. This letter is all about a city he found after hearing some of the local stories. It's made of gold and located near some oddly shaped lakes; infinity symbols and perfectly cut squares. And apparently, he left the exact location hidden in Iglesia del Triunfo." That was the oldest church in Cusco, and Caeli apparently liked what she'd heard, judging from the fact she was shuffling in her seat like an over-energetic toddler.

"A city of gold, South American Conquests which places the letter around the end of the Incan period, the statuette possibly being a depiction of Inkarri... it all points to Paititi." Holy hell, were we actually... *no*. "The only thing that doesn't add up is how old that fucking statuette is."

"We can figure that bit out later," Hunter said, maybe a little too quickly for my liking, but he had a point. That part wasn't important right now. "Malakai definitely understated the amount of gold that would be in this place, and Nylah didn't give it enough precedence either."

"Well, neither of them lied. Paititi is a lost city of gold, that implies there should be more than enough to go around," Caeli said. She didn't seem overly convinced that moving on from the topic of the statuette was a good idea, but she'd done it anyway.

An entire city made of gold? What would we even be able

to do with that much? Even if we sold it all, what would we do with our fortune? Buy a nice house, reliable cars, new identities... I could start my life over again. I could give Caeli the stability she'd never had, but always deserved. We could live a normal life without stealing and treasure hunting ever again. We could live like the father-daughter duo I'd viewed us as for years now.

"But they also said it's a place of power. I know Nylah told us to get there first and destroy it, but what if they're already there? Nylah found that letter for Ryne *four years ago*..." Hunter stated, which made me raise my eyebrows. Ryne had known about this place for four fucking years?

"Kid..." I trailed off as I looked over at Caeli. How did she not seem the least bit worried right now?

"We only just found out," she said to reassure me. It didn't work, because I knew it wouldn't make a difference to her plans. If she wanted to find this city of gold, then she would; threat or no threat.

"Are we still going?" I asked, just in case she was going to put our safety above money. I couldn't fault her if she didn't, I usually had my priorities around the same way. She'd learned most of her bad habits from me, and that was one of them.

"It's an entire city of gold, Vince. I don't see how we couldn't." And that was the answer I'd expected.

"Ryne will have people all over it, or in it. If it was just gold, he might leave it unattended, but he would never risk a place of power." Hunter pointed out, and it only made me wonder one thing; how did the kid know so much about Ryne? I looked at him through the rear-view mirror again and saw the concern etched on his face. He looked almost haunted.

"All we need to do is make a detailed plan and sneak in and out without being spotted. We use the destruction of the place of power as a distraction, and in the commotion, we take what we can and leave." She made it sound so simple, so achievable, and yet I couldn't help the feeling that it wouldn't be like that at all.

"Might be easier said than done," Hunter said as he continued to read the letter. "The city is completely underground. The only ways in and out are through tunnels carved into the sides of a huge square formation in the middle of the forest." That sounded like it could be an issue.

"Then we make sure we don't fuck up the plan. I'm not giving Ryne a pass on this one. With that amount of gold, he could do anything he wanted, and if this place of power is real and he gets his hands on some conduits... it would be reckless to hand it to him on a silver platter." Caeli made a good argument.

If we looked at the situation from a moral high point, then we were potentially the only thing standing between Ryne and control over the world. It was a nice addition to lining our pockets comfortably enough for the rest of our lives.

"He already has places of power under his control. Nylah said her brother already went through his incitement, so maybe handing him another pool won't make a difference."

Hunter argued. A *pool*? Something was off.

Now that I was paying more attention to the newbie, I'd realised that something wasn't right with him. I couldn't put my finger on it, which was why I hadn't told Caeli yet, but this was another thing to add to the list. Only people who had intimate knowledge of conduits knew that these places of power were pools of water, ones that conduits walked into so they could jumpstart their powers. I only knew because of Caeli... so why did this kid know?

"Do you actually want a good pay cheque or not? Because if this is getting too scary for you, you can stay behind." Caeli's voice came out as a dark warning. It was a tone that I'd only heard a few times before. And even though I felt she was taking the interrogation in the wrong direction, I would let it be. "We can leave you right here in Rome, if that's what you'd prefer. Hell, it's what I'd prefer. That would mean I wouldn't have to share shit with you, or worry about keeping you alive on top of everything else I do."

Hunter shook his head. "No, I want to do this. I just need to make sure we're all aware of the dangers here."

I couldn't shake the feeling that Hunter was attempting to divert us from Paititi for a reason. What the fuck did this kid know?

"I'm aware of the danger, Hunter. Just trust me when I say that I could protect us with my hands tied behind my back." I wished I could say Caeli was over-exaggerating, but the one thing I'd always trusted her with was my safety. No matter what we walked into, she would get us out in one piece. She always had, and always would.

"I hope so, because if we get caught, I won't be able to do shit." Maybe Hunter simply meant he wouldn't be able to break out of cuffs, or fight with his hands out of action, or that maybe he didn't do well under that kind of pressure.

But I felt it meant something else. I just didn't know what.

Chapter Twenty-Two

SILVER ARMOUR

Hunter sidled towards me; his gold eyes wary as I sighed during his obvious approach.

Vincent had talked to me after we got back to the hotel. He felt Hunter was hiding something big, so I had become more than wary of him. I mean, the fact that I was apparently attracted to him was a red flag that I couldn't ignore... I had a type.

"What is it?" I asked as I dropped my pen into the middle of my notebook and slammed it shut. He flinched at the action, which was for the best.

What happened in the Vatican had to stay at the Vatican. It was just a strange thing that occurred because of the proximity in the closet... and the fact that he had those

190

golden eyes and that annoyingly beautiful smile and those muscles and-

He cautiously sat down next to me. "Well, since we're stuck in the air for the next few hours together, and Vince wants me nowhere near the cockpit, I thought we could talk."

There was only one row of seats, since the plane was designed to carry cargo more than it was meant to carry people. It had never been an issue before, but right now, it was more than a problem. It meant there weren't any other seats I could retreat to, aside from the co-pilot's seat. Vince preferred to be alone up there during flight though, so that was only an option for if I got desperate.

"Talk about what?" I moved as close to the window as I could, shifted the notebook from the small pull-down table onto my lap and pushed the table closed again. It would be best for if I needed to make a quick escape, especially since he was too close.

I couldn't have a repeat of the closet, not when my body had already threatened to overheat because of his proximity.

"Me," he said, as if it was the simplest answer on the planet.

His hands shuffled around on his lap before they settled into prayer hands tucked between his powerfully built thighs—okay, *no*. We weren't thinking like that. He had perfectly average thighs, not even close to being muscular enough to hold me up against a wall effortlessly.

My tongue darted out to lick my suddenly dry lips. *Fuck,*

this was going horrendously.

"I just wanted to say I understand why you don't trust me."
I highly doubt that.

"Well, I don't need your acceptance, and I certainly don't
want it." I moved to stand, my right hand on the armrest in
preparation to push me up, but his hand latched onto my
wrist. I froze.

His hand was warm against my skin, *too* warm, and it sent
jolts of electricity up my arm. *No.* This was similar to what
I'd felt in that closet, and I *couldn't* feel that. So I took a deep
breath and readied myself to say my usual threat. I never got
the chance to.

"Before you say 'let go of me', please just stay for a few
minutes and hear me out." He locked his eyes on mine, and
I hated the fact that it made me want to listen. "I want to
explain everything to you." He wanted to...

I swallowed hard and tucked myself completely against
the wall of the plane. The metal was cold on my back, but
cold was what I needed to keep my sanity. He only let go of
my wrist after I nodded, to confirm I would hear him out,
and my skin burned in his wake. I quickly tucked my arm in
front of my chest just to make sure he knew I didn't want to
have this conversation.

Even though deep down I *did* want to... I couldn't let him
see that.

"Hurry up then," I told him. He nodded as his eyes shied
away from me.

It must be bad if he couldn't look at me like normal.

He did it more consistently than Vince. It was a constant, something I'd become used to over the last few days. So why wouldn't he look at me?

"The reason you think Hunter Black isn't my real name is because it's not. You were right."

I could feel my heart beat in my chest, could hear it thunder in my ears. My pulse had sped up, my entire body burned, but not for the same reasons as before. No, this was a *bad* burn. A burn that made my stomach turn to acid.

"You swore on your dad's soul that-"

"Yeah, I don't give a shit about him." Was that supposed to make me feel better? It was something he'd used to make me trust him, a thing that he said to make me *believe* him. Not that it had worked, but that wasn't the point. "If he could have died because I lied to you, I still would've done it."

That was something I could circle back to. For now, I had to worry about myself. I had to focus on the fact that he'd lied to me and figure out where to go from there. The only reason I would care about his messed up family would be if there was a good reason for what he'd done.

"You're the one who made the rule of no manipulation... because you were fucking *projecting*." I sat up straighter in my seat, but kept as much distance from him as I could. "If Hunter isn't your name, then what is?"

"I can't tell you." I scoffed at the response. "It's the best way to keep my sister safe." Maybe I should have been happy that I was right, but instead the acid in my stomach became painful. "She's not actually safe, she's... she's being held by the cult that my parents got involved in. They idolise conduits, just like Templum does. Our ancestry implies we could be of magical blood, so they won't let her go, not easily, at least."

"Magical blood?" The question was enough to prove I didn't believe his story. The second someone dragged conduits into an explanation, it was always hard for me to think it was real.

"Conduit... specifically lamia." I shook my head as my jaw clenched. Vampires? Really? Was I honestly supposed to believe this was the *true* story?

"Why does everyone believe in this shit?" I whispered as I ran a hand over my face.

"Because it's real, Caeli. I've seen it all for myself, more than once while I was stuck with them." He untucked his hands to run them through his soft curls. "They let me go because they tested me and don't think I'm a conduit, which makes me worthless to them. My sister, on the other hand..." But why would he have to keep his identity secret to keep her safe?

"They put a price on her, and if I can pay it, then they'll let her go. When I got out, I was on my own for the first time in my life, and I had no options to make money, not the amount I need at a fast enough speed, anyway. Going after artefacts and selling them to the black market, or trying to find a lost treasure seemed like my best options. My parents were obsessed with history and told us stories about lost treasures, so I figured I could use that knowledge to my advantage. I was at that museum in Lima to find something that could lead me to Paititi, something that proved it existed, and I guess you could say I succeeded."

Should I believe him, or not? He sounded genuine, but he'd already lied to me about his past and swore on someone's soul that it was the truth. It didn't matter that he didn't like his father. It was still a tactic he'd used to get me to believe him... and I'd almost fallen for it. There wasn't any way I could believe it this time either, not yet. Not until he could prove to me that he was telling the truth. Not until I saw it for myself.

"Why didn't you tell me this from the beginning?" I asked, because even though I didn't believe him, I could tell that his sister was truly in danger. It was hard to mask that kind of fear, or fake it, and it was all I could see in his eyes. "You know who I am. We could have saved her by now, we still can-"

"No. Even you couldn't win against them, Princess. The amount of guns and easily swayed men they have at their disposal is astounding. Skill can't beat that much stupid."

What was I even supposed to call him now? If Hunter wasn't his real name, and he didn't like being called *American*—which I didn't understand since he still called me Princess—what option was I left with?

"Aren't your parents some of that stupid if they're part of the cult?" Well, that came out wrong.

I looked down at my twitching hands. Only my fingers moved through the familiar motions, and I knew if I allowed myself that my hands and arms would follow. If the time ever came, I would *need* to.

I loathed the movements and loathed the fact that they worked just as intended. The Order had drilled them into me for a specific purpose; to calm me, to control me and my emotions. They regulated me, even when I didn't want them to.

"Yes, and no." I looked up at Hunter as he spoke. Apparently, he still couldn't focus on me. "They became part of the group because they were fascinated with conduits. They wanted to prove they existed without any form of doubt. Mum realised too late that these people thought more than that. They think conduits are lost gods or the descendants of them. But there's nothing I would describe about being a conduit that's god-like."

Hunter looked up at the roof of the plane and took a few short breaths. Since he'd handed me the opportunity to, I stared at the curve of his throat and his Adam's apple that bobbed every few seconds.

"My sister is dispensable because she's a lamia. She needs another conduit to have any power to use. If this group can get enough money together, they could buy what they really want. They could get their hands on a devorator, or a custos, something more in line with their twisted idea of a god."

Devorators were also known as witches, a type of conduit that used the energy of the earth and became addicted to using it. While it threw me off that he used all the archaic terms for the conduits, that wasn't where my focus had directed itself.

"*Buy one*?" I asked, and his head levelled out again. His eyes landed on mine. The molten gold displayed concern and sadness.

"Human trafficking exists for all types of people. There's a hidden, and elite, market for conduits. The fucking assholes who run it never get caught." He furrowed his brow as I processed the information. "You should know that. You're supposed to be a conduit, right? If what Malakai said was true, at least."

"It would be true if conduits existed..." I smiled, shook my head, and ignored the lump that formed in my throat. "But they don't." I shuffled in my seat so I could face Hunter a little better without twisting my neck anymore.

"How many people need to tell you that you're wrong?" He asked, and I regretted turning to face him. "Is your ego that fragile that you-"

"No, you don't understand." I cut him off. This had nothing to do with my ego. This had nothing to do with *him*, but I guess if he was going to stick around, then he probably deserved to know why I had such a problem with conduits. "If conduits exist, then... then it means that what the Order attempted to do with me... well, it would have worked. Hansen said I was their experiment, and I told him the truth when I said he was right."

"Okay, so they experimented on you. If you're a conduit, then they were just trying to boost your power." Fuck, he really *didn't* understand. "They wouldn't be the first who've tried, and they sure as hell won't be the last." I rolled my eyes and took a few more slow breaths. If there was ever a time to tell him exactly what I was, now seemed to be it.

"They didn't just experiment *on* me, Hunter, I *was* the experiment." Maybe if I emphasised the words I needed him to listen to, then he might understand. He might see what I was trying to tell him.

The consequences of what the Order had done with me would run so much deeper than if they had just tried to boost my power.

"I'm not meant to exist." That was something I'd always known, something I'd always felt in my bones—*I wasn't meant to be alive.* "I was never conceived by my parents, and I was never carried in a womb."

Hunter was going to be the second person I'd told all of this. He would be the only person, aside from Vince, outside of the Order who knew. He better not make me regret it.

"They made me in a test tube, from the broken DNA of a long dead woman and filled the gaps with a powerful witch they have in their tanks. They grew me in an artificial womb, spent I don't know how much money to make me. And then they never so much as gave me a name. They did all of that for a reason."

"Why would they..." he trailed off, and I saw the realisation sit in his eyes.

They made and raised me to be a weapon, and it was the reason I didn't want to believe conduits existed. It wasn't ignorance, because I knew conduits were real. But if I admitted that magic existed and that it was possible to gain it, then I had to admit they succeeded. Ignorance didn't fuel my denial; it was the nightmares sparked by what I knew would be the worst potential outcomes of my existence.

"Truci... they tried to bring back the truci." And there he was, using the archaic terms again. That wasn't what I was used to, because even the Order used the English variants.

"The woman they desecrated is believed to be one of the most powerful grims to have ever existed. She single-handedly destroyed cities for the Ottoman Empire and consumed so much power that she died at nineteen," I explained. He seemed to understand what that meant.

Every conduit had consequences to using their power, and for grims it was their life. Every use of magic shortened the time they had, and that was the reason they weren't around anymore.

"If the Order succeeded with their experiment—if they succeeded with *me*—then they've resurrected the most dangerous conduit type to ever exist."

Malakai had been right four nights ago; I couldn't admit conduits were real, not when doing so had such dire consequences.

Grims had died out because they devastated everything they touched, through shadows and darkness and disease. And even if they didn't use their power, there was the fact they heard the voices of spirits who endlessly hounded their only connection to the living. Between the burning out of grims and the rate of suicide, the conduit had died out. The last known grim had caused the Black Plague because they'd lost their minds to the spirits, to the darkness...

I couldn't become that.

"You can't ignore something just because it scares you. People will use it against you, the Order will and Templum and..." he trailed off.

It seemed he finally realised I knew everything he'd said, but couldn't bring myself to care. I hated to admit it, but fear had ruled over me since I knew what my life meant. While I was constantly stuck in that fear, it didn't mean I wasn't capable of protecting myself or the people around me.

"They *are* using it against me. *Malakai* is using it against me. He brought it up in Romania to tell me he knew, that he *always* knew." My hands gripped onto my notebook with such tension that my knuckles had turned white. "Even when we first worked together, and I gave him an alias, he knew it was all a lie. He knew who I was, and if that's the case, then Templum is working with the Order just like I assumed."

"What were you doing with him back then?" His eyes flicked towards my fingers, which made my grip tighten even further.

"He hired Vince and I, but we were double booked so we split up. We shouldn't have, because Vince should never have accepted that other contract." I tried to steer the conversation away from Malakai, but the look in Hunter's eyes told me I wouldn't get away with it. Not this time.

"Malakai hired me to steal some shit for him. I completed

the job like I always do... and then I realised they were watching me. It wasn't until after I'd completed the contract that I realised he was part of Templum Gratiae. If that was the case then there was every chance he was feeding information about me to the Order of Shadows, since the two organisations like to help each other out every now and again. I lead him into a trap, left him with some people he's fucked over before, and left him for dead."

"How did you know they were talking to the Order?" Was that the only part he was worried about? Did he not care about the vengeance? Or the way I had screwed someone over so badly that they could have died and I wouldn't have batted an eye? Why was he focused on me knowing if the Order was involved?

"I didn't, not for sure, but there's a long history of them working together," I explained. "Even the slightest of possibilities is enough for me to-"

"They really fucked you up, didn't they?" Hunter cut me off again, and all I did was close my eyes.

Saying the Order had fucked me up would be the grossest understatement of the century, but I didn't know another way to summarise it. There wasn't really another way to say they tortured me under the guise of strengthening me. They'd filled my veins with unknown liquids that made my blood feel like fire for days afterwards. They'd made me kill the other kids I'd thought of as siblings; if I didn't—if I was close to throwing a fight and letting myself die—they would kill the kid for me and then they'd use water in whichever way they chose to do so.

But sure, they'd simply *fucked me up.*

"You could say that," I whispered.

I felt my fingers let go of the notebook and begin their circles again. If it didn't work so well to calm me, I would never do it again. If it wasn't a necessary step to ease my nerves, then I would scream at the fact I still couldn't break their conditioning after eight years of freedom.

"They're the reason you're afraid of water."

I took another deep breath and stopped myself from crying. I couldn't do that. Not in front of Hunter. He wasn't safe... even if some part of me said he was. I couldn't trust him, especially because something in me screamed to do so.

"When they started training me, they set up punishments for if I screwed up or talked back or failed." My eyes stung even though I told myself not to cry. Was I really going to let him in like this? Let him see me like this? *I didn't even know his name anymore.* "They drowned me, waterboarded me..." I was. I was going to tell him.

Why was I going to tell him?

"If it was a way to use water against someone, they did it. They poured boiling water on me, submerged me in water that was too hot for too long. I can't have baths or hot showers. The heat reminds of that burning, of feeling like I was cooking inside of my own skin."

I couldn't bring myself to look at him. Not when I knew all I'd be able to find in those gold eyes of his would be pity. It was how Vince looked at me when I told him, so this would be the same. It was the only possible response.

"My father lost himself to the cult..." Hunter's voice reached my ears, but I didn't look up. This would just be some spiel about what he went through, or another attempt to convince me to trust him. "They had their own punishment for the kids who disobeyed orders or requests, or who were just too much like kids can be. They locked us in chests, small enough that you have to curl up inside to fit. The amount of time changed depending on how *severe* your actions were. My father did that to me until three years ago." My eyes finally lifted.

He didn't look at me with pity, nor I with him. It was understanding. This was why he was claustrophobic, and why he didn't like his father.

"What happened three years ago?" I thought it was safe to ask that question, that we had opened up enough that I could push a little further.

If I was willing to give him the leverage of my past over me, then it felt reasonable enough that I could ask about his past, too. The weight that constantly sat on my shoulders had lifted slightly at my admission, so why wouldn't I give him the opportunity to do the same?

"It doesn't matter. What matters is that he stopped, but the nightmares didn't."

The weight that had floated from my shoulders crashed back down, heavier than before. It made my body tense to try to carry it, to act like everything was fine—but it wasn't. None of this was fine or fair.

He still stared at me, as if he thought it would help me continue to open up to him, but it wouldn't.

This was all a mistake.

I'd handed him some of the most vulnerable parts of me on a silver platter, and he'd taken it all without the promise of returning that vulnerability. He was too close. I'd *let* him get too close.

If he'd asked me anything about my past—anything about me and what or who I was now—I would have told him. Had he asked how I felt about our current situation in actuality and not how I was acting, I would have answered honestly.

I would have told him whatever he wanted to know, and he couldn't tell me anything about him? He couldn't tell me his damned name? Or why they stopped locking him in a chest?

"I just told you..." I trailed off as I pulled my notebook against my chest. "I just told you what I am, why I am the way I am, *who* I am even, and you can't return any of it?"

Why did it hurt so much? Was it because I'd opened up to someone only to be rejected? Or was it specifically because it was *him*? Was it because I thought we were similar—that he might actually be able to understand me—and I still wasn't enough?

This was Dallas all over again... except a thousand times worse.

"I have shit to protect, the same as you do," he said. I stood up and refrained from simply running. He had shit to protect? And what about me? What about protecting myself? Did he even realise what I'd done? "What do you want from me?" Was he kidding?

He stood up, his body a mere few inches from mine, almost as close as we'd been in that damned closet. That was where everything had gone wrong.

Fuck. It hadn't just been my mind or body playing tricks on me.

I felt something for his asshole.

"What do I want?" I asked before an empty laugh left my lips. I didn't even know what I wanted, but *this* wasn't it. This *emotion* wasn't it. "I just let you in and if you'd pushed, I would have..."

No. I couldn't give myself away, although it was too late. The way he looked at me told me that much, but maybe I could weaponise it against him.

"I let you see beneath my *silver armour*." I used his own words against him, the ones from four days ago, when we agreed to work together. "I let you in, and now I don't even know what the fuck your real name is. You're the one who wanted to talk, and I shouldn't have..."

"Caeli-"

"Don't." What had I done? "Please, just *don't*. I've done this before, not this badly, but I... why can't I fucking learn?"

I tried to walk past him, but he blocked my path.

Damn it, was he trying to get stabbed? I might not have a knife on me, but I still had my pen, and I knew how to wield it.

"Please-"

"No!" I froze as the word left my mouth. It was louder than I'd intended. *So much louder.*

Maybe I should have apologised for the outburst, but I wasn't sorry. He'd made me feel cornered, trapped, and the only way to free myself was to attack. It was all I knew, and it had always worked. There was no point in changing a tactic that worked for me.

He stepped away, his eyes trailed to the floor as he mirrored my perfect stillness.

"Just leave me alone, *American*," I hissed as I walked past him and into the cockpit.

Vince side-eyed me as I curled up in the co-pilot seat. Yes, I was desperate enough to be where Vince wouldn't want me just so I could keep my distance from *Hunter*. And yes, Vince would know something was wrong.

He wouldn't tell me to leave, like I knew he wanted to, but he continued to look at me like he wanted an explanation. I couldn't give him one.

"Not now." It was all I could say, and he tilted his head to the side in acknowledgement. It wasn't agreement, but acceptance.

Once we landed in Cusco and were in a hotel, I knew that the acceptance would be over, so I would have to figure out what I was going to say. Because while I would have every chance to convince him I wasn't in the wrong, it was still likely that he'd side with the American.

And that he'd tell me exactly how *I* had fucked up.

Chapter Twenty-Three

EMPATHY AND UNDERSTANDING

"Kid, we need to talk." And so it begins, the father-daughter lecture I didn't want or need.

"No, we don't," I replied as I threw myself onto the bed closest to the door. The room seemed secure enough. There was only one window next to Vince's bed to worry about, and the cleanliness was better than most other places we stayed at.

"Caeli..."

He looked tired. One of his hands was stuck in his blond hair as if he was trying to physically hold the last dregs of patience in his body. Maybe he didn't understand the consequences of the conversation I'd had on the plane with Hunter. He probably hadn't heard what was said, and therefore didn't understand the scope of what I'd done.

"He admitted that what he told us was a lie, including his name. And when I handed him everything about me, everything I've been through, and everything I am, he didn't have the decency to hand me everything about him. What would you have me do, Vince? Pretend it didn't hurt like a fucking shot to my stomach? You want me to just move on?" I threw my hands to the sides as I stared at him.

"I want you to forgive him, Caeli." He could not be serious right now. While I'd expected him to take Hunter's side on this, it still hurt for it to happen.

"I'm not having this conversation with you..." I trailed off.

The skin under my eyes was heavy, as was that permanent weight on my shoulders. I pushed myself to sit up on the bed, in spite of the heaviness that held me down.

This was getting exhausting. It felt like I just kept giving pieces of myself away, and I wasn't leaving anything for myself.

"I'm not asking you to have a conversation about it. All I'm asking is that you listen to me, for once." I turned to look at him. He removed his hand from his hair so he could fold his arms over his chest. Damn it. He really was about to pick Hunter's side on this.

"Fine." My voice was hollow and blunt. He either didn't notice the lack of emotion or didn't care; given the circumstances, I assumed it was the latter.

"We already suspected it was a fake name-"

"And he tried to convince us it was real, swore on his *dad's soul*, which he got around because his father was an abusive piece of shit." That was too much emotion. I definitely needed to take that down a notch. "When you two were trying to convince me to let him work with us, that was the argument he made to get me to trust him. If that's a lie, then who's to say what else is? What if his sister doesn't even exist and she's just another detail to give his story more depth? To make it more believable or to make sure I don't question it?" I argued and ignored the pointed look he gave me. I'd always been good at multi-tasking.

"You said you'd listen," he said in response. I bit the inside of my cheek; maybe a physical way to stop myself from cutting in would work. I doubted it, but it was worth a try. "You'll get your time at the end, I promise. Just hear me out first."

I shuffled on the edge of the mattress as I continued to stare at him. He only broke eye contact after I mimed zipping my mouth shut and throwing away the key.

"We assumed Hunter was a fake name, so that's not surprising. And before you get the idea in your head that I trust him, after what he pulled in Romania, he is still on thin fucking ice with me." I rolled my eyes, but nodded nonetheless. "All I'm saying is that we have the potential for an ally here, and we desperately need one. If you tell me there is absolutely no part of you that thinks we could ever trust him, even after he eventually tells us everything he can about himself, then we can cut all ties with him after this hunt. Deal?"

Vince had posed it as a question, but I knew better. This was him telling me what was going to happen under the guise of giving me control and a choice. I nodded so I could play my part.

"Good. So, do you think you could eventually trust him? Keep in mind that you're the one who fought to keep him working with us, and that you opened up to him on the plane ride over. So don't lie."

Fucking asshole.

I closed my eyes for a moment to help myself think.

Aside from not knowing his name or his full history, what else could I even go on? All I had were his actions since he'd started working with us. They—and his unplanned reactions—were all I could trust to be real.

"Can you count? There's three of us against your precious Templum."

That was the most I'd ever been thrown off by anything in my entire life, and all it had taken was eleven words. It implied he wanted to stay. It implied that he was on my side. But they were words, and I couldn't trust a damned thing that came out of his mouth.

So maybe I could use the broom closet to gauge him. Maybe I should listen to my heart that had been loud enough to deafen me the entire time we'd been stuck in there together. But then again, that was my body telling me what to feel. It wasn't factual and I couldn't trust it when it had screwed me over so many times before. When it came to other people, my gut feeling was always wrong...

Although *that* could be an argument to make. I was so against trusting him, and my gut always told me to do the wrong thing with people. It told me I could trust Malakai, and so I did before he put me in my place by showing me who he truly was. The same thing had happened with Dallas, but so much worse since I had given him my trust without a single reservation. Then he threw my glass heart on the ground and shattered it. If my gut told me *not* to trust Hunter... then maybe I *should*.

"Caeli..." Vince snapped me out of my thoughts and back to the real world, to the present, where my hands were gripping the maroon duvet beneath me so tight that I'd lost feeling to my fingertips.

"It'll depend on if he tells us everything or not. I can't make a decision without knowing. You know that. Whenever I think I finally know someone, they show me I don't know a damned thing. Everyone aside from you, obviously." It took everything in me to loosen my grip on the duvet, and I gave myself a brief reprieve from the questioning by looking at the grey ceiling before I looked back at Vince.

"How about after Paititi you make your decision? That sound like a fair compromise to you?" Once again, it was a question that wasn't a question. So once again, I nodded to play my part. "Good, now talk to him. You need to apologise." Apologise? There was no way in hell I was going to do that.

"What for?" I asked as I stood up to unpack my bag.

"For the way you snapped at him on the plane ride over. I might not have heard anything else, but I heard *that*." He sounded bored, not that I could blame him.

"Vince, I'm not apologising. I told him about the Order-"

"I could bet good money on the fact you told him nothing but the barest details about the Order. You probably hardly scratched the surface." This was why I didn't let people get close to me, because I was apparently easy to predict once you knew me. "Reflective of how you likely told him what you could without breaking down; he probably told you everything he could without giving his identity away. Maybe you could do that thing we practiced..."

Oh no, not *that* thing. Anything but *that* thing.

"Empathy and understanding?" I screwed my face up as I asked the question for two reasons.

The first was because I hated having to do the whole empathy and understanding thing. It was fucking exhausting. The second was because I hated when Vince was right.

"Empathy and understanding," he confirmed. Okay, let's give a shot then.

Of all the billions of people on the planet, I should be able to understand why someone would need to play their cards close to their chest. Of all the people in the world, I should know how important it was to fly under the radar when you need to stay hidden.

Damned fucking *empathy and understanding.*

"Fine, I'll go. But only if you find a helicopter by yourself tomorrow." It was a pitiful bargain, I knew, but as long as it sounded like I was doing this as a favour to him, then it would be fine.

We were going to need a helicopter because the lakes where we were heading weren't large enough for the plane to land on, and I hated shopping for the damned things.

"I assumed that's what was happening in the first place, so that you and Hunter could go to this church and see if the next clue's there," Vince replied.

Well, that didn't help make me feel like I was doing him a favour. But I guess as long as I didn't have to source the amphibious helicopter, then it was a win for me.

I redid my ponytail as I sighed and zipped my bag shut again.

"Okay, I'll talk to him."

———•○•———

Alright, well here goes nothing.

I knocked on the door to Hunter's room. It slowly opened and my hand fell limp at my side.

What was I mean to do now that his golden eyes were staring down at me?

Had he always been that tall? Or did he just seem bigger because I had to apologise to him? Because he had the power for the current second?

"Can I help you with something?" He asked, and I nodded slowly. He could help me, in a round-about way.

"I was wondering if I could come inside; I don't really want to talk about our plans out here," I replied. For a moment I thought he wouldn't let me in, that he might actually slam the door in my face, which would be a warranted response, but then he backed away from the door and left it open for me.

"What's this plan, then?" He crossed his arms over chest once he closed the door behind me, his body leaning against the wall as either a form of comfort or intimidation. I didn't know which it was, but if it was the latter it wouldn't work. Not on me.

"Vince is going to find us a helicopter. I found the lakes mentioned in the letter from satellite view online, and they're not big enough for the plane, so we need a different way to get there. We, on the other hand, are still going to Iglesia del Triunfo together. We need to find whatever clue Mr Lopez left behind there. It might just give us the upper hand on Templum and we could use all the help we can get on that front."

"Is that all?" He pushed off the wall to reach his bag, which was open on top of his bed.

"I'm sorry. Was I interrupting something?" I asked with an empty laugh. Maybe it was an attempt at trying to lighten the weight that pressed down on me from every conceivable angle in the room. It didn't work.

"No, I just want to know if that's all you came to talk to

me about. If it is, then I... look, I'm exhausted and I want to get a half-decent night's sleep before tomorrow." Well, that seemed fair enough. I needed a good night's rest to catch up from the last few days, too.

"Okay," I replied as my hands began moving in circles. I had to do this, or Vince would talk to Hunter tomorrow and find out that I hadn't. "Look, the words I'm about to say don't come out of my mouth very often, so please take that into account when I say them." I hoped that intro would be enough to get him to listen, to sway him back in my favour, but it seemed to have the opposite effect.

"Are you going to apologise, Caeli? Because we both know it'll be bullshit. Your opinion of me hasn't changed, and it never will. I'm starting to understand that now." He didn't even look at me as he spoke, his eyes focused on his clothing as he unpacked and chose what he would wear tomorrow.

"Why is it so important to everyone that I like you? Or trust you? I think it's reasonable that I don't, especially since you've already lied to me once about everything. How could I trust you when I don't know your real name, or who you're running from? Would you be able to look me in the eye right now and tell me you trust me?" I asked, a grin on my face. It was a valid point, and it should have been a straightforward answer from him.

I should have won the argument... but he didn't move a muscle.

He seemed to be frozen in time as he propped both of

his hands on the bed, his eyes locked on his open bag. His cheeks flushed, and I saw him flinch as I took in a sharp breath.

Fuck, he *did* trust me.

Chapter Twenty-Four

LET ME CATCH YOU

Why would he trust me? I hadn't done a damned thing to earn it. How *could* he trust me? I lied whenever it suited me, manipulated people when I needed and killed those who got in my way. He watched as I shattered Hansen's skull. He'd seen me at my absolute worse, why... *how*?

"You can't be serious..." I trailed off as I retreated a step towards the door. How could he trust me? All I'd done was fight against him at every chance I could. I hadn't given him a damned thing to work with. "There's no fucking way that you could trust-"

"You've protected me more in the last week that we've known each other than anyone I've had in my life for years." He cut me off, but his voice lost power with each new word,

217

until he simply whispered the next five words and I felt something shift within me. "Of course I trust you."

His eyes finally found mine, and they searched for something I wasn't entirely sure I had.

"I haven't protected you." What else could I say? What other argument could I make? He shouldn't trust me, because I wasn't someone to trust. I put myself first, with the singular exception of Vince and his safety.

If he trusted me then... well, I wasn't sure I'd ever be able to reciprocate it. All I could do was argue that he was wrong, that his thought process was wrong, and that his assumptions about me were *wrong*. I had to prove that trusting me was a bad idea, and then get him to recant his admission.

"You have, whether or not you realise it, and whether or not you intended to. I saw the look in your eyes at the Archives, when that kid grabbed me. You were going to kill her because she took me—because she endangered *me*." I rubbed my arm and broke eye contact with him before I gave too much of myself away. "You're protective of what's yours. You told me that, and if you didn't want me to stick around, then you've had a handful of opportunities to leave me for dead. If you didn't want me here, you would have screwed me over like you screwed Malakai and Dallas."

Fuck.

"Don't insinuate anything." Well, my argument had already fallen apart in my hands, but I wouldn't give up on it. Not yet. I could come back from this minor setback. "I protected you because if you died on my watch, then Vince would never let it go. He'd constantly remind me of the *idiot* American I let die because I wasn't competent enough to keep him alive." That didn't sound like denial. Not in the slightest.

As I looked back up at him, however, I knew my words had been pointless. He wasn't looking at my face. His eyes were focused on my hands that had curled as I'd spoken, to keep them occupied and my heartrate steady. It was as if he knew what the movement meant. He watched me as if he knew I'd just spat out blatant lies. How did he know my tell?

"You're used to being around people who can't read you, but I can." *Fuck.* I tucked my hands in my armpits as I crossed my arms over my chest. An obvious move to both cover my fidget and cut my body off from him. This was not going the way I'd planned; not in the slightest. "And I'm sick of seeing one thing from you and hearing something completely different come out of your mouth."

He walked over to me and stationed himself a mere two feet away. Was he really able to tell? Had he been able to tell what I'd been thinking in that closet?

"Do you even want me to trust you?" That was an easy question to answer, but I still hesitated.

"No, I don't." It wasn't a lie, but it wasn't the whole truth either. It was somewhere between the two, where it summarised what I felt but gave no context to it. If we were going to continue working together, then maybe I would have to suffer through some more honesty. I could do that,

219

surely. "I don't want you to trust me, because if you do, then you'll stay. And if you stay, then you'll inevitably get under my skin like a parasite..."

I saw him flinch at the comparison, but I couldn't stop to ask why. If I stopped, then I wouldn't start again, and this was important for him to know. "If you do that, then I'll eventually return the trust you've given to me. And if I do *that*, then I leave you in a prime position to hurt me." His eyes averted from me once again. What was he thinking?

"You want to trust me, I know you do," he whispered. His eyes reached for mine once more, and I made sure to stay focused on him. "But I understand why you don't, why you *choose* not to. If our situations were reversed, then I wouldn't trust you either, so it's fine. I don't want you to apologise for what happened on the plane because it was a reasonable response. It just hurts to not be able to do anything about it."

His eyes averted from me before he scratched his arm hard enough to leave risen skin. "I can't change your opinion of me because I can't tell you everything until I know my sister is safe. Your opinion is based on the idea you have of me, and I'm the one holding back from fixing it."

He was wrong. While my opinion *was* based on the idea I had of him, it was more than just what he'd told me. What I thought of him wasn't solely founded on what he'd said. It was *me* and my understanding of him. Whether or not I wanted to admit it, we were similar. I hated it, but at the same time I... I *didn't*.

"If Vince was in danger, then I would do everything to keep him safe too, so I understand why you're keeping things from me." Ice. My stomach felt like ice. "I understand the weight that's sitting on your shoulders, more than anyone else might be able to. If you..." Damn it, I was about to do this. I was about to make everything so much harder for myself. "If you share it with me, then I can help you carry it."

Fuck. I actually liked this asshole. If he pushed me into it, I might've admitted that I trusted him. That I... *shit.*

"There's no weight on my shoulders. That implies I have control over my life," he said. A laugh echoed from his throat afterwards, and it was the kind I knew all too well. It was one you used when you had to cover what you were really feeling, when you had to conceal how bad it had all become.

He took another half-step towards me. "It just feels like I'm stuck in freefall, rushing towards the ground without anyone to stop me or slow me down. Instead, I'm just gaining speed; spiralling and slipping faster through the darkness without anything to grab onto or anyone to help me. And I don't know how much further I can fall. I don't know how long I have to do this before I collide with the earth or someone *catches* me."

I understood that feeling, too. It was all I felt throughout every waking moment with the Order. You couldn't carry any weight if you weren't grounded to do so—if you didn't have the ability to make decisions for yourself.

"Then let me catch you."

The words slipped out of my mouth faster than I could repress them—faster than I could think them over. I said them before I could weigh the consequences of them and decide if they were worth saying.

Judging from the look on his face they were worth it, but I still wasn't sure if I regretted them or not.

I untucked my hands from my armpits and uncrossed my arms, instead busying my palms by rubbing the sides of my legs. And then I kept talking, so he didn't have the opportunity to ask questions.

"If you trust me, after whatever happens at Paititi, we can go and save your sister. The second we're done taking the gold and destroying this place of power, we can save her so you can feel like you're standing on solid ground again." And in the process of getting her, I might just kill Hunter's father for what the man had done to him.

"I told you, even *you* can't-"

"Do you trust me?" I cut him off and kept my eyes completely locked on him.

In response, he let out a sigh and closed the distance between us—crushed the two feet of air into a mere few inches. There was a moment of quiet, where I felt his breath fan over my face and his eyes scour me for some kind of reaction. He wouldn't get one. Not yet.

"I asked you a question." I felt my whispered demand catch in my throat. So much for not giving a reaction.

At least he couldn't tell that my fingertips tingled as he brushed my hand with his own. What was he searching for?

Why was he searching for something?

"I trust you," he whispered back, and I heard the words catch in his throat too.

His eyes watched where we touched, where he continued to run his fingers over the back of my hand. The touch made my skin burn, made my blood run hot and my heart beat so hard it threatened to shatter my ribs.

"God, I trust you more than anything," he breathed.

And then he pulled that hand away from me, and my body grew cold again. Usually, that cold was what I wanted. I preferred the chill of indifference and calm over the heat of emotion. But right now, as my throat ran dry, I knew I didn't like this unique cold one bit.

"But I know what these people are like," he said. While he *had* stopped touching me, he *hadn't* moved away. Why was he still so close? "You can't win against them."

"You don't know what I'm capable of," I told him, and he raised an eyebrow at me. Damn it, why did that make it harder to breathe? "All I'm asking is that you have a little faith in me, and maybe I could prove my worth to you at Paititi."

"Prove your worth?" He asked, and I nodded in response.

"Look, I don't trust you—" my hands rubbed together before I could stop them—"but I believe that you're terrified for your sister. And you're right; I protect what's mine. Whether or not I trust you yet doesn't matter, because you've opened up to me as best you can so..."

I tilted my head back so I could get a better look at him, so

I could be sure he listened to my every word and understood the weight of them. "You *are* one of mine now, and your sister means the world to you, so that means she's one of mine, too. I'd go to war for my people."

My chest tightened at the way his golden eyes darkened, and I lifted my chin just a fraction more. I was well aware of how the action could be read, especially as my eyes flicked between his eyes and then down to his lips.

Did I really want him to kiss me or was I just... *no*. This wasn't just because we were standing too close, this was something I wanted.

There was something about him, something I couldn't place or understand, but this felt *right*, even when I didn't know him. My ability to breathe fell away as his eyes dipped to my lips, and I realised he smelled like peppermint.

He still had gum in his mouth, and in that moment I wondered if he constantly had some in his mouth to distract himself. If he told the truth in the closet, then the thoughts he had were far worse than my own... what if the gum was a way to alleviate the burn?

I didn't want it to be alleviated. I wanted to know exactly what he wanted. I wanted him to tell me, and I wanted him to *show* me. Imagining wouldn't be enough.

I needed to know what his lips would feel like against mine, what they would feel like on my neck, hovering over my pulse and as his teeth grazed my skin.

"Caeli..." he licked his bottom lip, and I saw those sharp canines again.

What if he'd lied about not being a conduit? What if *he* was a vampire, like his sister? What if his thoughts would have him burned at the stake because he wanted to bite my throat and drink from me? Why wasn't I averse to that thought? Why was I okay with the fact he might have lied to me once again?

"I can't do this." He took a step away from me, and to cover the feeling that I'd just been punched in the stomach, I did the same. Too strong. I had come on *far* too strong, and I'd completely misread the situation. "Not like this." Not like... what did that even mean?

Did he not want this? That was fine. If he didn't want it, then neither did I.

"You don't have to be one of my people." I backtracked my words, just so I could take control of the situation again. I *needed* to take control again. "You can tell me what you choose after Paititi." I took a step towards the door. "Otherwise, just be ready for the church visit tomorrow." I turned away from him so I could pretend the air in my lungs didn't burn like acid with each breath.

I was *never* going to tell Vince about this.

"Is that all I need to be ready for?" Hunter asked as I rushed towards the door and placed my fingers on the cold metal handle. I couldn't bring myself to look at him as I blurted out my next words and walked out of the room.

"Nothing exciting should happen tomorrow, so yes. That's all."

CHAPTER TWENTY-FIVE

THE ELUSIVE SAMAEL ELDRIDGE

"What do you think we're looking for?" I asked before I sipped the coffee that Hunter had bought for me this morning. It was a truce gift similar to Romania, an olive branch between us, and it was one that I had accepted happily. To say I hadn't slept much last night would be an understatement.

After the events of the night before, it was too hard to close my eyes and drift off to sleep. Whenever I tried, the things he'd told me ran through my mind, or I imagined him standing too close to me again. It was hard to pretend that what happened last night hadn't, but I knew it was best for my sanity and his.

We didn't need the complication of whatever threatened to happen between us last night.

"I don't know," Hunter replied, his voice a little blunter than his usual tone. His eyes flashed towards me as we walked through the crowded streets of Cusco.

There were too many people on the sidewalks, almost too many for me to be comfortable, but with Hunter next to me, I could breathe relatively easily. The fact that I was with him, mixed with the comfortable clothes I'd chosen for the day, helped to keep me somewhat relaxed for once.

"Maybe it will come to us when we're in there," I replied, my spare hand smoothing the front of my black t-shirt.

I'd taken the risk of grey sweatpants in the rather warm weather of Peru during the middle of the year. We should be back at the hotel before midday, and this was the most comfortable way to keep my scars hidden. That—along with my white Air Jordans—really showed how comfortable I was around him.

I was always careful with what I wore, because if I needed to run or fight, I didn't want my clothes to prevent me from being able to do so... but I guess I trusted Hunter more than I would ever say. Not enough to let my hair down, though. That would stay tied back in a ponytail until I knew who he was.

"Are you okay?" I asked as I saw how tense his shoulders were—how rigid his entire body was next to me. Was this because of what happened last night?

"I'm fine. I just didn't get much sleep last night." His fingers clasped his coffee cup far too tight for that to be the whole truth, but I'd let it slide. He was probably worried about his sister, and thinking about what we might be able to do to get her out of the cult after this.

"Neither," I said as I looked at my paper takeaway cup. "I definitely fell asleep at some point, though. Vince was gone when I woke up. I didn't hear him leave, so..." my brow furrowed as I took another sip of coffee.

"Is that odd?" Hunter asked as he looked at me with concern in his eyes. I nodded my head and looked away from him.

"He always makes sure to say goodbye before we split up, even if it's only for a day." I tried to ignore the tightness in my chest as my spare hand tapped against my leg. "Maybe he thought I'd be fine because you were in the next room over."

I didn't really believe the pitiful explanation I'd come up with, but it was the best I had. If he was taken then I would have woken up; he would have made noise and I would have stopped them. Or they would have tried to take me instead, since I was closest to the door and that was the point of me being there.

"Maybe." Why was he being so damned callous? I didn't like how hollow his voice sounded, not in the slightest.

"You're worried about your sister." I voiced my assumption, and his eyes reached mine. Once again, they tried to search for something, and if I knew what they were trying to find I would have shown him. I would have given him whatever he looked for. But he didn't search for long, instead he turned his attention back to his coffee.

"Yeah, last night just..." he trailed off, but I understood what he hadn't said. Digging into the thing you kept buried inside you always threw you off and made the pain fresh again. That's what we'd done yesterday and last night. And add onto that the fact I'd given him hope in his situation...

It was probably a stupid thing to have done on my part, but I was confident I could help him.

"We'll get her out, I promise." I didn't break promises, it was why I made them so rarely, but I knew I could keep this one. No matter who it was, how many people or guns they had, I would get her out.

He nodded before he looked at our heading. Iglesia del Triunfo; the first church built in Cusco. While the outside didn't look like much, the interior was adorned with gold, and it seemed like an ironic place to leave a clue for a city made of the stuff.

"I know you'll get her out, I just..." he stopped walking as we reached the main door to the church. I turned my attention to him, solely to him, even though he just stared at his fingers as they rested on the door handle.

"Hunt..." He flinched at the nickname. Maybe it was because it wasn't his real name, or maybe it was because something else was going on.

"You remember the code words, right?" He asked, and it made something in my stomach fall through the earth.

Something was wrong.

Something was *severely* wrong.

"Of course I do..." I risked a touch to his shoulder, a blatant attempt to force him to look at me since I'd never initiated unnecessary contact between us before. It didn't work though, and instead of helping, he seemed to tense under my touch. "What's actually going on here?" My hand fell from his shoulder to my side again.

"I know you don't trust me, but I need you to promise that you'll remember everything I said about my sister. It's true, all of it." His voice dropped to a whisper, and it filled my stomach with acid.

I couldn't make that promise. It was impossible when something hit me in the chest; a feeling I couldn't place but understood the overbearing weight of. He'd done something.

Trusting him had been a mistake.

I took a step away from him, away from the church, but he looked over his shoulder at me with pinched eyebrows.

"You can't back out now, you can't walk away, or bad things will happen to all of us." His voice was still quiet as the realisation fell on me like a tonne of bricks. He'd betrayed me, but I didn't know the extent of how bad yet. Maybe it was something small, something that we could move past. "I'm so sorry." Sorry? He was sorry? If he was sorry, then he didn't have to do this.

He pushed the door open and walked in and—only because of the blatant threat he'd made—I followed. He didn't look back at me.

The second we crossed the threshold the warm expression I was used to seeing on his face withered away. Beneath it was a cold and emotionless exterior.

Hunter focused on the front of the church, where gold adorned the wall that was covered in depictions of Jesus... and a group of men stood at the altar. They were all dressed in black Templum robes.

There were a few of them with their hoods down, and they were the ones I recognised. Malakai, Ryne, and Nylah. Every one of the assassins, minus the three I knew, all pointed their guns at the same target. Not me, *no*, but I wished they were. Instead, they all threatened the out-of-place man in the middle of them. The one dressed in a bitterly familiar salmon pink shirt amidst the sea of black.

"Vince..." I whispered as the coffee in my hand slipped out of my grasp and hit the ground next to my foot. When I looked down at it, I saw the pale brown liquid had splashed over my fucking white shoes.

That coffee had been an apology, an olive branch, and I thought it was for past actions. It hadn't been. It was for this; to either ease the blow or make it worse. While I didn't know the true intention, I knew the false sense of security I'd felt with Hunter made me question my intellect on every fucking level.

Vince was right; I *never* trusted the right fucking people.

I slowly turned towards Hunter before I stepped away from him and the coffee spill I'd just made. This entire time I thought he was trustworthy, that my gut had been wrong like it always was. He'd convinced me he hated Templum just like I did... but he was one of *them*.

The only possible way this situation could be worse was if he'd been part of the Order. I guess I could see that as the only positive right now, because even this shitty situation could somehow be *worse*.

"I knew I couldn't trust you," I whispered, and I could have sworn he flinched at my words. And I could have sworn his Adam's apple bobbed with a gulp as his expression continued to be cold and emotionless.

The situation wasn't adding up to me just yet, though. While I understood he was a Templum assassin, I didn't understand how his sister could be connected. There was something obvious I'd missed. There had to be.

I realised what that something was as Ryne walked towards us down the aisle between the pews.

He'd lied about not being a conduit. He was a vampire as I'd suspected last night, and I'd already been handed that information on a silver platter. Nylah told me that her brother was a vampire... how fucking stupid was I?

"Well done, my child." Ryne's voice echoed through the church. The words reverberated off the walls and threatened to shatter my skull.

I wanted to scream, to throw up and stab everyone who came within arm's reach. I wanted to run and kill everyone who got in my way, but there was nothing I could do. Not when they had Vince at gunpoint. Not when they had my entire world held hostage.

All I could do was stand and stare as Ryne embraced Hunter like a father embraced a son.

"Thank you, father." The person I had come to trust whispered, hardly loud enough to be heard.

It was almost as if he didn't want to—*no*. I wouldn't read into his response because he'd just shown me his cards. He'd shown me the path he'd chosen.

The reason he never told me his real name was quite simple.

He was the *elusive* Samael Eldridge.

And *me*?

I was a fucking idiot.

Chapter Twenty-Six

LITTLE PARASITE

My stomach felt like it was full of acid strong enough to burn through my body and turn me into nothing more than a pile of melted flesh on the floor.

My throat burned with bile as Ryne let go of me. He rested his scarred hands upon my shoulders as if he gave a single shit about me—as if he was actually proud of what I'd accomplished. The hurt in Caeli's eyes was enough to send that bile into my mouth, but I couldn't let it out. Nor could I let the discomfort and disgust show.

Samael Eldridge was the dutiful and stoic eldest son of Templum Gratiae's priest, so that was the part I played. I was meant to be the ideal image of my father's assassins, to be better than all the others and always do exactly as I was ordered to.

So far I'd been able to continue the act, because the threat of the chest or Nylah being succumbed to the same fate was enough to keep me in line. It helped me practice my acting skills, though. I had to learn how to cover the fact that I wanted to kill my father—that I wanted to burn Templum to the ground for everything they'd done to me and my sister.

"You've done well, *little Parasite*, and completed your Pilgrimage much faster than any of us could have anticipated," Ryne said. Each syllable shot through me like a bullet, but I made sure not to recoil at the pain.

If Caeli was as smart as she'd made herself out to be, she'd likely pieced together why I'd flinched last night when she compared me to a parasite... or maybe I'd been lucky and she hadn't noticed. I doubted it, though.

"I aim to please," I replied, my voice rough as I forced the words out of my mouth.

This entire mission was meant to be easy. It was supposed to be simple, and I was meant to complete it without trouble. Instead, I realised how screwed I was the moment I had Caeli pinned to the museum wall back in Lima.

"You've got to be fucking kidding me," Caeli whispered, too quietly for Ryne or anyone else to hear. But I could, even if I couldn't afford to look at her again and show how sorry I was through eye contact alone.

Instead of focusing on her, and the fact she was likely tearing herself to pieces over how she didn't see this coming, I looked at my sister. Nylah blinked twice fast and then twice slow, so I returned the signal. We were both okay, and we were both unhurt. We were good—for now, at least.

There were things I'd told Caeli that had been the truth. Yesterday I'd chosen my words carefully so she would believe my story. I made sure there was the right amount of verity to the lies so that when the time came she might *understand* my situation. I didn't expect forgiveness, but I hoped for simple understanding.

The cult holding my sister hostage was this one. It's just the fact that they would *never* let her go that I'd omitted and lied about. Everything I'd told her about my father was true, everything he'd *done* to me... the only thing I hadn't told her was why it stopped three years ago. But if she remembered what Nylah had said back in the Archives, then maybe she'd already pieced that together too.

That's if she was thinking about me at all, which would be a shock if she was. If I was in her position, I wouldn't waste a single second on me. There were more important things to worry about. Her focus was likely on Vincent, on how to get him out, reflective of how mine was on Nylah.

"Caeli Venatrix..." Ryne finally let go of my shoulders to turn his full attention to Caeli. I had to tense my body to stop a shiver from racking my spine. "Do you know how long we've been after you, *One*?" *One*... why did that feel worse than when he called me *Parasite*?

"I assume since I left the Order." Caeli's voice was blunt, tired... *hollow.*

What the fuck did you do, Samael?

"No, it was long before then." Ryne inched towards her, and there was nothing I could do about it. At least, nothing that would simultaneously keep Nylah, Caeli, and Vincent safe. There were too many guns here. Even if I had any power stored, it would be useless with the amount of bullets they'd get through any one of the three people I wanted to keep alive.

"Don't tell me you're one of those conduit fanatics, Ryne. You're better than that," Caeli replied, her voice remarkably steady as my father stood directly in front of her.

I knew my father, knew how much he revered conduits and how he desired to control them. It was why I wasn't surprised when he ran a finger along Caeli's jaw. She was unnervingly still, like a predator stalking it's prey, completely unflinching as Ryne took hold of her chin and forced her eyes onto him.

Fuck, I wanted to rip out his damned throat for touching her. It was the same visceral reaction as when I *knew* Hansen had started to touch her, when my forehead started to burn all those days ago...

She wasn't *theirs* to touch.

"I'm not a fanatic, child; I'm a realist." Caeli's eyes flashed with silver licks of flame and I wondered how my father could still be so close to her with a steady heartbeat. "If Victoria succeeded with you, then you're worth more than anything else on the face of this planet. I know Victoria. She wouldn't have kept you alive if you were a failure."

Ryne finally let go of Caeli's chin and I had to consciously unfold the fists I'd apparently made. I had to keep calm and think clearly, which I'd already learned wasn't my strong suit when someone touched her. I had to stay focused so I could find a way out of this situation. There had to be one, and I had to get us all out alive.

"Well, maybe she would have kept me imprisoned in a tighter cell if I *was* a success." Had they actually kept her in a cell? Fuck, *no*, I had to focus.

"Do you honestly think you escaped of your own accord?" Ryne asked, and I walked away before I opened my mouth and screwed us all over. My feet carried me towards the altar, towards the men holding Vincent hostage and my sister standing at the edge of the group.

"You think they let me go? You didn't see the trail of bodies I left behind on my way out to know that doesn't make sense." Caeli's voice echoed through the church, which meant I couldn't escape it.

Even from my new distance her chai scent still wrapped itself around me. At least I was far enough that it wouldn't send me half-blind like it did last night when it looked like she'd been about to... *fuck*, what would have happened if I'd let her kiss me? Would I have told her the truth? Or would I have just made this entire situation worse?

"The person who let you out, do you remember him? The second in command?" Ryne asked as I reached my sister. I only turned back to watch the interaction once I was close enough to brush my shoulder against Ny's. "The only person you might call a father?" The devorator she'd told me about—the one they used the DNA of to fill the gaps of the woman they'd pulled out of her resting place.

"He didn't let you out as an act of kindness to his daughter. It was an order." My father continued speaking, and something hit me in the chest at the new information. She hadn't told me how she escaped the Order. "This has all been an elaborate test that you've passed with flying colours, but now they want you back. And on top of that, they want you to have the power you're destined to control. If you cooperate, I might give you a better option than being handed over to the Order like a prettily wrapped gift."

I looked at my brother and watched as he smirked at the words. So he knew the entire plan, just like how he'd known what Caeli was the entire time she'd been on Templum's radar. What other information was being held from me? I'd only found out what Caeli was on the flight from Rome, when she'd told me everything and I... well, I *hadn't*. Maybe I should have. Maybe I could have saved us the trouble of this entire shitty situation if I'd just told her.

But it had been too much of a risk to do so.

"Are you going to allow me the choice between one form of imprisonment and another? How very generous of you." Caeli didn't seem the least bit interested in the offer. I could tell that much from her body language alone. She stood as stiff as a board. Her eyes stared daggers right into my father's soul.

"No, it's the choice between imprisonment or working for me." My father was a bloody idiot if he thought he would get

Caeli on his side. She'd had her taste of freedom, and she would do whatever it took to keep it.

"Fuck you, Ryne." That was the exact response I'd expected. Anything less and I would have been disappointed.

"Are you okay?" I whispered to Nylah, who nodded, even though she was entirely focused on Ryne and Caeli. I didn't blame her, because if I was right, then Caeli was our only way out.

"I thought that might be your response, *Shadow*, but I thought I might give you some time to think about changing your mind." Ryne was really doing his best to sway Caeli. It was almost a pity that it wouldn't work.

"Is the plan going to work?" Nylah asked in a whisper as I followed her lead and focused my eyes back on Ryne and Caeli.

"I sure hope so..." I replied, and saw her nod again through my peripheral vision.

"You can wait until after your incitement to give me your final answer," Ryne said to Caeli, who's expression was still cold and empty. "By then, you'll have all the power you could ever hope to wield at your fingertips."

Caeli shook her head, and a familiar smirk played on her full lips. What I wouldn't give to know exactly what was going on in her head, to tell her telepathically that I needed her help. I just needed to tell her I'd do everything possible to help her now Nylah was back in my line of sight.

"If I get the power everyone seems to think I can wield,

240

you wouldn't be able to stop me." Caeli made a valid point, but it was one that didn't matter to Ryne. He thought he could control conduits, but that's only because the ones he had in Templum were used to his abuse and would do anything to avoid it. He hadn't met the force of Caeli before.

"Maybe not, but Samael could." I couldn't. There wasn't any power left in me. I'd have to drink the blood of a handful of incited conduits before I had any hope of standing against a truci. "Or Nylah, once she goes through the incitement with you. A truci and a custos working together, nothing would stop the two of you." Ryne's tactic was better on that front, but even playing to Caeli's greed for power wouldn't work. Not this way, at least.

"How the fuck are you going to convince her?" Nylah whispered. She'd probably seen the pure rage that seeped from Caeli, and the concern was a fair one to have because I didn't really know how to do it.

It was supposed to take longer to get here, to get back to Cusco, but Caeli was... she was just *too good* at what she does. She was too fucking intelligent, and it had made the 'not getting emotionally involved' part of the plan even more difficult than it should have been.

"I've planted the seeds," I replied in a hushed tone to match Nylah's. "I just don't have the details-"

"What are you two whispering about?" Malakai spoke loud enough to end every conversation in the church. The question forced everyone's eyes onto Nylah and I.

"I was catching up with my sister, who I haven't seen in a

while. We were trying not to disturb anyone," I answered.

My eyes flicked towards Vincent to confirm he was okay before I settled on my brother, who seemed far more observant compared to normal. That wasn't a good thing for us.

"He just asked if I enjoyed the auction, since it was the first time I'd left the compound for a couple of years," Nylah added. I had to refrain from smiling at her choice of words. They made the story more believable, but they also gave Caeli more information about our situation. God, she was smarter than I was by a long shot. "If everyone needs to know, I thought it was boring. Even the theatrics weren't enough to keep me interested." Nylah looked to Caeli, who was still focused entirely on Ryne.

Getting her to focus on me long enough to communicate anything was going to be harder than I thought. Add onto that how difficult slipping the code words into sentence would be and it would be a damned miracle if I could convince her to help us.

I was the one who came up with the bloody words for this *exact* purpose, and yet I still picked something that would be more than difficult to work into a conversation that would need to involve mild threats. *Colours...* for fuck's sake, I was an idiot. I had to work out how to fit colours into a conversation naturally, and I'd have to work it out fast.

"Yes, I heard all about those *theatrics*, Caeli. Personally, I would like to avoid any moving forwards. Will I have to cuff you to do that, or will you behave?" Ryne swayed the conversation back to the topic at hand, which was actually a good thing for me. It meant that Ryne still questioned Malakai, and I could use that to my advantage.

"Well, you do have the only person I care about at gunpoint." Caeli spat the words at Ryne. If she had control of the situation, she would have gutted him already, and I would have held his hands behind his back to make it easier for her. "I'll fucking *behave* as long as you keep threatening him, and you know it."

"I'm glad we see this from the same point of view, because I would like you to follow my instructions very closely." My father was still focused on Caeli, on who he thought of as a new possession. A new *weapon*. "We're all going to take a short walk to some cars. From there, we'll get to our helicopters, and we'll head into the National Park, straight to the location of Paititi. We'll split you and Sinclair up for the air travel, but you'll see each other when we land again."

"I want to fly with Vince-"

"You aren't in a position to negotiate, *One*. You will do as I say, or Sinclair won't be flying anywhere ever again." Ryne threatened, so she backed down. Literally. She retreated two steps from Ryne as her face turned to stone. Was it the threat that forced her away from him, or being called a number instead of her name?

"If you're worried about being surrounded by strangers, don't be. The three who did this to you will keep you company and answer any questions you might have. Samael!" I stiffened as he called my name, and I touched

Nylah's shoulder before I walked back to them. "You can escort her to the car."

I nodded before I led Caeli out of the church. Once we reached the black SUV, we had a split second to talk. It wasn't long, but it might be the only opportunity I'd have to communicate with her. That opportunity turned to smoke in my hands as she clearly saw the same excess of time. And of course, she jumped on it first. As I expected, she used it to remind me of her previous threats.

"I warned you what I'd do if you ever hurt Vince," she said.

Her silver irises were as hot as white flame, and it almost made me take a step back. *Almost.* But just like every other time she'd looked at me with pure anger, there was an idiotic conflict of interest in my brain.

The reasonable, self-preserving side of me screamed that I should run and protect myself. And then there was the irresponsible part that thought she was the most beautiful creature I'd ever laid eyes on. It whispered as it told me to be consumed by her inferno.

"But just in case you forgot, I'll remind you, *Samael.*"

Her saying my real name forced that war in my head to it's overdue end. The reasonable, self-preserving side laid down it's weapons in surrender and the irresponsible part claimed victory.

Burning in her hellfire it would be.

She tilted her head to the side as she hissed out her next words at me. "I'm going to cave in your fucking skull with my bare hands."

Why did I find that attractive? What was wrong with me? Was it because I'd watched her do exactly that to Hansen?

She'd been covered in blood, and the look on her face when she'd done it... if that was how I went, then that was fine with me. I'd give anything to be a source of solace for her. She could have my life if that's what she needed.

Fuck, I was beyond screwed.

And no amount of gum would help distract me from that fact anymore.

CHAPTER TWENTY-SEVEN

A TOOL TO BE USED

My breaths were quick and staggered.

I could hardly get any air in my lungs, not when I was stuck in the helicopter across from Hunt—*no*, not Hunter. *Samael.* His stupid gold eyes monitored my every breath as I tried to think of a way out of this. But there wasn't a single way out of this. Not yet.

Nylah was stationed between her brother and another assassin I didn't know the name of, while I was stuck next to Malakai. The only missing member of the Eldridge family was Ryne, who no doubt had Vince at gunpoint on the helicopter behind us.

"It's been a while since all three of us were last together. How are my brothers doing?" Nylah asked, which meant I was about to listen to a conversation I wanted nothing to do with. Maybe it was a jumpstart to the torture that awaited me after this incitement business.

"Fucking fantastic," Malakai replied, his warm skin tone slightly pale. He clearly still had his fear of flying.

How had I not noticed the similarities between Malakai and *Samael*? Or between him and Nylah when they had stood next to each other in the damned Archives? I knew I wasn't great with faces, or names or reading people, but fucking hell, how dumb was I?

"Better, now that I know you're safe," *Samael* told his sister, his right hand held by both of hers in her lap. It was the same hand he'd brushed against mine the night before. It was the same hand that made me question my standpoint about him. And it was *that* damned hand which made me think about... *fuck.*

"Same," Nylah replied. Her fingertips tapped against the back of that dangerous hand in a rhythm. A consistent tapping of twice fast and twice slow. It meant something to the siblings, but I had no idea what.

"How long are we meant to fly for?" Samael asked his brother, who shook his head.

"Under an hour," Malakai responded far too bluntly.

Now, while I didn't want to listen to their family reunion, I didn't have a choice. But I could use it to my advantage. If they were going to talk openly and casually, then they might let something important slip through the cracks. I'd take whatever leverage I could get my hands on.

"And how are you holding up?" Samael asked, still focused on his brother. I did my best to make myself look busy and stared out the window over Megantoni National Park, where Paititi was located just north of Cusco. The trees stretched as far as my eyes could see, a comforting sea of lush green.

"Like you fucking care." Well, that was a fun response I couldn't ignore.

When I turned back around, I saw Malakai glare at his brother, a bitterness in his eyes that he hadn't even shot at me when I fucked him over two years ago. He truly hated his brother, and this conversation seemed like the best way to figure out why. It would be a good thing to use against them, to create a little more chaos. If I could spark the fire that threatened to explode in front of me, I could ruin what little familial bond was left between them. That would benefit me greatly.

"You're my brother, Mal. Of course I care." And that was definitely unstrained and extremely believable.

"Don't waste your energy," Malakai responded. What the fuck was going on? "We have more important things to focus on."

"Like what? Your mockery of a Pilgrimage?" Well, I guess Samael agreed with Malakai; it was best to focus on the *important* things. I had to refrain a smile, because there wasn't a way I would let Samael elicit one from me—even if I was entertained by the direction this conversation now headed. "The Pilgrimage you've been trying to complete for three years? The one that keeps being extended and twisted-"

"The only reason my journey continues is because our father sees promise in me-"

"No, it continues because you consistently fail him. The only reason you've succeeded this time around is because he got *me* involved." Samael ripped his hand away from his sister as he spoke and rested his elbows on his knees to get closer to his brother.

Malakai went rigid next to me, and something in the air shifted as the frail bond between them snapped.

"You should not speak of our Heir in that-"

"Brother Koen, stand down." Malakai cut off the other assassin in the helicopter with us.

"You sure you don't want him to fight this battle for you? Because delegating *is* the only thing you're good at." Normally I would have pushed the situation to explosive levels of anger, but it seemed that with Samael involved I didn't have to. In a regular situation, I might have implied that I slept with one or both of the brothers, added an extra level of betrayal and jealousy. Maybe—just this once—it was best to keep my mouth shut and let them bury their relationship while I stored the information away for later.

"How about you stay focused on your role, Samael? You are a tool to be used, nothing more and nothing less. You are just a *Parasite*," Malakai hissed. There it was again. Samael flinched at the word—at the *name* he had been called.

But this time he went completely silent, which was how I

knew something was severely wrong.

All he did was stare at Malakai, who had gone even more pale. Was he afraid? Shit, he *was*. He was terrified of Samael... now that I could use to my advantage.

Now, as for the nickname, if you could call it that, I wasn't sure how to utilise it. It could be something to make him shut down, or it could be a way to learn more about him. If he was truly a vampire, and he hadn't lied about the fact that the cult he and his sister were in viewed vampires as less than other conduits, then maybe—*no*.

I'm not doing this. I'm not giving him another chance. He made his bed and now he must lie in it.

If I made it through this incitement, he would find out why his choice had been a lethal one.

"Sam, what colour would you say the sky is today?" Nylah asked to change the subject after a few moments of bitter silence. "And be as specific as you usually are." He was usually specific with colours? Was that why he—for the love of fuck, *no*. He wasn't my problem. He was a grown man, and a possible vampire. And he could take care of himself. "Would you say it's azure blue?"

Azure? As in the code word—*no*.

"Azure is too bright. The blue is dark today, more like a sapphire."

I slowly looked towards Samael. This had to be some kind of sick joke, a way to rub in the fact he and Templum had won. It had to be to prove that he knew what he'd done to me, that he knew exactly how close I'd let him.

"And what about the storm clouds on the horizon?" Nylah asked, and I looked at her fingers as they tapped her leg. Twice fast, twice slow. It meant something, it *had* to, and there was a reason she still did it without Samael to notice it. It was for me. It had to be for *me* to see.

"They're the same colour as Caeli's eyes..." Samael replied, his eyes locked on me as I noticed his hands move in a bitterly familiar pattern. It was *my* pattern. "Plain old *grey*." Grey? Were they asking for my help?

My eyes flicked back down to his hands, that still ran in the same circular motions. The point of his movement was to prove that I had the right idea of the situation, and Nylah's was to give me a way to communicate back to them without saying a word.

But *he* had lied to me. *He* had endangered Vince, who I didn't know for sure was even still alive. I wouldn't know until we landed, and I laid eyes on him again. Samael was the reason I was in this damned mess to begin with. But I'd promised to get his sister out of whatever they were stuck in...

"What are you two doing?" Malakai asked, but I knew the words weren't directed at me. He must have felt the control of the situation slip from his fingers, and now he needed to claw it back through whatever means necessary.

"You know what you did by calling him that name, Malakai. I'm trying to make him feel better." Nylah cared about her brother, and it was obvious that he cared about her, too. If he hadn't lied, like he said he hadn't, then she was in danger.

But there was for certain one part he *had* lied about, and that was the option he had to buy his sister out of the cult they were in. If she was a guardian, as she had told me in Archives, then there was no way they would ever let her go. There was no simple way out for either of them, not together at least.

So if that *was* true, then how long had I been a part of their escape plan for? Because while Templum had tasked him to become a friend to me, to make me trust him and help them take me down by destroying me from the inside, I think he'd actually used the situation to his advantage. He'd been careful with his words. He'd made sure to get close but hadn't let me cross the line with him last night...

I should know how that all works, because it had been the exact method that Dallas used on me a year ago. But not Samael. He'd protected me.

"I can't do this. Not like this."

If he was meant to tear me apart, he should have let me. If he was truly one of them, he should have jumped at the opportunity to let me attach myself to him and let me fall to pieces when he would betray me. Instead, he drew a line, a boundary, and saved me from the hurt. The only reason he would have done that was to get me to *actually* trust him in the aftermath of his betrayal.

"It's not a *name*, Nylah. It's what he is." Malakai turned towards me. He had a grin on his face, like he'd just figured out how to grind me into dust. "Did he tell you?" I raised an eyebrow in both interest and a lack of care. Whatever he was about to tell me didn't matter, and I felt I knew exactly what it was he was about to say.

"Samael here isn't just an assassin, but a conduit. He's a lamia. A bloodsucking vampire... and do you even know what the real plan is for you after your incitement?" So my assumption was correct. Samael was a vampire, and that meant everything he'd said about the conduit type being *ungodly* had been from personal experience. He'd told me so much, and I hadn't even noticed that he'd let me in on how he felt about himself and what he was.

Maybe I could have feigned concern or shock at his question, but I didn't have the energy to. And maybe I could have pushed for him to speak, or let out a weakened word that showed I was afraid. But I wasn't, and Malakai didn't need the encouragement to keep talking.

"Once you gain your power, you're going to be a personal battery for Samael."

Chapter Twenty-Eight

COMFORTING COLD

So I would be reduced to a power source for another conduit. *Great*, that's exactly what I needed, to be diminished to something even *less* than what I'd been with the Order. This was just so *great*.

"You don't have to use your power and suffer the consequences, and we still get to have shadow-magic in our ranks. It's a win-win for everyone involved," Malakai explained, but it was a lie. It wouldn't end well for Samael, who would have to deal with the consequences of his own power.

If they forced him to drink from me, to use the shadows that everyone seems to think I could wield, then he would become addicted in a far different fashion to a witch. The issue was that while Malakai, and likely Ryne, thought I would be the battery, it wasn't quite that way around. I would be the energy source, *he* would be the battery. The only issue was that batteries degraded over time, and eventually he would need to drink me dry to use even a tiny portion of my power.

He was just as trapped as Nylah.

I looked over to Samael, who'd lost the colour in his face. Did he think I cared? Did he think I would blame him for what he was? Or that I would hold it against him? Maybe he did, because it sounded like that's what Templum had done to him for years. *Parasite...*

"I'd have to survive the incitement to worry about that happening." It wasn't the first time I'd come face to face with my mortality, and the thought of death didn't scare me. It was something I'd accepted years ago, and I hadn't expected to make it this far. I'd always lived on borrowed time, especially since I found out how I was made. I wasn't meant to be alive, so why would it matter if I died?

"You'll go through your incitement with Nylah. The statistics of survival, even from centuries ago, have always dramatically increased when people go through their incitements together. That survival rate spikes again when they're balancing conduits. Nylah is a custos, you're a truci. A guardian and a grim. It can't get more balanced than light and dark together." Fuck. If Malakai spoke truth then it was more than likely that I would survive these next few hours, and that I'd come out of it with the power I didn't want.

That meant I would lose to the Order and everyone else who wanted to see the grims resurrected.

Shit. I was going to *lose*... but maybe I didn't have to do it alone.

Me, Nylah and Samael. We all needed each other to get out of this alive... and maybe if I helped them, then I could keep up my streak of unbroken promises.

I took three deep breaths as I thought about my options. Either help the siblings and have a greater shot at getting out alive or take my chances of getting Vince and me out without backup.

This wasn't just about me, it was about them and Vince. I didn't have to work with Samael at all once we were done here. We could part ways after we made it to a safe distance.

I looked over at him then. He was still too pale, too focused on me. He was waiting for an answer, but so was Nylah. So I gave them one.

I tapped on my thigh, twice fast and twice slow.

And I felt my stomach turn to comforting cold.

———◦◦◦———

"Are you going to be okay?" Samael asked, and my breath shook in response.

We stood in the open side door of the helicopter, and all I could see in front of me was the lake we'd landed on. There was only one way to reach the shore, and that was to swim.

I'd known it was how we would have to get to land. It had

been part of the original plan, but the initial thought was that I'd be doing it with Vincent and *Hunter*, two people I trusted to help me through. Now I was separated from Vince and left alone with Samael *fucking* Eldridge as my help.

"I'll be fine," I whispered as I rubbed my freshly uncuffed wrists.

What confused me the most about this entire situation wasn't the fact that Malakai had left Samael and me alone on this thing, but the concern I could see clear as day in his gold eyes. It was as if he actually thought of me as a person instead of the only option he had for freedom.

"I am actually afraid of enclosed spaces," Samael whispered back, and I slowly looked up at him. Was that why Nylah had been holding his hand on the flight over? "There were things I didn't lie about, and when I told you what my father did to me, that was one of them." The helicopter had been small, so maybe it had pushed his limits and Nylah did all she could to help him through it. "I know you weren't lying about being afraid of water. I could hear your heartbeat, so let me help you like you helped me in the Archives."

He could hear my heartbeat? Did that mean he could hear whenever it raced? Whenever I thought about—*no*. What was wrong with me?

"I didn't help you, I-"

"Sure, you didn't try to distract me by asking me to describe how you smelled. *Not at all*." Right, maybe it had been a little obvious, but that didn't mean he had to bring it up.

He sighed as he ran a hand through his hair, which I didn't want to read too far into. I didn't know what his body language meant outside of the persona he'd shown me. I didn't know what was real and what was a lie.

"We're the only ones here, Princess." And what was the point of calling me that? "Everyone else is on shore to make sure it's safe. You *can* talk to me." Could I now?

"Is that why you've stayed back to watch me?" I asked, my eyebrows furrowed as I glared at him. "Was it just so we could talk? I already told you I would help without saying a word. Do you realise how much of a risk-"

"They have no reason to think this is anything other than a captive getting used to their new captor. Like Malakai said, you're supposed to be my new power source, so..." It seemed he was unable to look at me again. If past experience meant anything, it was likely a trait of his guilt. "Ryne said you'd have a choice, but that was a lie."

Ryne, not *my father.* He distanced himself from his own blood, from all of his family except for Nylah. If everything he'd said about his past was actually true, then I couldn't blame him for doing so.

He rested a hand on the top of the doorframe, and it took everything in me to continue hating him. The sunlight reflected off the water and took away any shadows that should have been on his perfect face. If I wasn't careful, I might let what my body wanted overrule logic. This man couldn't be trusted, no matter how beautiful his features were.

"Besides, I'm the only conduit here aside from you and Ny. The others are back at the compound, so they aren't put in danger now that you're involved. You haven't been conditioned to follow orders, so they think you're the only risk in this situation. I've been programmed, so they're not concerned about me."

"Malakai is," I replied, shaking my head as I turned towards the edge of the water, where the other assassins were clambering onto land. "He thinks something is going on."

"My brother is a fucking idiot, and Ryne knows it. We all do." That didn't make me feel any better about any of this. "He won't say anything to Ryne because he knows that if he wants to bring up a theory, especially one about me, then he has to have evidence. He learned that the hard way." And what the fuck was that supposed to mean? Had he done something before that threatened Templum?

"What if he's recording us? That would be all the evidence he'd need."

"He's not intelligent enough to think that far ahead." And that didn't help my confidence, either. In fact, that might have just made my anxiety worse, because he didn't seem worried about any of this in the slightest.

My shoulders tensed as I saw Nylah pull herself out of the lake. How was Samael not worried about the incitement? His sister could die, and he didn't seem phased about it. It didn't make sense, because if all of this was for her, then how could he not be worried?

"You and Nylah will be fine for your incitement if you're concerned about that," he said, as if he read my mind. More likely he had read my body language, since it seemed he could do that without an issue.

"I'm not worried about that. It's the water." I attempted to redirect the conversation. It was the only option I had left to distance myself. While I was more than willing to help him and Nylah break away from Templum, that was where the relationship would end. Working together afterwards wasn't an option, not when I couldn't trust him to tell me the truth.

"Okay, well, if you were worried about the incitement, I would tell you I *know* you're going to be fine," he said as I looked over at him once again. "You and Nylah are the two most stubborn people I know, and with you going into it together, there's no way you'll fail the Entity's trial."

The Entity... it had been so long since I'd heard that word. Eight years, to be exact. Aric had told me that the Entity was what I needed to appease, what I had to keep happy. It liked balance. That was why you were more likely to survive the incitement when you entered with another conduit of a different kind.

"If we find a guardian to go through the incitement with you, then you're guaranteed to survive. The Entity hasn't had a grim in hundreds of years. If you play your cards right, then you may end up being it's favoured."

I didn't know what terrified me more, the thought of gaining power or being the focus of the Entity's attention.

No one knew what it was, or what it was truly capable of. All we knew was that it's where the magic came from, that it had created the pools and chose who received it's power.

My shoulders relaxed at the mention of it, and at the thought of Aric. He'd been the only one of the Order of Shadows personnel who treated me like a person instead of an object or a weapon. While Vince was who I saw as my father, Aric was the closest I had to the real thing, and having to leave him behind had been the hardest part of running.

But if what Ryne said was true, then that was another lie. Aric hadn't released me because he wanted me to be free. He'd done it because Ashford instructed him to. Why couldn't anyone just be who they said they were?

"And what would you say to someone who's about to swim through a lake when they're deathly afraid of water?" I asked as my eyes settled on the lake's surface. Maybe if Aric had cared about me, then he would have done something about all the torture...

And maybe if I focused enough on the water, I could pretend Vince was next to me, and not the person responsible for putting me in this position.

"I would remind that person that their father is being held at gunpoint, and if they let their fear get the better of them that the bad guys won't hesitate to shoot him."

My breath hitched at the words, but only because he was right. If I froze out there, if I did anything other than what Ryne instructed me to do, it wasn't me they would hurt. It was Vince.

While I had been fishing for a response a little more supportive than what he'd given, making sure I knew something worse could happen worked too. I nodded at him to prove I'd heard, and that I wouldn't let my fear get the better of me. Not my fear of water, at least.

We waited in silence for an assassin to signal to Samael it was safe for us to come to land. Malakai was aware of my fear of water, just the same as I knew of his fear of flying. The only difference was that I'd never use someone's phobia against them the way he had done to me.

The entire reason they held me behind was so they could get Vince onto land without me pulling any stupid moves. If I was honest, I would admit it was a smart move, and that was why I was worried. It was the reason I wasn't as confident in Malakai's lack of future planning as Samael, because if he had forethought this, then there was every chance that Malakai also had a plan to prove that Samael wasn't loyal to Templum.

If he did, then this entire situation was so much worse than what I thought. It would mean I was ten steps behind *Malakai* of all people. Hell, I'd be more than ten steps behind because I wasn't even on the same path.

"Why didn't you just tell me who you were?" I asked when I realised Vince wasn't even on the shore yet. The question was all I could ask, because it was the only thing I couldn't figure out. I looked over at him and saw his eyebrows were furrowed.

"I couldn't risk-"

"I would have helped you."

Chapter Twenty-Nine

I LIKE THOSE ODDS

Samael shook his head at my certainty. How could he not believe that I would have helped him?

"You would have killed me." The certainty in his voice made me question myself for a second. Yes, there might have been a chance I would have avoided all possible risks and killed him without hesitation, but it was so slim it was near non-existent.

"No," I said without any doubt. "I know exactly what it's like to be stuck in an organisation you're terrified of. If you'd just told me the truth at the beginning of this, we wouldn't be here." I held his gaze so I could prove I wouldn't back down from the argument.

I was right, and I knew it. It was a long shot to say any of this to him, but I hoped it might force an apology from him. I would even take a half apologetic look.

"There was no way to tell when they could hear us and when they couldn't. It was the only way to keep Ny safe." And yet here we were, talking as if we were in a secure position to do so.

I shook my head as I looked forward and finally saw Vince's blond hair floating above the water as they directed him to the lake's shore. I understood the need to protect those you cared about; it was why I wouldn't be able to hold this against Samael if he told the truth from this point forward. But I could still be pissed at how everything had turned out.

"I would have found a different way," I told him as I kept a watchful eye on my father. While I could understand what he'd done, I still wanted him to admit that it hadn't turned out well for anyone involved. "We could have taken Nylah from the Archives, or the auction. If you had just trusted me like you said you do, we wouldn't be stuck in the middle of a forest with all of us at risk of getting shot and your sister about to go through her fucking incitement."

"Like I said before, you and Ny will be fine," he told me, which made me shake my head. Of course, he wouldn't even acknowledge anything else I'd said.

"You only think that because you know what to expect from an incitement," I argued. "It's different for everyone, and we probably won't have it as easy you." Maybe I shouldn't have said that, because no incitement was ever easy, but it definitely proved what I thought of him.

"It wasn't easy..." he trailed off as he looked down at me with a smirk on his face. "And are you really going to let yourself fail when you know I passed my trial?" Damn it.

My jaw popped. While I didn't know what was true and what was fake about him, I hadn't been afforded the luxury of a false persona. He knew how to get me riled up, how to make sure I survived what was to come.

He'd made it a competition, and I didn't have to say anything for him to know I was grateful for his words. Nor did I have to confirm that they worked just as he intended. They only worked so well because it wasn't Hunter Black I was competing against anymore. This was *Samael Eldridge*, the one person in the world who might actually be a worthy opponent.

"What was your trial?" I asked, half wanting to know what to expect and half wanting to know what I had to beat. To win I just had to survive something darker than him, which should be simple enough given my history.

"I had to accept my anger at my father for killing my mother in front of me. In the trial, I killed the dream version of him, and allowed myself to feel that bottled pain." Fuck. That was almost as messed up as my childhood. "The trial is something that you need to accept. It's an emotional imbalance that you need to rectify in order to keep control over your power. If you freeze, or deny it, the Entity will see you as unbalanced and, therefore, unworthy. You won't come back out of the water, and your locked power is leaked into the pool for the next person."

Shit, I didn't really need the reminder of what the worst possible outcome could be today, but he'd given it to me anyway. My heart hammered in my chest as the weight of what was to come slammed into me. Emotions weren't my strong suit, but I'd have to figure them out in the next hour or so, or I would end up dead.

Before I could make myself look like an idiot and ask for advice, Vince made it to the shore. An assassin signalled to Samael while ten others directed their guns towards my father.

"Are you ready to swim?" He asked me. His golden eyes latched onto mine as I nodded. "It's going to be the four of us against forty of them."

I took a deep breath as I readied myself to jump into the water. Forty of them? That was more than I thought there would be.

"I like those odds," I said before I threw myself into the water.

Chapter Thirty

EASE UP ON THE THREATS

"Are you alright, kid?" Vincent asked the second I helped Caeli from the water.

In all honesty, I hoped the man was speaking to me, but I knew better than that. Vincent wouldn't so much as spare a glance at me after what I'd done, and I understood completely.

I'd fucked up with Caeli, which meant I'd absolutely fucked up with Vince. They both cared about each other more than they cared about themselves. It was how their relationship worked to keep them both alive. While it would be hard work to gain back what little of Caeli's trust I had, it would be even harder to earn Vincent's as well. It would take a damned miracle for either of them to want to speak to me again after we got out of this.

If we got out of this.

"I've been better," Caeli hissed through her teeth, which reminded me I was supposed to be holding her hostage. I was supposed to be in control of her, not holding her arm gently as I shamelessly stared at her body through her soaked black shirt.

Maybe my job would be easier if she didn't smell like fucking *chai*. Or maybe it would be easier if she didn't look at me with death in her eyes, which never affected me the way she likely aimed for.

Now was not the time to get distracted by those eyes of molten silver. I had to proceed carefully, and not just for my sake, but for the sake of Ny and the other two people I considered allies—even if that consideration wasn't reciprocated.

"Malakai, you studied the maps. Take us to Paititi," Ryne instructed as I let go of Caeli's arm. My fingers tingled and ached at the broken touch, but I hid the feeling as the group followed Malakai through the trees.

The quiet walk that followed was more than enough for me to spiral into a deep well of regret. It was far too easy to overthink everything Caeli had said in the helicopter, and therefore too easy to conclude that she was right and I was entirely wrong.

The only reason I hadn't apologised to her was because it would mean I'd have to admit that I'd made a huge fucking mistake. And I'd have to admit that mistake could cost us our lives.

When I responded so bluntly to her saying she would have helped me—when I said she would have just killed me had I told her everything—I'd only done so because it was the only avenue I had left.

But now I realised I was wrong, because I hadn't accounted for the generosity and understanding that she'd already showed me. I'd simply focused on her paranoia and self-preservation, the things that she'd already ignored by continuing to work with me.

While I hadn't intended to get close to her—my entire plan relied on *not* doing that—I don't think I'd quite managed to distance myself.

I felt like I knew her, at least enough to read her body language and understand the basis of who she was. I knew she would have listened to me if I'd told her everything, and that she would have believed every word I told her. She had been in a similar position, imprisoned with the Order until she was fifteen, and the idiotic argument I'd made was that she wouldn't have cared...

What would have happened if I'd told her the truth? What would have happened if that admission had been recorded and shown to Ryne? Sure, we might have planned to get Nylah out at the auction or the Archives, but then she would have been at gun point just like Vince. Hell, our situations were so similar that both Nylah and Vince would even get shot for the same reasons. If Caeli or I crossed a line then our family would pay the price.

This was the safest option, right? For all of us? Especially for Ny?

Fuck, I didn't even know anymore. I knew that what I'd seen Caeli do was just the tip of the iceberg, but what if it wasn't enough?

"Sam, are you okay?" Nylah asked, her voice quiet as she crept up next to me.

"Yeah, I'm just tired," I answered, which wasn't a lie.

I'd hardly slept the night before, and it had caught up with me. There wasn't time to rest when I was too busy overthinking every way today could go wrong. I'd thought over every action and reaction, and some of my predictions had already come true.

Ryne had allowed Caeli to walk next to Vince. While it might have been misconstrued as a nicety, I knew it was to remind the Shadow of what was being held over her. It was to remind her that if she so much as thought about breaking free that they would take Vince away from her permanently.

It was the same reason that he'd allowed Nylah to catch up to me.

"Fair enough..." Nylah trailed off.

Her topaz-coloured eyes that reminded me of Mum glittered in the sunlight, completely focused on Malakai and Ryne as they walked side by side at the head of the group. They were too close, and it put me on edge.

What if Malakai realised what had happened on the flight over? What if my brother had pieced all of it together, just like Caeli thought he had?

I'd always thought that Caeli's denial of conduits had been naïve, but now I'd done the same thing by denying that Malakai's intelligence. It was almost too much to think that he could pose a threat. If he beat me then I would be defeated by my little brother, the one who'd always been lower ranked than me. He was the one who always needed to prove himself, not me...

My thoughts stopped in their tracks as Nylah squeezed my hand, a brief but purposeful contact that I nodded my thanks for.

This wasn't the time to be unsure of myself, it wasn't the time to spiral over what could happen or what I'd already done. I had to be focused. It was the only way I would have a chance to act if an opportunity ever came for us to run.

An opportunity wouldn't likely come until we were back out of Paititi and above ground. By then we would have new powers to weaponise against Templum.

Paititi was an underground city, one we would be trapped in if we tried to free ourselves too early. When observed from the sky, there was a square formation visible through the trees, near the oddly shaped lakes mentioned in the letter from Andres Lopez.

That part had been true, what I'd read from it, but the clue leading to the church had been a lie. That was simply what I'd been told to say, to get her to a secure location while she was completely oblivious to danger.

Templum didn't need direction to where the creviced entryways were located on the side of the formation, because while the city of gold had been lost to the world for centuries now, it hadn't been lost to them. They were the ones who created the statuettes a hundred years ago, but back then they'd been used as a trial for those who wished to join Templum.

Ryne just saw the opportunity to utilise them once again, just to get Caeli to the most concentrated place of power on the planet.

No conduit had been dunked into the pool below Paititi for centuries. The Order of Shadows had paid more than enough gold to make sure it was saved for the grim they wanted to create. Caeli had been over a century in the making; it had just taken until the last few decades for the science to catch up and allow it to happen.

Our small group of assassins and hostages filed through an entryway, and we were stuck in that single line as we wound into the depths of the earth. The tunnels were so dark that I wouldn't be able to see my hand if it was an inch away from my face without our torches.

"What do you think these mean?" Nylah asked. I looked at the paintings she had taken an interest in on the tunnel walls.

"I think it's a depiction of Inkarri," I answered, even though I looked at Caeli. She had done the research on this place, not me, so she would be able to give an in depth answer. I'd seen the amount of paper she'd carried in her bag.

"The paintings tell the story of Inkarri and his retreat into

Paititi, which was where he fled after he created Cusco and the Q'ero." Caeli took over just as I thought she would, and my blood boiled at the warning look my father shot her. "Inkarri is a folktale, one related to their king, Atahualpa. He was the last effective Incan emperor before the Spanish killed him during their conquest. That means they made these paintings after that, which tells us that the people who lived here still had ownership of it, that they didn't lose their home." And of course she'd figured out the rest of it as well. I should have known how easily she'd put two and two together after she saw this place in person.

"Where are they?" Caeli asked as she turned to face my father, who's look of anger had settled into one of calm tranquillity. Had he slipped up before? Had he shown emotion when he hadn't meant to?

"They were dealt with two centuries ago," Ryne answered. The words turned my insides to acid.

Even though I'd always known what happened here, hearing the way my father said it didn't feel right. It was almost as if Ryne thought the people who lived here, who kept their home hidden from the savagery of the world, were a cancer that had needed removal.

"And was it your people who *dealt* with them?" Caeli asked as the line moved again. The torch in her hand shook as she spoke.

Was it anger that made her usually surgeon-steady hand tremble? I hadn't noticed her shake with anger before, but then again, I'd only known her a week and hadn't seen her *this* angry.

"The records state it was a team effort, one between Templum and the Order of Shadows in order to have complete access to the pool below the city. You know the Order wished to resurrect grims the moment they went extinct? Plans for you specifically started two centuries ago, and securing a place for your incitement had been at the top of their list." It sounded so simple, as if they hadn't committed genocide just to create a weapon out of a human being. One that wouldn't come to fruition for two hundred years after the bloodshed. "The Order has paid us well to take this place and to keep it under control. The pool hasn't been touched since we took it, making it the strongest place of power in the world. If all goes according to plan today, you and Nylah will be the strongest conduits in history."

"And the Sabamantiari people? This is their land-"

That was all the proof I needed to know that she would have helped Nylah and I'd just told her the truth. Fuck, I *had* screwed this up.

"We have an... *understanding*. They don't get in our way, and they get to keep their lives." Ryne's voice was so indifferent that it made me question how we could be of the same blood. But just like every other time that thought ran through my head, the simple answer echoed through me. *Mum.* I couldn't imagine how I might have turned out had she not slipped out of Templum when I was born. I could have turned out like Malakai... or, more likely, I would have turned out worse.

"God, I'm going to enjoy killing you," Caeli said, and it made my heart jolt. Her words were loud enough for everyone present to hear, but no one was worried by the threat. It wasn't surprising, but her tone made me believe she *would* get her hands on Ryne one way or another.

It created a conflict in me I hadn't expected, but only because I wasn't sure if I wanted to simply watch Caeli kill Ryne or if I wanted to do it myself.

"If you kill me, then my men will kill Vincent. I would choose my words a little more carefully, if I were you," Ryne warned, and I watched as Caeli's shoulders tensed once again.

"Maybe just ease up on the threats, kid," Vince said. She looked over her shoulder at her father before she looked at me, and those dangerous eyes were filled with silver flame.

"They won't kill you, not yet. Doing so would take away the only thing holding me back," she said as her eyes burned through me. The message was clear, so I blinked my understanding.

She didn't give a shit about me or Nylah. She only cared about Vince. It wasn't her backing out of the deal; it wasn't her rescinding her help. It was just a simple reminder of where I stood on her list of priorities. It was her simply saying that if she had to choose between helping Nylah and me or saving Vince's life, that she wouldn't hesitate to do the latter.

"Yeah, well, I would rather we didn't test..." Vince trailed off, and I wasn't entirely sure why until I realised the light around us was soft and golden instead of harsh and artificially white.

The line filed out from the tunnel and basked in silence as we took in the new surrounds. Sunlight flowed through the city from skylights dug through the earth and illuminated every surface in the enormous cavern we stood in. The abundance of light was simply because it reflected off every golden faced building in front of me.

We'd reached Paititi, which meant our time was running out.

CHAPTER THIRTY-ONE

I HOPE SHE SHOWS YOU MERCY

I hadn't been here before, but I'd seen the pictures in the Templum records. None of those pictures did this place justice.

This cavern was the main one, if I remembered correctly. It held the market, the gathering spaces, and the places of prayer and worship. To the right, I could see the beginning of the housing district, where homes had been carved into the earth and adorned with gold. I would never lay eyes on that section of the city, not when we were going even further underground.

The entrance to the maze beneath the city was through

a golden archway. The pool was down there, and so far it hadn't been found by any of the assassins we'd sent down. It seemed that only an unincited conduit could find it, to be drawn to the power in that pool, and now we had two to lead us down.

"Welcome to Paititi," Ryne said. I risked another look to Caeli, who stood in awe of what was in front of her.

Her lips were parted just slightly, the same way they'd been last night when I almost gave in, but this time her heartbeat was steady. Her hands continued to tremble as she put the torch she'd been given into the pocket of her already stained, and still damp, sweatpants.

My own fingertips tingled... so maybe it wasn't anger that made her shake—maybe it was our proximity to the place of power.

Back when I'd been taken to the pool in Romania, my entire body shivered until I absorbed the power into myself. This one hadn't been touched for two centuries, possibly even more. How much had the power grown for her to be so affected when we were still so far from it? Especially when Nylah seemed completely normal? Unless it was because she was the first truci in hundreds of years...

"We still have far to go," Ryne gestured towards the arced opening that lead to roughly cut stairs and pure darkness. "Nylah and Caeli will follow the pull they no doubt feel in order to lead us down to the pool."

Nylah looked at me with wide eyes before she moved to the front of the group. With the new distance between my sister and me, I realised I'd been using her to keep my focus.

There were too many people around me, and all of us being in a marginally enclosed space meant my senses would soon be overwhelmed. Between everyone's different scents and heartbeats, it had been the familiarity of Nylah next to me that helped block out the others.

"I want to stay with Vince," Caeli argued, which warranted a laugh from Ryne.

"Vince will be perfectly fine next to Samael," Ryne replied. I followed the implied instruction and walked to take Caeli's place by Vince's side as she was pushed to the front of the group next to Nylah. Malakai also left his station next to our father to accompany Caeli and my sister, which meant he had some kind of plan he wanted to enact.

But I couldn't focus on that right now, not with all the unfamiliar sounds and smells. I had mere minutes before I'd start to lose my self-control. I had to pick one heartbeat to listen to—one scent to entirely focus on—and I had to do it soon.

Vince was now the closest person to me, so maybe focusing on his scent of musk and sea salt would be the smartest idea, but the man's racing heart wasn't going to help calm me like I needed. Nylah's heartrate was just as fast as Vince's. There were only a handful of slow heartbeats that could help calm me, and out of those few there was only one scent I'd want to lose myself too.

And, of course, the one person I wanted to hone in on had to be the furthest away from me.

Even with the distance, Caeli's addictive scent and her slow, meditative heartbeat had already calmed me enough to take in the situation around us again. Maybe I should have focused on *anyone* else, maybe I shouldn't have allowed the part of me that wanted to be close to her to control my actions. The only issue was how impossible she was to ignore.

All I could do was watch as she took out her ponytail and ran her fingers through her still damp hair. How many times had I imagined doing that exact action? How many times had I wondered what her hair and skin would feel like against my fingertips? Would she be warm or cool? And how many times had I imagined her neck against my lips? Her warm blood flooding my mouth?

It was the entire reason I had to chew gum around her, because it was the only thing keeping my mouth busy when I looked at her. It was the only thing that stopped me from doing what I wanted to... and it was a necessary precaution after I pinned her against the wall in that damned museum.

From that moment on I couldn't stop the thoughts or the impulses that ran through me near every second of every day. What would she think of me if I let my impulses get the better of me?

I'd drawn a line; there was no way in hell that I'd do what those parts of me told me to. I couldn't when she didn't know who I really was.

But that hadn't stopped me from learning what I did about her. It hadn't helped ease any of that burn in my body to have her on top of me, or under me, or however she might want to have me.

Maybe she'd want me to pin her against the wall, just like we'd been when this all started. Or like we'd been in that closet in the Archives, when her heartbeat had been so loud and fast that it almost drowned out the sound of my own. How close had I been to kissing her neck then? *Too* close.

I ran a hand over my face and took a slow breath. This wasn't the time to get distracted, it was the time to focus on our fucking situation and not what could have been. Her heartbeat was the calmest, so I would have to listen to it. And her scent of chai and all the things I've ever desired would have to keep me grounded, instead of making me remember the dreams I'd been having every night for the past week.

I looked back at her, and saw her hair was still out of it's usual ponytail; it made me realise I hadn't seen her with her hair down before. Without ever asking about it, I knew why she constantly had it up. It was simple to understand that the dark onyx strands that ran to the bottom of her shoulder blades would end up in her face if she got involved in a physical conflict.

Her paranoia lead her to believe that a fight could come at any second, and right now was one of those times when she might need to do something at a moment's notice. So why hadn't she put her hair back up?

It had to *mean* something.

Which meant it was a signal.

Caeli was thinking about our escape. She had to be.

Unlike me, she had likely come up with a plan and decided that now wasn't the optimal time to escape. Leaving her hair down was a signal to the people that knew her, to show that she wouldn't take action.

Malakai was as observant as a brick wall, so there was no way he'd know what she was doing. Ryne hadn't been around her before, so he wouldn't know what was normal for her and what was different. It was only Vince and I who knew that the second she'd tie her hair up that we'd all have to fight like hell for our freedom.

"Look at what you've fucking pulled us into, Rookie," Vince said, which made me look at the man. Rookie?

"If you say so, Brooklyn."

"I do say so, Rookie."

He was communicating, showing he understood what had happened and why. It also implied that Vince wasn't holding my past against me, and that while he might not forgive me, we could work together. Or maybe I was reading too much into it.

"I don't know what you're talking about, Brooklyn," I replied. But maybe it wasn't enough. Maybe I had to say something more specific and personal to show that I understood what Caeli was doing, too. I'd have to mention her specifically, but maybe I could do it using one of those childhood nicknames he'd told me about in the same conversation we came up with those nicknames in. "Your little Demon made this decision all by herself. This was all her plan."

Vincent narrowed his eyes at me, as if it was an action that would help him see through any bullshit I could be spitting. But then he relaxed his shoulders and turned to look at Caeli and Nylah at the front of the group.

"I hope she shows you mercy, kid," Vince responded.

It was the end of the conversation. I knew that much. It meant that he was happy to work with me, that he understood why I had to do what I'd done. So I'd gained the temporary allyship of both Caeli and Vince to help Nylah and I get out of Templum.

Now all we had to do was force Caeli and Ny through their incitements that could potentially end in their deaths.

What could go wrong?

Chapter Thirty-Two

I'D NEVER INCINERATE MY STANDARDS TO ACCOMMODATE YOU

I didn't know how to get us out of this situation, and if I was honest, the others probably didn't either. The meticulous plan I'd made had gone down the drain, and now there was no form of cohesion or direction. I hated that lack of control, the lack of knowledge over how this would all go.

It shouldn't have gone this way. It wasn't meant to end with Caeli and me going through our incitements. I wasn't meant to gain the power that would cost me everything I held dear but still desperately needed. The truci weren't meant to be resurrected alongside me.

We were supposed to get as far away from all of this as possible, with Sam and I being able to start from scratch without having to deal with Templum ever again. But with each step I took, the weight of knowing it wouldn't end that way fell harder onto my shoulders.

Ryne would never let two conduits walk free of his grasp. Especially not a custos and a truci. Especially not when we had to follow our connection to the place of power through a maze of skinny tunnels that we couldn't escape from.

We had to follow the gut feeling that tugged on us a like a string. While the power that emanated from the pool felt like a comforting hug to me, warm and welcoming, I knew Caeli didn't feel the same.

Her entire body was tense. Her hands had been shaking since we walked into the tunnels from the surface, and that tremor had seemed to slowly take over the rest of her body. Surely I wasn't the only one who'd noticed that every step of our descent seemed to make it all remarkably worse for her.

"You know, Nylah, after this you're going to have many opportunities available to you," Malakai whispered as he walked close enough for his damned hand to keep brushing my arm. I understood the dark tunnels we continued to weave through were slim, but he didn't have to be that close to me.

"Like what?" I whispered back, determined to do one thing and one thing only; end this damned conversation as soon as I could so he would leave me alone again.

"Chances for growth, and to climb the ladder."

I took a slow breath and refrained from rolling my eyes. Something in my gut told me the exact direction he was about to take this conversation in, and all I could do was hope that feeling was wrong.

"What makes you think I'd want anything more than my position as a researcher?" I asked as I angled my body to walk closer to Caeli. While I'd hoped it would deter him from being literally stuck to my side, it didn't work.

"Because you're a custos, and on top of that you're a Dawson. Clarissa always wanted to be more than a researcher; it's in your blood to crave more than a desk job," he replied. I glanced at him. Even though he'd mentioned my mother's name with no form of empathy, this conversation was really heading in the direction I thought it would. "This isn't just your incitement. Today also marks the completion of my pilgrimage."

"I wish I could say I cared, but I'm currently being marched to my death-"

"I doubt that's how this will end," he cut me off. Caeli's hand brushed against mine as he spoke. It was the strangers attempt to show she was there to support me. It made me feel slightly more confident in myself, because it implied Caeli would help us out of this after all. "You're going to survive the incitement, so you need to think about what your next steps will be. You can't continue on as a researcher, not when you have the power of a custos at your fingertips. Caeli will be a power source for Samael, but we could trust you to use your power."

I could have sworn I heard Caeli growl at the words, at her being reduced to fuel. But that didn't matter right now, not when Malakai had made a valid point. I hadn't thought too much about what would come next for me, because beyond my wish to no longer be in Templum, there wasn't much of a plan at all.

"What are you trying to offer me?" I asked, faking interest in whatever recruitment tactic this was. But I couldn't hide the disgust I felt when he said his next words.

"We could have a place for you... *I* could have a place for you."

I almost tripped over.

Well, my naïve hope had just been crushed by those chilling words. I knew he would 'have a place for me', but that place felt so undoubtedly wrong that I had to confirm my suspicion.

"A place by your side, I assume," I said. He stared at me, and his honey-brown irises made me sick to my stomach.

"We can work together. You could rule Templum with me and change things for the better. I'm offering you the position of the Priestess, Nylah." That nausea more than doubled, and I had to swallow down the bile that threatened to projectile vomit from me.

"There's never been a Priestess," I said as I placed a hand on my abdomen. It was a pitiful attempt to ease the way my stomach tumbled.

For the second, I wanted to pretend that the implication behind what he'd said didn't exist. I could focus on one thing at a time, like the fact that a Priestess wasn't a position within Templum. Not one that I knew about, anyway, and I knew nearly everything about the organisation. Knowledge was the best weapon, and I wanted to destroy Templum so definitively that they couldn't even think of recuperating.

"There's been a few of them, actually. The only hitch to it is that they have to be married to the Priest in order to have the title." Maybe I couldn't ignore the part that made me sick anymore.

"Please tell me you're joking," I begged. It was futile, because I knew he wasn't.

I'd known for months how he felt about me. No matter how much he treated me like nothing more than a burden for him to carry—especially after I manipulated Ryne into letting me join the mission to get Caeli to Paititi—I'd always known it was simply an over-correction to cover his true feelings. It had always been easy to read the emotion in his eyes when he stared at me. It was a constant hunger that shouldn't exist.

"You're my brother," I pointed out, but he just shook his head.

"No, Samael is your brother. There's no blood shared between us."

Malakai was fucking delusional. Even if we weren't family, he was still six years older than me. I'm only seventeen, this was... I couldn't just let this slide.

"If you have to pull a technicality to justify something like incest, then it definitely crosses a line," I said. Even if we didn't get out of Templum, even if I had to be stuck in this damned organisation for the rest of my life, I would *never* allow myself to be married off to this asshole. "I'm not even going to toy with that idea, Malakai, and you knew I wouldn't. It wouldn't matter to me if we shared a brother or if we didn't, because I would never incinerate my standards to accommodate *you*."

The only sound that echoed through the tunnel, aside from the shuffled footsteps behind us, was Caeli's melodic laughter. It was such a light and pretty sound to come from someone I knew had the capacity for extremely horrific acts—I'd seen the evidence of her capabilities through photographs.

Because of that, I had to look at her, to confirm the sound had definitely come from her. It was hard to describe the discomfort in my stomach as I saw Caeli's body shake with the dissonant laughter that sounded similar to chimes being caught in the wind.

"I don't remember you being a part of the conversation, Caeli," Malakai said, as if he thought it would offer him any form of control over the situation. Caeli's silver eyes turned towards Malakai, the metallic colour of her irises sharp enough to cut through skin.

"I've been stuck in this damned conversation since you walked up here." Caeli kept her voice to a hissed whisper, the same volume as the rest of the conversation that had taken place between Malakai and I. "Did you honestly think I wouldn't listen when you were standing less than an arm's length away from me?"

"No, but I thought you might know your place."

In that moment, I was glad I was stuck between them. If Caeli had attacked Malakai like I knew she wanted to, then there would be no chance for escape. They could bicker all they wanted, Caeli could throw verbal threats all day long if she so desired, but the second that she'd attempt to kill one of them...

Not that what happened was much better. Caeli could have wrapped her hands around Malakai's neck, and it might have had the same response.

Instead of violence filling the tunnel, everything dipped into a darkness as thick as tar. All the torches flickered out at the same time. The impossible night surrounded us for a split second before it evaporated again, as if it never existed.

But the way my heart sat in my throat told me I hadn't imagined it. The way Malakai's eyes widened told me it had truly happened. And the way Caeli's were still pitch black as she glared at Malakai told me where the darkness had originated from. The ink-like colour slowly seeped away from her irises, almost as if it didn't want to leave her...

"We must be getting close if you can draw on it." Ryne's voice echoed through the cave, and a shiver ran up my spine at how calm and comfortable he sounded. It was as if the display of impossible power didn't terrify him like it should have. It was as if he didn't feel a heaviness in his chest, or taste a bitterness in his mouth like I did. "You couldn't draw on the power before your incitement, Samael."

I looked over my shoulder to find my brother, who studiously stood guard over Vincent Sinclair. If we weren't stuck in this horrible position, I might have been excited by the fact I was in such close proximity to Sinclair and the Shadow. I'd followed their escapades for the last few years as part of my workload in Templum, and it was no secret between me and my brother that I held them in more than high regard.

"I'm a lamia, father. I need blood. I don't have any power of my own to draw on." Samael reminded Ryne, who didn't seem to care.

When Sam had first gone through his incitement, he'd been the centre of attention. Everything that happened in Templum had been tied to him. Everyone who hired us wanted to see or pay for the lamia in our ranks. He'd never wanted that enthrallment. Now Ryne had Caeli in his grasp, and she was going to full weight of his intrusive obsession whether or not she wanted it.

"Yes, but Caeli can. Imagine what our Shadow will be capable of by the end of the hour, and what you'll be able to steal from her, little Parasite." I'd forgotten about the nickname that Ryne had given to Sam until today. It wasn't overly original. There had been records of lamias being called such since they'd been discovered, but it didn't make it any less harsh to hear.

"I'm glad you have this illusion of control, Ryne, because it won't last much longer," Caeli said, a new venom present in her voice. Everyone in the tunnel froze at her words, and

I couldn't figure out why she'd said them or why she'd used that tone. Sinclair was still being held at gunpoint, so it was dangerous to push Ryne... especially when it seemed the venom was because of what he'd called Sam.

"It's no illusion, Shadow, not while we have Sinclair," Ryne replied, which made my breath hitch. I, personally, didn't think this was the best time to threaten the Priest, but maybe Caeli understood him better than I did. It wouldn't take much to do so. I never understood him. I was just good at manipulating him into thinking I was weaker than I was.

"That won't be of any benefit to you when you can't see anything." So that was Caeli's plan, for her to use her power once we go through our incitements. If only that helped to make me feel a little more comfortable in the situation.

"I'm not worried about your powers; you can't control them," Ryne said as he walked once more. The movement prompted the rest of the group to trudge forward, so I followed suit and moved towards where the pull in my stomach told me to go again.

"What makes you think that?" Caeli asked, her eyes focused on the path ahead of us.

"You can't acknowledge your emotions. The Order specifically trained you that way so they could manage you after your incitement," Ryne replied.

Emotions helped clarify the output of a conduits power, the clearer the emotion the better the control. If a conduit didn't have the ability to regulate their emotions, then they wouldn't have a leash on their power.

Caeli seemed like she wanted to argue, to threaten Ryne a little more and make him rethink the situation we were all in. Unfortunately, there wasn't time left to try.

We'd found it.

"Oh, my god..." I whispered as we turned a corner in the tunnel. I turned off my torch, since it was no longer needed, and felt my heart sit in my throat.

We couldn't stall anymore.

"Shit," Caeli hissed.

We'd reached the pool.

The water glowed an bright blue and illuminated the otherwise dark cave with iridescent light.

If I didn't know any better, I might have described the pool as beautiful, or an impossible wonder of nature. Instead, I knew it had the potential to kill me, that whatever the Entity was that fuelled the magic of our planet might deem me unworthy of wielding it.

I looked back over my shoulder to find Sam's gold eyes and the stoic façade that had glazed over his face. He was as terrified as me, although it didn't show on his face.

Even though we'd both prepared for this moment, even though he'd told me what to expect, the thought that I might not walk out of that pool alive made me hesitate... but I turned my attention back to the water and took a step towards it.

I either took my chances of survival by going into that pool, or I faced certain death by not doing so. That meant this was it. The deciding moment of whether the Entity thought I should live or die.

And there was only one way to find out which it would be.

CHAPTER THIRTY-THREE

TO RESTORE BALANCE

I'd never seen something as horrifyingly hypnotising as the pool. Never had I laid eyes on something so hauntingly wynorrific, and I knew there wasn't even a chance of seeing something like it again.

The water glowed with it's own source—a power I didn't quite understand which only made it all the more terrifying. The colour illuminated the faces of everyone in the cave, and when I locked eyes with Vince, I saw the light was the same colour as his irises. *Azure*. It only made his fear more obvious.

"I can't do this," I whispered as I looked at Nylah, who'd taken an uncontrolled step towards the pool. Only Nylah could have heard me. The water had everyone else distracted by its perfectly still surface and it's haunting beauty.

But to me, this place didn't feel right. Something told me to run as far and as fast as I could, but I couldn't. If I did, then Vince would end up dead, just as Samael and Nylah would. But my body was filled with equal parts acid and ice, and I didn't know which was more important to listen to.

"You have to," Nylah whispered back, but her voice was different than it had been before. There was something hidden in her undertone, as if it wasn't truly her words that had left her mouth.

"I can't," I replied. I tried to back away a step, to begin my retreat, but Nylah's hand wrapped around my wrist to stop me. Her fingers were impossibly cold, and while it *should* have worried me, it didn't.

"You have to, or they will kill your father." The words didn't shock me back to reality like they should have. They couldn't when it sounded as if hundreds of voices flooded from Nylah's throat all at once.

I looked over my shoulder at Vince, to communicate that I needed to run—to figure out if he had lived a life he was happy with because I couldn't do this. I *couldn't* do it.

"You need to go in together so that you may both come back out again."

I looked back to Nylah, who's irises were no longer the colour of topaz crystals, but the phosphorescence of the pool. Something had control over her, and it wanted her to go in the water that was so still it looked like blue glass. Whatever that something was filled my entire body with an icy feeling, like the one I got in my stomach when I was doing something right.

That something... it had to be the Entity, didn't it? If that calming cold had always been from it, then... what did that mean?

I knew the Order made me to do this, to become a grim, but it still felt wrong to be here. It felt *wrong* for the Entity to want me to be here.

"She cannot do this alone," the Entity whispered through Nylah.

Why was it trying to convince me to go in that water? Did it not realise that I wasn't meant to be here? Did it not know that I wasn't meant to be alive?

"I..."

What could I even say to make it understand me? What could I do to convince the Entity that giving me the power I'd been created for was a bad idea?

"You just have to submerge yourself. The water will do the rest. Don't make her do this by herself. This is the only path to restore balance." Restore balance? How could this restore balance?

I looked back at Vince, who stared at me with pure concern in his eyes. The expression didn't ease the sinking feeling in my stomach, nor did the weight of everyone else's eyes on me. Did they not see what was happening? Could no one see that something had a hold of Nylah? Their attention should be on *her* and not me.

"It's time, Caeli." Ryne's words vibrated through the

cavern. That same cacophonous echo of voices beneath his tone sent a chill down my spine. Was I the only person who could hear it? Was I the only one who could hear the damned whispers?

Nylah took a step towards the pool and pulled me with her. There wasn't a choice in the matter.

I *had* to go in, and I *had* to dip my head beneath the water's surface. I'd have to submit to the Entity that already had a hold over Nylah, and hope it decided I could control the power it wanted to bestow unto me. I had to, not just because the Entity told me to, but because if I didn't then Ryne would kill Vince.

I took a step forward of my own, my eyes locked on the eerily still water. Every fibre in my body told me to run, to not go in, but every part of my mind screamed the opposite. I needed to follow the pull, to do as I was being told, to make sure that Vince lived and I could get out of this alive.

If I went in, then I could take the power I needed to make sure everyone who'd ever hurt me would regret doing so.

"Everyone here is about to witness history being made," Ryne said. His voice was back to a single modulation. "You all get to witness the inversion of extinction."

The words reached me as my foot touched the edge of the water. I couldn't let my fear get the better of me. Like Samael had said—if I did, then they would kill my father. Fuck, I couldn't wait for this to be over.

I took a step into the pool, and then another. And another. I walked in until the water reached my waist. It was cold, but not *too* cold. It was the perfect temperature, like what I showered in, and it stopped me from thinking I was back in the Order. But it couldn't stop the lump that formed in my throat.

Ice filled my stomach, as if to reassure me that this was the right decision, but now I knew the source of that feeling I wasn't sure I could trust it anymore.

My wrist was still in Nylah's icy grasp, acting as a lifeline as we turned to face each other in the water. The Entity had let go of her, and I could only tell because that blue glow in her eyes was now gone. Without it, her eyes filled with pure terror, and I could see how her body shook in the water.

Nylah's dread wasn't the same as mine, that much was obvious. She was simply terrified of death, whereas as I felt... how could I still feel so *wrong*?

The blatant wrongness of my life was something I'd felt for as long as I could remember. It was as natural to me as the feeling of my limbs being part of me. But being in this water, it felt so much worse.

The power that flowed around me in the blue acknowledged my existence. It writhed against me as if it knew I shouldn't be there, but wrapped around my legs like it didn't want me to leave.

The power and the Entity knew that grims were gone, and both knew that I was just an inferior imitation of what had been the most powerful force of magic on the planet. Surely they both knew that I had been manufactured in a fucking laboratory, toyed with and engineered to fit the exact vision

300

that the Order had for their ideal grim.

How could it want me here? How could it want *me* to restore balance? What the fuck was that supposed to mean? What did it have planned for me?

"Are you ready?" Nylah asked, her voice back to normal as it rippled over the surface of the azure water.

"No..." I whispered back, watching Vince, who had somehow tempered the fear in his eyes. I didn't know how he'd managed it, but I appreciated it nonetheless. "But I don't have a choice." I added before I turned my attention to Nylah's brother, who also hid his fear behind a false wall of bravado.

I took hold of Nylah's hands and looked at her. We would do this together because we *had* to. The Entity wanted us to do this as one, and if we went against it's wishes, we wouldn't make it out alive. We would do this together, so that when we came back out again, we could have enough power that the guns pointed at us and our loved ones wouldn't make a damned difference.

We would do it together so we could both be free, and so the people we cared about could be as well. I would never have to fear the Order again...

"On three..." I said as we sank to our knees in the water, our heads hovering just above the surface. My body tensed at the feeling of the water against my skin, but I couldn't let it affect me. This wasn't the time to freeze in fear. "One..." I spared one last look to Vince, and tried to ignore the way my eyes stung and my vision blurred.

"Two..." Nylah squeezed shut before they opened again, and that glow from before had returned as any acid left in my body shifted to ice. Whatever this Entity was, it didn't just have Nylah in it's grasp anymore. It had me too, and it was doing everything it could to make sure I was comfortable.

"Three."

We whispered at the same time, our voices melded together with the echo of the other being with us. And before we could sink into the water of our own accord, we both blacked out and our bodies slipped into the water.

We were at the mercy of the Entity.

Chapter Thirty-Four

I'M NOT AFRAID OF YOU...

I opened my eyes and found myself in an unfamiliar house. My bare feet were on cream coloured carpet next to a well-worn couch covered in dog fur. On every available surface were pictures or potted plants.

This wasn't just a house, it was far too lived in and far too warm and welcoming. This was a *home*, something I'd never really seen with my own two eyes before.

"Nylah..." I trailed off, since she wasn't anywhere that I could see. There was a strange feeling in my stomach that told me she was close, but I just couldn't see her.

"What are we going to do when we wake up?" She asked, walking out from the hallway that no doubt lead to the bedrooms of the home.

"I don't know. All I've got so far is a way to communicate with Vince and Hu—*Samael*." Fuck, that was still going to take me a little while to get used to. "My hair is currently down, and when I put it up, that will mean I'm about to do something. You'll need to get ready when I do that, okay?" I responded as I walked towards the fireplace where a flickering flame lived.

Seriously, where was I?

"I can't use my powers," Nylah whispered. My plan didn't rely on Nylah using her power. I couldn't put her through the possible hell of losing the only family she had left.

I squatted in front of the fire and reached my hand towards it, but there no warmth came from it. Now that I noticed I couldn't feel it, I realised I couldn't feel the carpet beneath my feet either. Why couldn't I feel anything?

Nylah walked to stand behind me as I put my hand directly in the flame. I still felt nothing.

"I can't risk-"

"I know," I cut her off as I stood up and looked at her. "You won't have to, because I'm going to use mine." I made my way into the rustic dining room.

"I thought Ryne said you weren't a threat, that you weren't raised to feel your emotions. If you can't feel your emotions, then you can't control your power. It's how it works." I was well aware of that fact, but it was something I wasn't overly concerned about.

"He's conveniently forgotten that I haven't been with the Order for eight years." That was all I could respond with, because while I knew it would help, I wasn't sure it would be enough.

Vince wasn't necessarily the most helpful with emotions, or being mentally stable, but he did his best. There was only one way to find out if his best had been enough. It was a pity it had to be tested in a situation where success meant living and failure meant death.

"Besides, the incitement might help with that," I said.

"How?" Nylah brushed the dining table, a gentle caress of her fingertips against the varnished wood. It was like this place was familiar to her...

"Your brother told me that the point of the incitements is to help you accept an emotional imbalance from your past. It forces you to work through something that would otherwise keep you from holding authority over your power," I said as I wandered over to the pictures handing on the wall being the table.

They showed a family of four. Mother, father, son and daughter. All of them were focused on the camera, with huge smiles plastered on their faces as they held each other. They were so comfortable around one another... it made my chest burn with something I hadn't really felt before.

Was this jealousy?

"Sam never went into the details of what happened in his trial, but he summarised it by saying he had to accept his anger at Ryne for killing Mum," Nylah said. Her shoulder brushed against mine as she looked at the same photo that made my mouth go dry. "If he had to accept his anger, then

I need to accept my grief."

"What makes you think that?" I asked as I saw tears sitting in her eyes. If this place wasn't familiar to me, then it had to be familiar to her.

I looked back at the picture as the realisation punched me in the gut. The people in the photo, the *family* in it... it was the Dawsons. It was their mother and Nylah's father with an arm around each other. It was Nylah missing her two front teeth and Samael getting his hair ruffled by his step-father.

"Nylah..."

I turned to look back at the girl, but she was gone. Instead, all I could hear was the echo of children laughing and the thundering of chaotic footsteps as someone ran down the hallway.

"No! Help!" A small girl screamed, and I immediately ran towards the sound.

"Nylah!" I shouted. Panic ran through my body as I prepared to save the girl from danger, but there was none.

The heavy footsteps had been Nylah's father as he chased after the young version of Nylah from the picture. The squeals had been from him tackling her onto the couch and tickling her sides.

My ribs constricted painfully tight as I watched the interaction. My hands curled into fists as I forced myself to watch their joy. Was this what I'd missed out on? Was this what a childhood was meant to be like? It all seemed so foreign to me, the idea of screams of *happiness*...

Why were my eyes stinging?

"Unhand her, you vile beast!" A small Samael shouted, a roll of wrapping paper in hand as if he wielded a sword. He was on the cusp of being too old to play make-believe, but maybe he was doing it for Nylah. Maybe he was comfortable and happy enough that he would do anything to keep her entertained.

"Do you think you can win against me? You are nothing but a lowly knight, but me?" The father shouted as he let go of Nylah and stood up in dramatic slow motion. "I am a god!" He motioned for a fake attack, but was stopped before he could make it too far.

"No! Leave Sir Sam alone!" Nylah screamed as she stood up on the couch. She then threw herself onto her father's back, which elicited a look of discomfort on the man's face.

"Oh, you found my weakness, tiny one!" He shouted, still acting, even though I was absolutely sure he was in *severe* pain. "It is indeed my middle-aged back." He breathed the words out before he fell onto his stomach, as if he'd suffered defeat at young Nylah's hands.

"Are you okay, Daniel?" Samael asked with a laugh, watching as Nylah mercilessly sat on Daniel's back with a beaming smile on her face. The two front teeth that had been missing in that picture were grown in halfway. I wasn't sure I even remembered losing my baby teeth. It must have happened, but I couldn't... I couldn't *remember.*

"I will be after some strong painkillers and another visit to the chiropractor." The response was muffled, since Daniel's face was stuck in a pillow on the couch. "I might just need to lie here for a minute."

The front door opened, which granted Daniel some mercy as Nylah clambered over the back of the couch so she could run towards the door.

"Mummy!" She shouted as she ran, but the girl froze before she closed the distance.

"Hey sweetie, this is an old friend of mine. Everything's okay," their mother said as she walked in the door, but what followed her didn't look like a friend at all. It didn't even look human.

It was a living shadow, too tall to fit through the door without folding itself in half first. The only parts that helped it look even remotely humanoid were it's contorted limbs and the glowing red eyes.

"Would you like to go to your room, please? Maybe Sam could help you find that painting you made of the four of us and you could show it to our friend here," their mother said. She was terrified, but hiding it well.

Sam edged around the couch, and he didn't take his eyes off the figure next to his mother until he'd grabbed Nylah's arm and dragged down her the hallway. Daniel stood up off the couch then too, announcing his position to the monster in the room, which was likely the biggest mistake he'd ever made in his life.

"Clarissa, who-"

An all too familiar crack cut him off, one that echoed from the gun being held by the shadow monster next to Clarissa.

"Daniel!" She shouted as she ran towards her husband.

He'd fallen to the ground instantly. Blood pooled from him, spilling from where the bullet had torn through his chest without mercy to stain the carpet.

The shadowy figure let Clarissa run to the body, but only because it's focus wasn't on her. It stalked down the hallway, and I followed, wanting to stop it, but I had a feeling there wasn't a thing I could do to help.

This was a memory, a twisted one made from fear. The shadow wasn't a mysterious monster that came for the Dawsons; it was just the best way for Nylah to process what had happened. It was the simplest way for her young brain to process the trauma. I suppose in a normal childhood it was impossible to understand why a person would commit such a horrific act.

The figure opened a bedroom door, where it walked to the children hiding behind the bed and took both of them by the arm.

"Let her go!" Sam shouted, not caring for his own safety in the situation and focusing instead on his sister.

The figure stayed silent as it dragged them all the way back to the lounge room, where Daniel's body was covered with Clarissa as she sobbed onto him. The woman's focus only shifted away from the body when a sickening scream tore from Nylah's throat.

"No! You can't take them!" Clarissa shouted, and without a second to waste the room filled with a blinding white light.

It was the only thing I could feel in the memory, the way that light both burned and froze as it hit my skin. She was a custos—a guardian. Nylah and Samael had told me the truth when they said they'd watched their mother use her powers. And Nylah hadn't lied when she'd said the consequences of Clarissa using that power had hit immediately.

I heard the window shatter and watched as the light in the room faded as quickly as it had appeared.

And then all I saw was Clarissa's body lying on top of Daniel's, completely still.

A sniper had shot her through the skull. Her blood mixed in with Daniel's, and together they turned the cream carpet to a scarlet red.

Nylah screamed again, and the sound was even more horrifying the second time around.

Samael was silent. All he could do was stare at the bodies in front of him.

It was the first corpses that either of them had seen. For her, it was both of her parents. For him, it was his mother and the one person he might have considered a father.

It wasn't just grief that Nylah had to work through. If it was, then the figure holding her arm wouldn't be shrouded in shadow. No, she had to work through her fear. I should know... it's exactly what I'd likely have to face for my trial.

"Nylah, can you hear me?" I asked as I walked over to the girl.

The scene seemed to be frozen in time. Samael wasn't breathing, and the monster didn't move. Only Nylah seemed to be alive, her breaths shallow and staggered as tears tumbled down her cheeks.

"Nylah, I know you're scared right now, but I need you to do something for me," I said as I knelt in front of her and took her tiny hands in mine.

Nylah's eyes tore away from the bodies of her parents to reach me, her bloodshot eyes wide.

"I need you to breathe," I instructed. Nylah nodded as she tried to suck in some air. "Now I need you to look at the monster next to you, and say that you aren't afraid of it. Tell it you're not scared—that it didn't achieve what it wanted." Nylah's eyes flicked towards the shadowed figure who's elongated hand still held her upper arm. "The entire point of taking you in this way was so he could make you afraid of him. You need to tell him it didn't work. Believing those words can come later, for now you can just pretend."

Nylah's hands shook as I held them, and I wasn't entirely sure if this was what the Entity had intended for me to do. I wasn't sure if this was how I was supposed to help Nylah, but what else could I do?

If whatever was testing us hadn't lied, then Nylah couldn't do this by herself. The Entity hadn't said it outright, but the implication was that Nylah wouldn't survive if she did this alone. We had to do this *together*.

"I should have done something..." little Nylah trailed off, which made me shake my head.

God, this kid was beyond traumatised, but she couldn't blame herself for something that Ryne had done. My eyes stung as I squeezed the girl's hands. She had to be around seven years old, and she blamed herself just as I did for my childhood.

Maybe the Entity was making a point. Maybe we were meant to do this together because our trials could help each other—because we were similar people. The only difference being that Nylah was young enough to heal, and I was beyond that.

"You were a child. It wasn't your job to do anything. Not this time. You did everything you were supposed to do. None of this is your fault. The blame is completely on the monster," I said. Nylah's empty eyes turned to that monster, still frozen in time as it looked over the bodies it had left behind.

"I'm not afraid," Nylah whispered, but nothing happened.

"Say it louder, and say it with your chest. Involve every fibre of your being." God, I hoped I was actually helping this kid. It would be the most wretched thing I'd ever done if I made this worse for her.

"I'm not afraid."

The image of the child in front of me flickered between the past version and the present on her knees. Surely that meant I was doing the right thing. Surely that meant I was helping.

"Nylah, you need to tell him you aren't afraid of him."

The small version of the girl looked up at me, but when I blinked, the child was gone, completely replaced with the version I'd become used to.

Nylah nodded her thanks and let out a slow breath as she let go of my hands. She then stood up and moved to be in front of the shadow monster.

"I'm not afraid of you, Ryne," Nylah said.

She spoke the words with strong enough conviction that I believed them, and as a result of them being said, the shadows finally melted away from the man. It was a slightly younger Ryne Eldridge, holding the arms of both Nylah and Sam as children. That had to mean that Nylah had separated herself from the memory. She wasn't stuck reliving it like she was before, which meant she had done what she needed to pass her trial.

"How did I let you rule my life?" Nylah whispered as she took a step backwards. She then looked over her shoulder at her parents, and moved as if she wanted to go over to their bodies, as if she wanted to say goodbye.

But the second that Nylah's foot hit the ground on her first step, the scene around us flashed in a bright white light.

CHAPTER THIRTY-FIVE

...OR MAYBE I AM

When the light faded, we were in a laboratory—one that I knew all too fucking well.

It was exactly as I remembered it. The only thing out of place in the sterile room of stainless steel and white tile was the woman tied to a metal chair in the middle of it all. I recognised the strawberry-blonde hair immediately, her head tilted down and that hair fallen in front of her face like a curtain. It had always been tied in a ponytail, so it was strange to see it down...

"Caeli, do you know this place?" Nylah asked as I finally stood up from my kneeling position. She stared at the metal contraptions and the confusing machines in the room. It must have been a shock for the girl to go from her childhood home, a place that comforted even me, and then immediately be thrown into what I knew as my version of that. The cold walls, all the freezing metal...

"It's where *she* made me." I walked towards the woman in the chair and took in the situation. What was I supposed to do here?

This situation was something I never thought would happen. I could never have imagined a scenario where I had the advantage over the woman who'd controlled my every waking moment—even from thousands of miles away and without a single order from her. Everything I did was because of Ashford. Everything I did was because of what she'd taught me and because of what I knew would happen if she caught me again.

"Victoria Ashford, I met her once..." Nylah trailed off. Her voice echoed off the cold walls, and the woman in the chair stirred with a deep inhale as she heard her name. "Why is she tied to a chair?" Nylah asked, but as I looked for the girl, for my only backup in the situation, she was gone.

This was my trial... and it seemed that I would have to work out what I needed to accept without Nylah guiding me.

"Come on then, *One*, do your worst," Victoria said. Just as I remembered, her speech was slow and purposeful, each word clear and careful just the same as my way of speech. She was where I'd learnt it from, through some twisted form of a mother-daughter relationship that was never even close to being the real thing.

Simply hearing her voice was enough to make me flinch,

to make me stumble backwards a step and reassess what I was doing.

"Still scared of me?" She asked.

This wasn't a memory, and my body hadn't shifted to the childhood version of myself. This was one of my fantasies—to kill Ashford and be free of the woman once and for all. This trial was testing me to see what I would actually do in this situation.

"Of course you're still afraid. It's how I trained you."

This trial was about fear, just the same as Nylah's had been. It was the only thing that made sense.

"I'm not afraid of you..." I whispered, but doing so felt wrong. It felt like a lie. There was no way I could say I wasn't afraid of her, because it was in no way true. "Or maybe I am," I said, and a dagger fabricated itself in my hand out of thin air.

I ran a finger over the edge of the blade. *Fear* was one of those unpleasant emotions, one of the difficult ones I put into my vault that should never be opened. It was easiest and safest to leave it there, shoved deep down where I could pretend it didn't exist. But it did, and it had affected every part of my damned life for the last eight years.

"It's why you won't do anything," Ashford said. She smiled at me as she tilted her head to the side. It was where I'd learned the move from, so it didn't surprise me she'd used it. "What if I get out of here, *One*? What if I send my people after you?" God, I was sick of those questions.

They were the same ones I'd asked myself for the past

eight years. They were what fuelled my pure terror of being found, my paranoia that I wasn't doing enough to stay hidden and out of their grasp. I had constant nightmares about it—about what Ashford would do if she ever got her hands on me again, or what she would do to Vince as punishment for everything I'd done.

I knew Ashford wasn't above killing him or torturing him in order to hurt me, and if letting me go had been part of her twisted plan, then she'd likely hoped I would attach myself to someone. It would make me easier to control, and I'd handed her Vince on a silver platter.

It had drained me completely, that constant fear. It was the reason I hid who I was, why I had to check a room multiple times over to make sure we were safe, why we never stayed in a place longer than two weeks at a time. I couldn't do it anymore. Samael had been right back in Egypt. This paranoia wasn't good for my health.

I rolled the dagger over in my hand before I took hold of the black handle, the grip exactly as Ashford had taught me.

I was sick of pretending I wasn't afraid—sick of pretending that nothing could hurt me. Most of all, I was sick of holding people at arm's length so they couldn't be used against me. While I'd never had a family like the one I'd just seen in Nylah's memory, I still deserved one. I'd deserved a *real* childhood, a real *life*, and this woman had stolen it all from me.

"Tell her you aren't afraid of her." Nylah's voice was nothing more than a disjointed echo throughout the laboratory, her body still nowhere to be seen.

I shook my head and closed the distance between myself and Ashford. My trial wasn't to convince myself I wasn't afraid of Ashford—that I wasn't terrified of the Order of Shadows. That was what I'd been trying to do for eight years. It was the entire reason I'd lived in denial over conduits and their existence. Samael had told me that his trial was to accept his anger at his father, and that he killed Ryne in his dreamworld.

He'd walked into his vault of emotions and come out unscathed... I had to do the same.

"Go on, *Shadow*, tell me you aren't afraid of me," Victoria said. I took a deep breath before I looked down at the dagger in my hand. The Entity had given it to me for a reason...

"I can't say that, because I *am* afraid of you." I put one hand on her shoulder for leverage and plunged the dagger into Ashford's chest. It sunk to the hilt between her ribs. "I'm terrified of what you could do to me, what you could take from me... *who* you could take from me." My eyes lifted to Nylah as she faded into view behind my victim, but I couldn't look at her for long. She wouldn't understand why I needed to do this—why I had to kill this version of Ashford.

So I turned my attention back to Ashford's green irises. "Everything I've done for the last eight years has been to accommodate that fear. Saying that Vince is the Shadow? The countless aliases I've made to cover my tracks? I'm tired of running and hiding, of feeling this constant paranoia that you're going to be around every damned corner I turn." I twisted the dagger as I put all my weight behind it.

"I won't keep doing it to myself," I said before I took another deep breath.

The weight on my shoulders lightened as I twisted the dagger once more and heard Ashford's whimpers of pain. "I'm not alone anymore, and I won't be powerless after I wake up in this pool of fucking water. *Water*... if only it was so easy to make myself less afraid of *it*."

I ripped the dagger out of her chest and took a step away. It was best to get some distance, so I could take in my work in all it's glory. Without taking that step back, I wouldn't have been able to watch the blood as it pooled onto the floor and see her face go pale at the same time.

"I dare you to come after me, Victoria. I *fucking* dare you. I might be terrified of you, but my rage will override it when the time comes. I can promise you that. You taught me *never* to break my promises."

Before I could get the satisfaction of watching the life fade from Ashford's eyes, everything around me fell from view and I was left suspended in darkness. Nylah floated in front of me, worry clear in her eyes.

She didn't understand what I'd done, and was rightly afraid that I'd failed my incitement. But the ice in my stomach told me I'd done right, that opening the vault to my fear had been what the Entity wanted.

Balance. It always wanted *balance*.

"Do you think we passed?" Nylah asked, and all I could do was take a gulp of air. While I was sure I'd passed, my chest had still locked up because of the fear, and getting air to my lungs was harder than it should have been.

There wasn't time to respond as the surrounding nothingness twisted and moved.

And I fell into a lonely, black abyss.

CHAPTER THIRTY-SIX

LIKE WISPS OF SMOKE FROM A DYING FIRE

My heart fell from my chest as Nylah and Caeli both fell into the water. They'd held hands and whispered to each other before the Entity recognised they were in the pool and took them for their incitements.

"Your sister will be alright, Rookie. She's stuck in there with the most stubborn person I've ever met. They'll make it, because if the power isn't given to them, then Caeli will take it," Vincent whispered. He must have noticed how tense my body was, how I'd held my breath the second the two of them had fallen beneath the surface of the pool.

I couldn't help thinking that Vincent hadn't just said the

words in a failed attempt to help me, but to convince himself that his child would make it out alive, too. It was probably for the best that he couldn't hear as well as I could, because the second Nylah and Caeli had been taken by the Entity, their heartbeats stopped echoing through my ears.

"How long does this take?" Vincent asked, loud enough for everyone in the cavern to hear. He covered his fear with impatience, probably to make sure Ryne didn't feel as in control as he wanted to. I wasn't overly sure it would work to throw my father off, but I was more than willing to let Vince try.

"Apparently when I did mine, I was only below the surface for a few seconds, even though it felt like hours-" I was cut off by the echoing sounds of people gasping for air, of people thrashing in the water and two sets of familiar heartbeats reaching my ears once more.

They fucking survived.

Immediately I locked eyes with my sister, who's demeanour had changed from before she'd entered the water. Even though she gulped down air like she hadn't tasted oxygen before, her eyes surveyed the room differently—almost as if she wasn't afraid.

Caeli, on the other hand, looked fucking pissed. That was a complete understatement, but I wasn't sure if there were any words to really encapsulate her anger.

No one spoke as the two of them caught their breath. No one dared to ask if the incitement had been a success. No one wanted to ask whether extinction had indeed been reversed and the truci had been resurrected.

In the silence, Nylah and Caeli waded back out of the pool, and the second she was free of the water, Nylah ran to me. I wrapped my arms around her shoulders, and every tense muscle in my body released as I let out a quiet exhale. I blinked back tears as I squeezed her hard enough that in a normal situation she might have joked I would break her ribs.

"Are you okay?" I whispered to her as she shook in my arms. I couldn't tell if it was because of the adrenaline or if it was because she was cold from the water.

"I think so," she whispered back. Good. As long as she was okay, then everything was going to be okay.

I opened my eyes to look at Caeli, who was frozen at the edge of the pool. Her wet hair clung to her shoulders, just as her black shirt clung to her skin again, revealing every shape of her body and how fast and deep she was breathing. She stared at Vincent, seeming to have an entire conversation with him without saying a damned word. Those eyes of silver flame then turned towards me, and they made my heartbeat drown out every other noise around me.

"I don't know about Caeli though, her trial..." Nylah trailed off, her voice hardly above a whisper as she pulled away from me.

"What about it?" Vincent whispered, staring straight ahead as he made sure his voice was also barely audible. It was for the best that no one thought we were talking to one another. It would raise suspicion.

"I didn't think she'd passed," Nylah answered.

"What do you mean?" I asked as my brow furrowed. I was still stuck on Caeli's form, and it seemed to be impossible to look away. It also seemed impossible to stop the shivers that ran down my spine from simply looking at her. *Don't tell me you're thinking inappropriate thoughts again, Samael. Now is not the fucking time.*

"She leaned into her anger. She didn't resolve anything. She just admitted she was afraid of Victoria Ashford, that she wouldn't hide it anymore. Then she *killed* Ashford..." Nylah told us.

I had to block out the ache that echoed through my body at being so far from Caeli. Why was my body doing that? And why was my heartbeat racing? Why were my hands curling and unfurling as my fingers realised they weren't touching her skin? *God, you are so entirely fucked, Samael.*

"It's different for everyone," I said to distract myself from the tug I felt that wanted to pull me closer to Caeli. "I didn't need to resolve anything. I just had to accept the anger that was boiling in me."

An unfamiliar feeling flooded my body at knowing that Caeli was the same as me—that we would both use our anger to fuel us to protect the ones we care about.

"But I'm glad you resolved whatever you did, that it wasn't simple for you." I added as I tore my eyes away from Caeli and looked down at my sister. Nylah nodded as she watched Ryne move towards the person I wanted to be close to.

"Do you feel like you've become what you were meant to

be?" Ryne asked, either not noticing or not caring for the fact that Caeli was hyperventilating.

"Yes," she hissed through her teeth, her eyes focused solely on him.

"Good, then we should head back to Cusco. Tomorrow, we'll take you to your new home," Ryne said.

"And what will you do when the Order comes for me? They won't let you get away with holding me hostage." Caeli furrowed her brow as she spoke. If I didn't know any better, I might have said I saw a flash of black cross her bright eyes.

"I'd like to see them try to take you from the compound, especially when our little Parasite is going to have your power." How could Ryne still be so calm? How could he think he had control right now? "Now, front of the line for you. If you promise to behave, then we'll let Vince walk by your side."

My heart skipped a beat. If I made sure that Nylah and I were near the front of the line, then we could be close enough to have a chance to escape. This was it.

"I promise I'll behave," Caeli said it so calmly that it almost sounded genuine. If her eyes hadn't turned to me, then I wouldn't have known she thought the same thing as me; this was our chance, and we had to take it.

It was the only thing that echoed through my head as we fed ourselves into the tunnels once more. The group of us walked in a single file as we made our way back to the centre of the city. The promise of a chance of freedom was the only thing that drove me forward.

I was separated from Caeli and Vincent by three Templum assassins, but Nylah was right behind me. If we used the tunnels to our advantage, then I could take out the three men without so much as breaking a sweat.

The shadows around us stretched. They reached up and climbed the tunnel walls. They encroached on the light that shone from the torches of each Templum assassin. This was Caeli's doing, but her hair was still down. It wasn't time to move. Not yet. But it was close.

"Behave, Shadow." Ryne's voice carried through the tunnel, so I looked over my shoulder to see exactly where he was.

He was at the very end of the line, almost as if he thought that the further he was from Caeli that the safer he would—*fuck*. My heart caught in my throat as I turned back around.

"You're the one who said I wouldn't be able to control my emotions, and therefore my power. It's not my fault you've put me in a stressful situation where if I make a wrong step, you'll kill my father, myself, or the both of us. What did you think would happen? What did you think I would do?" Caeli asked as the torchlight dimmed for a moment.

"I thought you might see the situation you're in, and realise you don't have the luxury of working this out. The Order taught you everything you need to know about harnessing this darkness, so it might be best for your *father* if you allowed yourself to remember it," Ryne replied as I looked over my shoulder at him once more.

My brother was next to him, his honey-brown eyes locked on me, similar to how I imagined someone watched a wild animal. He knew. He knew what was going to happen. There was one reason that Nylah and I had been allowed so close to Caeli and Vince, and it was because this was a fucking test. It was to figure out exactly where my loyalty lied, and I was about to fail that test horribly.

I turned my attention back to Caeli as we walked into a small cavern, one hardly big enough for six people to stand next to each other shoulder to shoulder, but it would have to do. *Surely* it would have to do, because we were running out of fucking time.

Caeli ran her nimble fingers through her hair and slowly dragged each loose strand into a ponytail as she stopped walking and turned to face Ryne.

"The thing is, Ryne..." she said as she wrapped a hair tie around her onyx strands. "The thing is that I *do* remember everything from the Order." She let go of her now tied up hair to lift her hands in front of her body.

The torchlight slowly dimmed, but this time, the shadows clung to the floor of the cave, becoming so thick that it looked like we were standing in a void.

"I remember everything they did to me, everything they *taught* me," she said as her hands twisted in familiar circles. It was the patterns and movements she repeated whenever she was anxious, when she tried to calm herself.

With each curve of her hand—with each delicate movement of her fingers—the shadows lifted from the ground. It was a thing of dangerous beauty, watching the darkness fight against gravity like wisps of smoke from a dying fire.

"So yes, I do remember them teaching me how to harness the shadows."

She tilted her head to the side as she slowly lifted her hands to her shoulder height. The tendrils of shadow reached towards the guns and weapons that each assassin either held or wore. The darkness wrapped around my legs, an unexpected warmth to it's touch that made a shiver run through my body.

It felt like they were there to protect me, almost as if the shadows thought I *belonged* to them. They slowly reached higher. They caressed my wrists and curled around my thighs and waist. *Mine*, they almost whispered to me, an echo of what I'd felt in my chest when Caeli had waded out of the pool.

"And I definitely remember how to *control* it."

Chapter Thirty-Seven

THOSE EYES WOULD BE THE DEATH OF ME

Caeli lazily dropped her hands and all the light in the cavern fought against her, but ultimately lost it's battle.

In the tar-like darkness there was the echoed sound of metal crushing, of men as they tried to breathe but failed to suck in the thickened air around them.

And then there was a sensation in my body, like I was being pulled by a rope. Not knowing what else to do, I followed that feeling as it directed me out of the cavern filled with choking night.

"Jesus Christ, kid!" Vincent shouted once we reached the light again, which only happened when we were back in the main city.

The golden light, while welcoming, felt nothing like the shadows had on my skin. A part of me almost wanted to run back into the tunnels, to feel their warm embrace once more.

"I didn't know it would..." Caeli trailed off, but we didn't stop running. We couldn't. Not when there were more of Ryne's men stationed throughout the forest in between us and the lakes. Not when there was still every chance we could get ambushed and not make it out of this alive.

"Could we get to the forest before we discuss whatever the fuck just happened?" I asked as I looked over my shoulder to be sure Nylah was behind me.

Had I really been that distracted by Caeli's shadows to not even check she was with me from the beginning? Yes, apparently so.

Fuck.

"I like that idea," Nylah said, her eyes looking up to the tunnel we had entered the city through. "Do we go back the way we came? What if there's guards-"

"I thought we didn't want to talk," Caeli hissed the words through her teeth.

Before I could retaliate, I saw her eyes squeeze shut for a moment as she sprinted. Right, truci. She could likely already hear the whispers of the dead, especially if they could sense there was someone to communicate with. And especially since this place was filled with death—of the erasure of an entire city worth of people.

"If there are men blocking our path, I'll deal with them."

Her tone was softer, but I realised it was a purposeful nicety on her part. She had corrected her attitude for us, and I would take that for what it was; a sign that she didn't hate me or Nylah.

"You need to be careful with your power, don't-"

"I'm aware of the consequences," Caeli cut me off, and her eyes landed on me for a moment. Right, of course, she knew. How could she not? "But the potential for a long life won't matter if we fucking die here today. Aside from that, I never said I'd use it, did I?" Well, that was a valid point.

I'd watched her kill a man twice her size with bare hands before. I don't know why I assumed she'd immediately use her power as a crutch, not when she didn't need it.

Probably because I knew that I'd use it without hesitation to make sure my people were safe, consequences be damned.

Hell, if she'd let me, I would have already latched onto her neck and drunk some of her blood so I could guarantee our safety.

The risk of addiction didn't matter, not compared to getting out of this alive. And addiction seemed like a genuine possibility when her sweet scent of chai had only become stronger since her incitement.

We sprinted through Paititi, back to the tunnel we had entered through, and I took one last look over my shoulder at the golden city.

God, what wouldn't I give to have a camera right now... my memory would never do this place justice, but then again, a camera wouldn't either. Maybe I could do my best to paint it, to put the magic of this place onto canvas...

Once I'd committed every detail to memory, we used our torches to find our way back to the surface, where only two men stood guard at the entrance to Paititi. They didn't last long against Caeli.

She ran behind them and snapped one of their necks. Before he could even fall to the ground, she took his holstered handgun and shot the other through the skull. He never even stood a chance, not against her.

"Vince..." Caeli trailed off as she passed the handgun to him. He nodded as he took it and felt the weight of the weapon in his hands.

"You..." she pointed at me. "Do you have a gun?" My stomach dropped.

The thought hadn't even occurred to me to take a gun from the helicopter before we jumped into the lake. I'd been so caught up in my fear for Nylah that I hadn't planned in the slightest, much like the rest of the situation I'd put us in. Fucking hell, what was I doing?

"For fuck's sake..." she whispered as she ran a hand over her face. "Are you *good* with a gun?"

"Yeah," I answered. My eyes were on the ground, since it was impossible to look at her.

How stupid did I have to be to not even think of grabbing a fucking gun? Caeli shoved the handgun from the second felled assassin into my hands, and I took a deep breath.

"Nylah?" Caeli asked.

Fuck, I hadn't thought ahead... how could I do this to

myself? How could I do this to *Nylah*?

"I..." Nylah trailed off, because weapons weren't a part of her training. I'd been completely unable to work it in because the risk of getting caught while stuck in the compound was too damn high. All I'd done was train her in hand to hand combat—close quarters with nothing but her own fists and feet. She was good, though, so we could use it to our advantage.

"She can pack a punch. She's not as strong as you, but..." I trailed off. It was a blatant attempt at lightening the mood, since that's what I was good for, but Caeli didn't seem to care for it as she focused on the bodies in front of her.

The two men had been lightly armed, which didn't make sense when they'd had the important job of guarding the entry. Why were they chosen for this? Ryne surely knew that two men wouldn't be anywhere near enough to stop us, to even throw us off for more than a handful of seconds...

Caeli patted down their bodies, feeling for hidden pockets that could hold concealed weapons.

"Will this do?" Caeli asked as she pulled a set of brass knuckles from the older assassin.

"Oh yeah, that'll do nicely," Nylah said. She took the weapon from Caeli and immediately slipped it over her fingers. It was a near perfect fit for her, that much was obvious from the way she closed her fist with a light smile on her face.

"Okay, we have to get to the lake-"

"Don't you want a weapon?" I cut Caeli off, who seemed

offended by my question. Why couldn't I learn to keep my damned mouth shut?

"That's all those two have on them. I'll get daggers later if we take down someone who has any, alright?" Caeli replied.

The silver in her eyes was as sharp as the weapons she mentioned, and it cut right into my core. Of course she would be fine without weapons, *she* was one after all.

"We have to get to the helicopters, which is where I'm assuming the rest of the men are concentrated. You said there would be four of us against forty men. Was that the truth?" She asked as she wiped her hands on her dirt-stained and still damp grey sweatpants.

I nodded. "Ten were with us below, but there would be another twenty to thirty men that have been stationed here for the last week. Ryne's been waiting for you to get here, so he's been prepared." Caeli seemed to process what I'd said and nodded slowly.

"Let's be generous and say there *are* forty of them. We took down two here, and I probably didn't kill all the ones below, so let's say I got half. That means possibly seven down, which leaves another thirty-three men. We can handle that, can't we?" She asked.

"Fuck..." I whispered as I ran a hand through my hair.

Caeli had been right when we'd been waiting on that damned helicopter. I should have told her who I was long before she found out. We could have worked something out, and maybe we wouldn't have ended up in such an impossible situation.

"That's not even nine each. We've faced worse odds than that before," Vince said.

I had to focus on my breathing. My chest was far too tight to suck in any air, and my head was spinning. What the fuck had I done? What I had dragged us into?

"I know *we* have, but I'm worried about the other two not being able to pull their weight," Caeli responded, and I saw her nod towards me and my sister.

"We can pull our weight," Nylah said, which was far more than I could even think of articulating.

My choices had so severely screwed us over. Would I ever be able to make up for it? For putting us all in harm's way?

"Can you? Can you pull your own weight? Because your brother looks like he might have a fucking panic attack in the middle of this forest and we don't have time for that right now," Caeli snapped, which made my eyes flick towards her.

Maybe I had tried to look intimidating without intending to, or maybe it was an attempt to make her speak a little nicer to me. It didn't work either way. Instead, she stormed over to me and looked into my eyes with a silver fire I was more than happy to burn in.

"I don't care if you have anxiety to deal with. Hell, I have more than enough of my own shit to work through. But now is not the time to deal with it. You are going to have to compartmentalise that shit until we're up in the air, just the same as me. Do you understand?" She asked, and I nodded. I understood *perfectly*.

"I can pull my weight. I can deal with nine people." I

pulled my shoulders back as I spoke and forced myself to breathe slowly as she tilted her head towards the sky. "Trust me."

"I don't trust you, but I guess I don't really have a choice right now, do I?" She asked, and she levelled her head once again. God damn it, those eyes would be the death of me. "I swear, you make one wrong step and I'll-"

"Kill me with your bare hands?" I cut her off, tilting my head to the side like she had a tendency to do.

She was right. We didn't have time for me to have a breakdown about my fuck-ups that had led us here. If we wanted to get out of here alive, then we had to rely on each other, and if even one of us fell short, then we'd all end up dead.

And I would be damned if I allowed myself to die before I earned Caeli's forgiveness.

"I'm glad I've said it enough times to get the idea through your thick fucking skull." Caeli's eyes were stuck on mine for another moment before she turned around towards the lakes.

It was both a relief and a source of pain to have her look away from me, but that was another thing I would have to deal with later. I had a feeling there was more to unpack regarding that than a simple form of attraction. I'd felt attraction before, but it hadn't been anything quite like this.

"Now, let's move so we can get back to Cusco before the sun sets," Caeli said as rolled her head around to stretch her neck. "I want to shower, crawl into bed, and sleep for three days straight."

Chapter Thirty-Eight

A LIAR, AN ASSHOLE

If my situation wasn't so entirely *fucked*, I might have enjoyed the forest we had to race through. If I didn't have to worry about keeping the four of us alive, I might have enjoyed the soothing green of the trees and the sound of the birds around us. Hell, if I wasn't worried about stumbling into assassins amid the forest, then I might have enjoyed the smell of the leaves around me that reminded me so entirely of Samael.

Samael... if only he hadn't turned out to be exactly what I thought he would be. A liar, an asshole... and someone who cared deeply about his family. Why did he have to be someone I could understand the motives of?

Damn it, he'd burrowed his way under my skin just like I

knew he would. *Fuck.*

"Great, now what?" Samael asked as we reached the edge of the water. I let out a slow sigh and did my best to keep calm, just as I had from the second I'd come out of the pool.

Whispers had followed my every step, ones that I knew no one else could hear, but it was something I had to deal with later. The same way I'd have to deal with the strange feeling that flooded my chest every time I looked at Samael.

That wouldn't happen soon, though. I'd already decided that much.

"Well, *genius*, we get to the helicopter and then get the hell out of here," I replied as I stopped myself mere inches away from where the water lapped against the soil.

My white Air Jordans were completely ruined. Aside from the obvious creases from running and the water damage from being forced into multiple bodies of the liquid, there was the rather annoying fact they were now a blended colour between earth brown and blood red. This was the exact reason I couldn't have nice fucking things.

"I kind of meant if they come for us before we're in the air, while we're sitting ducks in the lake." Samael made a half-decent point that I would have to take into account.

If Templum swarmed the shore before we were in the air, then they'd be able to shoot us dead without any form of retaliation.

"I'll stay on shore," I said as I glanced at Vince, who seemed unhappy with my choice. I could deal with that later, just like everything else. For now, I knew this was the best decision we could make. "You guys get to the helicopter. When I hear the engine running, I'll make my way."

Along our trek back to the lake, we'd taken out a collective of twenty-one more assassins. The idiots had been spread through the trees instead of focused on the edge of the lake.

I wasn't overly sure what their defensive plan had been, but I knew that whoever had made it completely underestimated my abilities. I also knew that by my count, if there were actually forty assassins here, that there were only fourteen left—not including Malakai and Ryne.

"We're not leaving you on your own..." Vince said, as if it was the obvious response. Maybe it was, but I'd be damned if I let any of them stay in danger for a second longer than they had to.

"Vincent can get to the helicopter. Sam and I can stay. We'll go once-"

The echo of a gunshot cut Nylah off, and the bullet tore into the water behind us. Well, whoever had shot at us was either a terrible shot or a terrible decision maker. Either way, they wouldn't live to make the same mistake again.

"Go!" I shouted as Malakai walked out from between the trees, a handgun pointed directly at me. Excellent, so the person who'd shot at us was both a terrible shot *and* a terrible decision maker. Good to know.

There wasn't enough time between him appearing from between the trees and the sound of water splashing behind me for Malakai to threaten my people. But there *was* enough time for me to take a quick breath so I could centre myself once again.

I could use my power, or I could use my bare hands. It wouldn't matter which I'd choose because I would come out on top either way. There wasn't any other option.

If I lost, then my people were dead. And as much as I might hate to admit it, if I saw Samael with a bullet wound through his skull, it might cause some emotional pain. I could blame his previous lies for that attachment later, but right now? I had a fucking immature brat I needed to tear apart with my bare hands.

"You should go. You've done enough for me and Nylah," Samael said as he crept into my peripheral vision.

I glanced over my shoulder to see Vince and Nylah as they swam to the helicopter. He should have been in the water with them, to put distance between himself and the fight that would take place on the shore. But he was by my side, and ready to help me against the remnants of Templum.

"I don't leave jobs unfinished..." I trailed off as Ryne walked out of the trees, surrounded by eight assassins. That must be all that was left, because I doubted he'd come and face me with any less than what was at his disposal. I must have gotten rid of more of them in the tunnels than I thought. "Besides, if I leave you here and you die, Vince will never let go of it, *Samael*."

I could have sworn he shivered as I spoke his name. It was such a visceral reaction that there was no way he could have known he'd done it until it was too late.

"No one else will care? Just Vince?" He asked, and I

understood what he was asking.

He wanted to know if I'd feel any kind of remorse if he died here today, but I'd already let him in far too close. I now had to play my cards close to my chest. There wasn't a possible way I could let him know that my emotions regarding him were complicated and that I'd need some time to work them out.

"Maybe Nylah would care too," I deflected as I looked down at my fingers.

Even though I wasn't calling on my power, it was as if I had dipped my fingertips in black ink. I'd read that shadows sometimes circled a grim, wrapped around their skin as constant protection against the world. In very few cases, the shadows settled beneath the surface and became one with their vessel.

I rubbed my fingertips together as I realised the shadows had claimed me completely. It meant the alias I'd used for the past few years was more than a nickname. I was now the Shadow because that darkness was a part of me.

Maybe that was the reason Malakai and Ryne hadn't moved forward yet. Maybe they realised they faced a person they couldn't control, who had allies that were just as impossible to dominate. The people who'd sided with me couldn't be afraid, not when they had the only living grim on their side. And they had Ryne and Malakai to thank for that advantage.

"You know I'm going to kill your brother, right?" I asked, loud enough for the remaining Templum members to hear me—loud enough for the mentioned brother to feel every syllable as I stared right into his honey-coloured eyes.

"That's fine..." Samael replied, and I could feel the cold anger flow off his body in waves. "It's *more* than fine, because I'm going to kill my father."

I had to hide the surprise I felt at the blunt calmness of his words. It wasn't a threat that came from deep within his throat. It was a cold-hard fact, something that couldn't be argued with. The others noticed the tone too, and I could have sworn I saw each of the assassins flinch.

Something about the entire situation felt off to me, like the fact that every Templum member we'd disposed of had gone down too easily. It was as if they were all amateurs trying to prove themselves...

"We still have eight assassins left-" I cut Malakai off as I sprinted—faster than I had ever been capable of before—and snapped the neck of one of the remaining guards before I shattered the skull of another within the space of a few seconds.

With the blood of my second victim painted on my face, I looked right at Malakai.

"I think that makes six, little brat," I replied as I slowly took the daggers from one of the newly dead assassins and noted where the remaining few were. Ryne moved away from the protection of the six guards as Malakai edged towards them.

This would be far too fucking easy.

"Everyone on me!" Malakai shouted, and Ryne didn't

argue.

Maybe the Priest of Templum thought he could take on his own son, which was a bullshit assumption to make. Ryne clearly hadn't taken into account the bottled anger that had simmered to Samael's surface. Either Ryne didn't realise or he didn't care, but that wasn't my problem.

I had a brat to take care of as well as his pitiful protectors.

I took on the six assassins at once. My body moved through the air like a ribbon, graceful and impossible to cut down. Every movement had a purpose, to either block an attack from one assassin or to make an offensive move on another.

I ducked and weaved, swung and stabbed, until I cleared a path to my intended target. I hadn't killed all of them, not yet, but they were unconscious for now, and that was good enough. The second Malakai was gone, I could easily deal with the leftovers.

"Do you realise how fucking pissed I am?" I asked as I readjusted my grip on the unfamiliar daggers and stalked towards Malakai. His eyes lit up with fear, just as they should. "My shoes are fucking ruined, and I'm blaming you for that, you fucking asshole."

I reached striking distance and listened to what my gut told me to do, which was to drop to a knee as he swung at my head with his own blade. It was a wild and desperate move, one that cost him precious time and energy.

Without wasting any of mine, I swung my body around and swiped out his feet with my shin. A smirk graced my face as I watched him fall to the ground, completely helpless against me as I knelt on one knee next to his chest and threw away all his weapons.

"I loved these shoes, Malakai," I hissed. "Now, they're not just stained with blood and soil, and they're not just filled with disgusting water and mud. They are fucking *creased*." I hovered a dagger over his throat. "So, now is the opportune moment for you to apologise."

"Apologise for what?" He spat through his teeth. It was an obvious attempt to cover his fear with anger. I almost felt sorry for him, at how easy he was to read.

"For backstabbing me, manipulating me, kidnapping Vincent and myself, ruining the lives of your own siblings and, most importantly, for ruining my god-damned shoes," I hissed back.

In response he fucking *smiled*. I'd always hated that smile. "No..."

Well, if that's the choice he wanted to make, then I wouldn't stop him.

"Fine, just remember, this could have been avoided." I took a second to find the exact location I wanted to slit his throat, but something made me look away for a moment.

It was a tug in my chest that told me to look up.

Chapter Thirty-Nine

MASTER OF PATRICIDE AND SUNSET PORTRAITS

The air around the lake was silent. Beyond my heavy breaths, there was a pure stillness that shouldn't have been there.

Where there should have been grunting and heavy breathing from the other fight that should have been taking place, there was nothing. No shots of a bullet leaving a gun, or the familiar slick sound of a knife plunging into skin. There should have been the sounds of moving water, because Ryne and Samael had fought at the edge of the lake.

The silence made my pulse quicken and my entire body go tense, so I made the mistake of looking up without killing Malakai first.

It was more important to me to make sure that Samael was alive than to make sure that Malakai wasn't. I could berate myself for that decision once we were a safe distance from this place.

I felt like my eyes were seeing things, but they weren't. I hadn't imagined it, I couldn't have.

Samael stood at the edge of the lake, an unfamiliar knife in his hand as he stood over his father's body. His chest visibly heaved as he ran a dangerous and calloused hand through his dark curls.

As the sun set behind him, his silhouette defined itself against the orange sky. All I could think was how much he looked like a perfectly portrayed god of death.

"Holy shit..." I couldn't deny it; this was the most attracted I'd ever been to a person in my entire life. That probably wasn't healthy for me, but I would let it slide. Just because I felt drawn to someone didn't mean I had to act on that pull.

And I wouldn't.

I *couldn't*.

"Right, where were we?" I asked as I tore my eyes away from Samael, the master of patricide and sunset portraits, to find an empty space where his bitch of a brother should have been. "What the hell?"

I stood up slowly and looked back at the assassins I'd already taken down. Out of the eight that had been on the ground, only five dead bodies remained. Fucking *damn it*.

"Where is he?" Samael asked, his deep voice right next to me. Hearing it so close after he'd stirred something in my chest... it sent an involuntary shiver down my spine.

"He slipped away," I answered. The trees gave away nothing. There wasn't even a set of footprints in the soil that I could use to track him down. *Fuck*.

"You let him get away?" Alright, that's *not* how this would go.

"Oh, I'm sorry. I thought I might check on you since you were awfully quiet back there and I felt a slight hint of concern over whether you might be dead," I snapped as I pointed a dagger at him. "He must have decided it was an excellent opportunity to cut his losses and run. It might be one of the smartest decisions he's ever made in his pitiful fucking life."

I pocketed my new daggers and took in the mess around us.

"He's going to take over what's left of Templum," Samael said. His voice was dark as he stared into the trees.

"Well, at least we know it's going to be terribly run and, therefore, be easy to dismantle at a later date. Right now we should head back to Cusco, before it gets dark."

I turned on my heel to reach the edge of the lake where Ryne's body would remain forevermore. He was on his back, his glass eyes focused on the warming sky. Stab wounds covered his chest, and there were too many to bother counting.

"I see you let out that anger of yours," I said.

My eyes shifted slowly from Ryne to Samael as he walked into the water in front of me. He gave me nothing in response, not even a look out of the corner of his eye to acknowledge that I'd said anything. He didn't even look at the body of his own father.

"I guess I'll go fuck myself then," I whispered as I froze at the water's edge.

One more swim and this would all be over. Just one more dip into a body of water and I'd be able to relax. But I couldn't get myself to move, not until I saw Vince's head pop out of the helicopter door. His blond hair reflected the orange sunlight while the blades whirred over his head and moved each strand of gold.

"Let's go, kid!" He shouted, so I took one last breath before I waded into the lake.

With careful breaths and my eyes completely focused on Vince, I swam as fast as I could through the water.

Even with him as my anchor, it was hard to force my body to ignore the feeling of the water fighting against me. It was hard to stop myself from freezing in the middle of the lake, and difficult to follow each stroke of my arms with another, but eventually I made it to the helicopter alone.

Vince helped pull me in, and once all four of us were buckled up with headsets on, he lifted the machine away from the water and into the air.

"So we were just in an entire city made of gold, and we can't ever go back," Vince said. I looked out the corner of my eyes towards him.

"No, the tribe who live in the area would never give us permission to come back, especially after what we've done."

I looked at my hands as I spoke and some form of guilt ran over me at what had happened.

If I hadn't been forced into going there, I would have asked permission before we went ahead. I would have told them we were there to help them fight back against Templum.

"I'm more concerned about the fact there was an entire city of gold and we're leaving empty-handed," I pointed out.

While I wanted to be respectful of the people we'd eventually steal from, it didn't mean I wanted to continue not having any money. Unfortunately, it was a necessity to live—and you needed a lot of it to stay hidden from organisations like the Order.

"Actually..." Nylah trailed off, so I turned to look at the girl. "When we first walked into the city, no one was really paying attention to me, so I used that to my advantage..."

Nylah reached into a pocket of her black cargo pants and pulled out some gold coins. There were only seven, but it was sure as shit better than nothing. They'd fetch a good price from a collector here in Peru, or maybe even a museum.

"And I might have grabbed some while you were leading us into the tunnels," Samael added as he reached into the pocket of his jeans and pulled out a few more coins.

"Yeah, me too," Vince said before he pulled out his own stash of gold pieces.

The sight of the gold brought a smile to my face, and I felt laughter bubble in my throat. Of course, between the four of us, we'd managed to get something of worth. If it had just been Vince and me, then it would have turned out differently. We wouldn't have made it out of Paititi alive, let alone with something to sell.

Maybe this whole *working as a team* idea wasn't such a bad thing after all.

Chapter Forty

THE MOST PROFITABLE OUTCOME

"So, what do you think?" I asked once Caeli and I were in a new hotel room.

I was completely focused on her as she did her rounds of the space, triple-checking the windows and the bathroom before she decided we were secure enough in our new temporary safe space.

As I had explained on the drive to our old hotel to grab our things; Templum had taken me when I'd slipped outside for a cigarette before our day started. It was something I wasn't meant to be doing anymore, since Caeli had told me over and over again that I needed to quit. Now that it was the reason

I'd been taken hostage, I might actually try to do so again.

Even though I hadn't been taken because she'd missed something, I knew her paranoia was likely in overdrive after everything that had happened today, so I let her do what she had to do. Easing her anxiety was something we could work on later. After everything that had happened to *her* alone, it was best to leave her be. All I had to do tonight was make sure she was okay—or that she *would* be.

"What do I think of what?" She questioned, her brow furrowed as she picked up her bag from next to the door again.

We'd agreed it might be best for her to sleep in her own room for the night. She needed space to decompress after today, and needed time alone to work out what to do about her new shadow magic, which I was still trying to wrap my head around. I'd always assumed that conduits *weren't* bullshit, and I always suspected she was one... but now there was evidence that I hadn't imagined the choking darkness back in Paititi.

Her fingertips still looked like they'd been dipped in ink. The colour had slowly faded, but it was still obvious enough to serve as a stark reminder that everything was about to change for us.

"Well, before we left for Paititi, we talked about trusting H-*Samael*. Now that we know who he really is and why he had to do what he did, do you think you'll be able to trust him?" I asked, and her body tensed at the words.

While Nylah and I had waited for the helicopter to warm

up, we'd watched the fight as it happened on the shore. It wasn't the first time I'd seen Caeli win a fight that should have ended in a loss, and I knew that it wouldn't be the last, either. However, it had been the first time she'd stopped her fight to show even the slightest bit of concern for someone else's well-being—not including me, of course.

"I don't know," she answered. It wasn't snarky or snappy, as I had expected. Instead, her voice had been gentle and genuine. "I just... the incitement was strange." Okay, I'm sure that tied into the topic of Samael somehow. I guess I'd find out in due time.

"How so? Nylah didn't think you should have passed your trial..." Her body tensed again as I spoke.

"Our trials were very different. Mine was based on what I would do in the future. It was based on accepting the fact that I *am* scared of Ashford and the Order, and accepting that I can't stay hidden forever. I have the people around me I need in order to stay safe, and I can handle it if she finds me. Nylah's was based on her past. It told her she needed to move on. I watched the memory of their mother being killed by Ryne. I saw the exact moment their childhoods were ripped away from them, and I had to convince Nylah it wasn't her fault. I had to convince her to not be afraid of Ryne."

Shit. Nylah had summarised what Caeli's trial had been, but hearing it from my kid was completely different. Being able to see how her body responded to just the memory of it showed how much it had affected her. The reaction made me rethink whether having her in a room by herself for the night was a good idea.

"On top of that, whatever decides whether you're strong enough for the power or not... it *spoke* to me." Caeli's eyes were focused on the floor as I edged towards her.

She spoke of the Entity. It was something I was vaguely aware of, something that no one really knew the details of. When I suspected what Caeli was, I did my research, and finding anything of note on the Entity was impossible. It just existed, and no one knew what it meant. I hadn't found any records of it speaking to anyone, however, so I knew that much was strange.

"It said I couldn't make her do it alone, that me doing the trial with her was the only way to restore balance... I know it was just trying to convince me to get into the water, but it felt like it meant more than that. It was like it wanted us to stick together afterwards. It flooded my body with that icy feeling I get when I know I'm doing something right."

"What are you saying, kid?" I asked as her eyes lifted to meet mine again.

This was all getting too confusing for me—a little farfetched—but there wasn't any possible way that Caeli had made this up. If she said the Entity spoke to her, then it had.

"I'm saying that I think the Entity has been watching over me for a long time. It's pushing me in the direction it wants me to go by giving me a bodily sensation when I'm on the right track. Every time I've made a decision that relates to helping Samael or working with him, my stomach turns to ice." Okay, if that was the case then it had been watching over her for years. She'd been relying on that sensation since I found her. "It wants me to trust Samael and Nylah, and it hasn't led me astray before. I just... I don't know if they'll want to trust us. They might want to make their own way in the world now that they're free, you know? I don't want to get in their way if that's what they feel is right for them."

Caeli had historically never given herself enough credit for her ability to empathise with other people. Yes, it was difficult for her to do so, and it happened rarely. But then she would unexpectedly pull something like this out of her soul and it reminded me she wasn't the cold-hearted killer she pretended she was.

"That's not just about trusting them, then. You want to join forces with them," I pointed out, almost unsure if that was what was going on. Never in my wildest dreams had I imagined she might actually toy with the idea of expanding our team.

"Yeah, I guess it is," she said. It was so nonchalant that it felt more realistic that I'd simply lost my mind. She was serious about this, and it was hard to keep a straight face, so I didn't scare her into rethinking her decision. "I'll want to talk to them first, to make sure that they want to work with us. It won't be tonight, though. We should all get some rest and discuss this first thing tomorrow over some coffee."

I nodded my head before we bid each other goodnight and she walked out of the room to make her way to her own.

This was the best possible outcome I could have asked for after today and the past week. If Caeli had more people to work with and trust, then the plans she made would undoubtedly become larger and more dangerous. If the siblings stayed, then the coming months—possibly years—would be the most entertaining for me yet.

And also the most profitable.

I chuckled to myself as I picked up my phone and smiled as I looked through my contacts to see who I could sell the gold coins to for a good price.

This was going to be fun.

CHAPTER FORTY-ONE

YOU'RE BEING AN UNCOOPERATIVE ASSHOLE

"You should talk to Caeli." My voice was quiet as my brother turned to look at me.

Night had just fallen over Cusco, and while I was more than ready to go to sleep, I knew our day wasn't finished yet. The day had taken a toll on me. I was drained from the constant fear that filled my body and then, on top of that, was the experience of going through the incitement.

"I don't think she wants to see me right now. She might like some space after everything that happened today," Sam replied as he ran a hand through his freshly washed hair.

I shook my head as I sat down on the second bed in the room, the one I'd claimed as mine for the night. There were no belongings I had left to get to, not when going to the hotel Templum had stayed at was far too dangerous.

So, I couldn't wear my comfortable pyjamas tonight. Instead, I was stuck with one of his shirts and a pair of his sweatpants that I'd had to roll the cuffs on so they didn't fall past my feet. First thing on the list for tomorrow was buying me some new things.

"Well, she might like to know what we talked about. Caeli doesn't seem like the kind of person who would wait for important information," I replied as I crossed my arms over my chest.

I'd already had a shower, warmed up my body and changed to be ready for bed. It was the first time in years that I could let my body fully relax, to know that I wasn't being watched and threatened with every breath I took. I actually couldn't remember the last time I'd felt like this, to feel like I was *free*.

"Why don't *you* tell her, then?" Sam asked as he mirrored my body language. I shook my head and bit back a smile. There was no way he didn't know why it would have to be him to have this conversation with Caeli and not me, but I could clarify for him if that's what he really wanted.

"Maybe because I'm not the one who infiltrated her life and lied to her. I didn't gain some of her trust before I threw it on the ground and shattered it into a thousand pieces." He flinched at my words, which put a smirk on my face. If you ask a stupid question, I'll give a blunt answer. He should have known that. "She still helped us in spite of that and you probably didn't even apologise."

"How do you know if I've apologised or not?" Well, that blatant deflection was all I needed to prove my assumption was right, but he wouldn't care if I threw it back in his face, so I would go with the other reason.

"Because you're my brother, and I know exactly what you're like," I said. While it was the answer he needed to hear, it didn't mean he would actually listen to me. I knew that much from experience.

"Nylah-" was he seriously still going to attempt putting this back on me? For the love of god, I did not have the patience for this, not after today.

"On top of you needing to apologise to her, you also think she's cute." I cut him off and tilted my head to the side as my smile grew.

He blushed.

He actually *blushed*, which meant my second assumption about this conversation was another correct one. Once again, I was the only person on the face of the planet who could consistently read my brother without fail. I'm a god-damned genius.

"I don't think she's cute." Well, it didn't seem like a lie, which meant he was being annoyingly specific about the word I'd chosen to use.

Maybe *cute* was the wrong word after everything I'd seen Caeli do, and after seeing the aftermath of previous situations that she'd been involved in. After all, I'd been there when Caeli had stabbed herself in the stomach, and that had been to merely create a distraction.

"Fine, you think she's *attractive*, then." I corrected my word use, and there was no further argument from my brother as his cheeks flushed a little darker than they had before. "You can't deny it because I saw the way you looked at her at the auction, and in the Archives, and in the church and-"

"Alright, you don't have to list every single time I've looked at her." Did he seriously look at Caeli like that *every single time* he laid eyes her? My god, it worse than I thought.

"All I'm saying is that when you live a life like ours, that it's hard to find people you can see yourself being with. I don't know exactly what you're looking for with her, but I saw how you changed when she came out of the pool. You think there could be something between you two, and I haven't seen you keen on anyone since..." I furrowed my brow as I realised how close I'd come to letting that cursed name fall from my lips.

Sam took a slow breath, unfolded his arms, and let them fall by his sides.

"Camilla?" He asked, and I nodded.

"Yeah, you know, before she-"

"I was there, Ny, I know what happened." He cut me off, and this time the smile fell from my face.

Camilla Fontaigne had always been a sore spot for Sam, but only because she hadn't been who he thought she was.

361

It was rough for him to come back from, but he'd managed it. It was the other reason he should know that apologising to Caeli was the best first step towards what we wanted to do.

"Okay, just... do you like Caeli?" I asked as I folded my hands in my lap and patiently waited for the deflection I knew would come.

"If I didn't like Caeli, we wouldn't be staying in the same hotel as her." And there it was.

"Alright, you're being an uncooperative asshole, so I'm going to follow my gut feeling on this one." I leaned forward and jutted my head towards Sam as I pointed toward Caeli and Vincent's room.

"The longer you leave this, the further she's going to distance herself. If you don't apologise to her, then she'll never let you in like you desperately want her to." I dropped my arm and relaxed my posture. Why did talking sense into him have to be so convoluted? "And also, she might not let us work with her, which would be bad because we're going to need to make money from this point forward, and this is all we really know."

If nothing else, then I could use the money argument and win some points towards my side of this. It seemed to have worked, since he rolled his eyes at me.

"I'll go in the morning," he said. Maybe he thought that was an acceptable answer and that I would leave the conversation there. He really should know better than that.

"No..." I trailed off before I stood up with my hands on my

hips. "You're going to go now."

He tilted his head back to look at the ceiling. "Fuck me, I forgot how bossy you are." He levelled his head again so he could meet my eyes.

It was obvious he held back a smile, but I didn't bother hiding mine. I was far too happy to be around my brother again to want to keep that joy from him. We'd been separated for the better part of a year. It had been too hard to see each other in between my responsibilities as a researcher and his as the prized lamia assassin.

"And I forgot how much of a coward you are," I replied. It could have been viewed as a tad harsh, but with stuff like this, it was the truth.

"That was uncalled for," he said as he picked up his jacket and put it on despite his arguments. He then made his way to the door and slipped his sneakers on.

"Your face is uncalled for." Oh god, that had just slipped from my mouth with far too much ease. Apparently it wasn't going to take any time for me to get used to saying whatever I wanted again.

I half-expected him to throw an insult back at me, but maybe since he was in his mid-twenties, he thought he was too mature to partake in the back and forth. Or maybe he just wanted to be nice for one night before we settled back into our old routine.

"Kill me now," he whispered instead, but he looked at me with a smile before he walked out the door.

In the new silence of the room, I took a deep breath.

It had been months since I'd been truly alone—since I'd had space to breathe and not need to use every spare second to plan how to stay alive. I settled my body on top of the bed and stared at the white popcorn ceiling.

"Caeli cannot do this alone, and neither can you. Together you will restore balance."

The voice from the pool echoed around me.

No one else heard it, I knew that much. But the way the words had hit me in the chest made me more than sure that they were real. It wasn't just talking about us doing the trial together, either; I felt like it meant we had to stick together. A custos and a truci were balancing conduits, and if Caeli had any hope of keeping control over her darkness, then she would likely have to lean on my light.

I closed my eyes as my body remembered the warmth of the pool and my ears remembered the comforting voice that followed me through the entire trial.

And then I fell asleep, without a single worry to my name.

CHAPTER FORTY-TWO

THE EXTREMELY BREAKABLE LINE

I took a deep breath before I worked up the nerve to knock on the door to Caeli and Vincent's room. I knew that if I didn't that Nylah wouldn't let me live it down, so it was best to just get it out of the way. However, what I hadn't expected was for Vince to answer the door instead of Caeli.

I probably should have known there was every chance the man would do so, but I thought that with Caeli's paranoia, she would have... *no*. I didn't know her well enough to make any assumptions. I didn't have the privilege of knowing her, not yet anyway.

Vince let me into the room with a silent nod, and the

second I was in, I scanned every corner and every window to know where all entry and exit points were located. It was habit, I guessed, to make sure any room I entered was secure. It was maybe the hardest thing to tone down when I pretended to be Hunter, but I'd still done it every time I walked into a room, without fucking fail.

"You're just as bad as Caeli," Vincent said, as he clearly noticed what I was doing.

"Yeah, I think I just hid it relatively well..." I trailed off. How was I meant to even start this conversation? I bit my lip. "Is Caeli-"

"Caeli booked a separate room for the night. She wanted some time alone, which I think is more than warranted after today. What's going on?" He asked as he crossed his arms over his chest and leaned against the table in the room. The way he looked at me was reminiscent of how the blue in his irises had cut through me after I nearly got Caeli killed in Romania... *twice.*

"Nylah said I should speak to Caeli, but if she needs some space, then it can wait until tomorrow." I walked back to the door, since I was sure that would be the end of the conversation, but my entire body froze when I heard Vincent speak again.

"No, it might be best if you talk to her."

I turned to look back at the man who had dropped his arms from his chest and instead shoved his hands into the pockets of his jeans. Was he serious? Surely not.

"She's in the last room on the right, but she's probably in

the shower by now, so she might not answer the door. You could probably go in and wait for her, though," Vince said. I nodded, even though it didn't feel real.

"Thanks," I said before I grabbed the door handle.

But I couldn't leave just yet. I had to know whether I had just one relationship to patch and fix or whether I'd screwed up so badly that Vincent thought I was a villain too.

"Um, did you ever... even for just a second..." *did you ever think I was truly one of them?*

I couldn't really spit out the words, not when just thinking about the theoretical version of me that was a true Templum assassin made me want to vomit. Thankfully, Vincent could read people easily, and seemed to know exactly what I wanted to ask.

"I mean, when I was kidnapped and had a bunch of guns pointed at me, I definitely thought you'd sold us out and fucked us over. While I was stuck in that church, waiting for you to arrive, I definitely thought Caeli had been right, and I was kicking myself for being stupid enough to trust you... but then I saw you with your sister." Vincent squinted his eyes at me, as if the man was attempting to read my mind. And maybe he did. "You're not a bad kid, Samael, and I always knew deep down that we could trust you. I'm just glad you proved me right and her wrong."

"And Caeli? What does she..." I couldn't put into words what I wanted to ask. Or maybe I could, but I simply didn't want to say it out loud.

"Just talk to her. She'll tell you exactly what she's

thinking." Well, that didn't help ease any of my concerns in the slightest.

"Yeah, that's what I'm afraid of," I said. Although there was something comforting about the way he smiled at me.

Surely if he thought I was about to get murdered by the Shadow, he wouldn't smile at me like that... and he said back in Paititi that he hoped Caeli would show me mercy. There was only one way to find out what awaited me, and standing here wouldn't give me the answers I needed. But it might be a good idea to say a last goodbye to him, just in case Caeli killed me.

"Thank you for everything."

Before Vincent could reply, I walked out the door and shut it behind me. I hated thanking people because it meant admitting that I needed help in the first place. It was just another thing to add to the list of what I had to unlearn from Templum, which was an ever-growing line-up of new issues I could find within myself. I'm sure Nylah would have plenty more to add for me, too.

I knocked on the door that Vincent told me Caeli would be behind and, as expected, I didn't get an answer. But I had been told that I could go in and wait.

I picked the lock to the door before I walked in and waited on the edge of the bed, my eyes staring at nothing in the space ahead of me.

It was only after the bathroom door opened that the thought occurred to me that *maybe* what I'd done was wrong. And possibly imposing. And I pieced all of that together from the look on Caeli's face as she stood in the now open doorway, wearing only a towel and a glare.

Why did that make my blood run hot throughout my entire body?

"What in the name of fuck are you doing in my room?" She asked after a few moments of painful silence. I had to rub my thigh for any hope of easing the sudden ache that filled my fingers, and to distract myself from how hard my heart hammered in my chest.

"I came here to talk to you," I answered. I stood up from the bed as she walked towards it, and I put some distance between us. Personal space and all that.

Damn it, I hadn't put any gum in my fucking mouth. And I was going to have to stop looking at her so I would have even the slimmest chance of hiding the fact that each passing second made me want to do a lot more than just *talk* to her.

"And me *not* answering the door didn't make you think you should *maybe* come back at a later time?" She asked. Her voice was tired, which could be expected after everything she'd gone through today. *Jesus Christ, Samael, you need to get your shit together.*

"Vince said I could wait in here if you were in the..." That had been an attempt at defending my actions, but as each word fell from my mouth, I realised how I might have actually made the situation worse.

"So, let me get this straight..." Caeli trailed off as she rubbed her forehead with one hand and adjusted the top of her towel with the other.

With her eyes squeezed shut, I had an opportunity to look at where she'd trailed her blackened fingers near her collarbone. God, I could look at her bare legs and... and the scars that covered her from head to toe.

They hadn't been obvious on her arms until now, when I could afford to pay attention to every detail that made her who and what she was. The Order must have done a lot more than use water as a torture device for her. They must have used knives and... what else could they have used to make those thick scars?

"You came into my room with only the permission of someone else who isn't even staying in this room?" She asked.

Right, yes. I should probably bring myself back to the present instead of where my mind had run to.

I had to focus on anything other than placing a kiss on each one of those scars. I had to focus on *anything* other than what it might feel like to run my fingers over her golden skin, or what her pulse might feel like beneath my lips or-

"Now that you say it out loud..." I trailed off and closed my eyes before I ran a hand over my face.

This was a bad idea. Or an idea that actually lacked any thought or input whatsoever. I think the thought of being in close quarters with her had just overruled any kind of common sense that should exist in my mind.

"I'll come back later." I turned towards the door, but hearing her gravelly voice made me freeze.

"Well, it's a bit late for courtesy now. You're already in

here." Was that tone almost... playful? "Just stay facing the door. If you even *think* about turning to look at me while I get dressed, I will slit your throat."

I didn't need to look at her to know she was serious about that threat, since I was sure she'd be more than happy to follow through on it given the opportunity.

"Fair enough," I said as I trained my eyes on the door and forced down every impulse that told me to flirt or to turn and watch her. Not that she helped the matter in the slightest, not when all I could smell was fucking *chai* and I could hear every movement as she pulled her clothes onto her body. On top of that was the deafening sound of her racing heart which seemed to be louder than my own.

And of course there had to be a small mirror next to the door, placed there for someone to check their makeup last minute before they left the room. All I could see in the glass was the reflection of Caeli's bare back, her roped muscles stretching as she pulled a sweatshirt over her scarred skin.

Did this technically count as turning to watch? No, there wasn't any turning involved, so surely it didn't count... right? Although the way my cock strained against my jeans told me it might count as something she *should* kill me for.

"What do you want to talk about?" What did I want to talk about? Why couldn't I remember?

She pulled her wet hair free of the sweatshirt collar. The movement was so simple and yet so distracting as she tilted her head to the side. The movement showed the arc of her slender neck and-

Fuck, she was turning to face me.

I couldn't still be watching the mirror. That would be a dead giveaway of the rules I'd bent and the thoughts that had overtaken my every last brain cell. Ignoring the fact I had a glaringly obvious hard-on, the only thing I could do was squeeze my eyes shut and tense my hands.

It had always been impossible for me to ignore how I was drawn to her, but since the damned incitement, it was becoming unbearably strong.

It wasn't just *me* that wanted her, but my power, too. I wanted my canines to pierce her skin; I wanted to know what her blood would taste like as it hit my tongue and-

"You can turn around, Samael. I'm fully clothed." My body shivered once again as my name fell from her lips.

Turning around as she had instructed would be difficult considering what my body was doing, and it would only be made worse by the fact I knew she hadn't put on a bra underneath that sweatshirt. How was I meant to think of anything else other than how well her body might fit in my hands?

I turned around slowly and opened my eyes to see she hadn't put her hair up, and nor did she seem to have any intention of doing so.

God, was she comfortable around me now? Did she trust me?

It helped to quell some of the burn that flooded every inch of my body, but only enough for my canines to retreat into my gums and my cock to relax. There was nothing that could stop the way my fingertips ached at the thought of touching her, or the way she held every particle of my attention.

While the closet in the Archives had been torture, this was so much worse—even with the distance between us. It was because she knew my true identity. That was the imagined and extremely *breakable* line I'd drawn in the sand between us, and now that line had been washed away with the tide of her. That line was the only thing that kept me sane in the damned closet; I wouldn't get involved with her because she didn't know who I was. But now she knew everything, and it was more than probable that she hated me.

"Nylah said I should come and talk to you about what we're going to do from here," I said.

I tried to keep my eyes on hers, but that was easier said than done when she kept dragging a finger over the collar of her sweatshirt. That wasn't something she was doing on purpose, surely. There was no way she was *purposely* making this difficult for me, not when she shouldn't know how she affected me. Or how *easily* she affected me.

"I was going to come to you tomorrow about that. I thought it might be best for us to get some rest before we jumped into it," she replied as she walked over to the small table in the room.

On it's surface were her ruined Air Jordan's... maybe I could buy her a new pair as an apology—once we started making some money, that is. I had nothing to my fucking name, nothing I could get too easily at least.

"That's what I thought would be best to do as well, but I

got told to talk to you and I follow orders, so..." I said as she sat down and stared at her shoes.

"Noted." *Noted?* That what? I follow orders? Why did that feel like something I didn't want her remembering? "Let's talk then."

IF THAT APPEALS TO YOU

Caeli gestured to the other seat at the table, one that I immediately sat down on. I kept a little distance between me and the table, because by relation it meant I was a little further away from her. I didn't want to seem like I was imposing anymore than I already had.

"First topic, it's a very important one..." she trailed off as she picked up one of her shoes. "Do you think it's worth trying to save this pair, or will the water damage be too much?"

It was strange to see her doing something so normal. And to see her doing it in clothes that were also normal. It was strange for her to act so perfectly calm and *normal*. I almost wanted her to yell at me, or hiss her words just as she had been for the last week. But it also felt nice to know that she was comfortable enough around me to let down her guard, and to display it with her hair and her clothes.

No one should be able to make a matching set of black sweats look as good as she did. And yet, there she was. It would be easy to think she hadn't been killing people only a few hours ago... and that I wasn't one of the people she'd wanted to gut.

"Well, you have water damage, stains, *creases*..." I trailed off.

She scrunched up her nose at the list of issues with her shoes, and it brought a smile to my face. How many little expressions of hers had I missed because I'd tried to keep my distance?

"You're right, there's no way to bring these back." She threw the shoe onto the tabletop and finally turned her silver gaze towards me. As she did so, my chest filled with air, as if it was easier to breathe when she looked at me. "I assume you're more interested in topic two of this conversation."

"What topic would that be?" I asked as I leaned forward and rested my elbows on my knees.

"It's an open floor opportunity for you to convince me you would be an asset to the exceptionally well staffed Caeli and Vince operation," she replied. She picked up her socked feet and put them on the tabletop. Were her feet always so small? "So, off you go." She gestured a hand for me to start, but I didn't entirely know what to say.

"What do you want me to do? Give you an elevator pitch?"

I asked. She raised her eyebrows at the option.

It was something I was used to doing; it was a part of selling my services as a lamia in Templum's ranks. Honestly, I'd hoped to never need to break it out again—to summarise my skills and abilities and my fucking kill count.

"Actually, that would be wonderful. Give me your best elevator pitch," she said as she leaned back in her chair completely. Her arms crossed over her chest as she tilted her head to the side. "Please keep in mind the fact that you've lied to me about your identity, put Vince in severe danger, and nearly got all of us killed." Right, so just a few things I had to make up for.

I wasn't sure if my elevator pitch would be anywhere close to good enough to warrant forgiveness and a place in her *operation*, but I'd have to give it my best shot. To begin with, I sat up straight, pulled my shoulders back and opened my body just as I'd been taught, and I focused my eyes on the wall behind her so I could pretend I was doing anything else other than reciting this bullshit.

"My name is Samael Eldridge. I've been a fully trained Templum assassin for seven years and went through my incitement to become a lamia three years ago. I could be of use to you through my-"

"Please stop," she cut me off. When I turned my eyes back to her, all I saw was a soft smile on her face. "They do not teach you people skills in Templum and it's *painfully* obvious. You're focusing on the wrong aspects of yourself and your capabilities for your target audience."

"How so?" I asked, maybe a tad bit defensive since I'd begun reciting the exact pitch that I'd used for years with a perfect success rate.

"Well, you're talking to me like I want you to protect me or to kill someone for me. I don't need either of those things from you. What I'm looking for is a person I can trust, someone I can rely on no matter how dark a situation might get." She had a point, but how was I meant to even prove that to her with a pitch?

"Vince and I aren't just partners in crime. We're family, and that's why we work so well together. No matter what happens, he knows I'll be there for him the same way I know he'll be there for me. If you knew how to adjust your elevator pitch for your audience, you wouldn't have focused on Templum. Instead, you would have focused on the relationship you have with your sister."

My back curved as my shoulders fell. I didn't know what to say. This was unfamiliar territory for me, after all. While I had to sell my services before, there was no chance I'd be turned down. I was the best that Templum had, and I was the only lamia in their ranks. Getting work hadn't been difficult.

"The purpose of the elevator pitch was to see where your people skills are, it doesn't have an actual impact on my decision. Knowing your audience is extremely important for generating business in this line of work, so it's something we're going to have to work on," she said as she pulled her feet off the table and stood up.

"What are you saying?" I asked. While I could understand

the implication behind her words, I wouldn't get my hopes up until I heard the right ones tumble from her mouth in the right order.

"I would like to keep working with you."

I had to sit in complete stillness for a second to process the words. This wasn't real, surely. How could it not involve any convincing or negotiations? Didn't she want something in return for her generosity?

"You do?" I asked as she moved to sit crossed-legged on the tabletop.

After everything I'd done, she shouldn't want to work with me. It was impossible. There was a copious amount of apologising and pleading and convincing that I was meant to do first... this wasn't at all how it was meant to go.

"Of course I do," she answered, as if the words were in any way believable.

Her silver eyes watched me impossibly closely, as if she was trying to search for a reaction. No matter how much attention she paid, she wouldn't find one. That was simply because there was no way that this was real. I must have died today, and this was the beginning of my torture in hell.

"Why?" There had to be something I'd missed, a piece of information so important it could sway someone as stubborn as the Shadow to give me a second chance.

"Because I've seen how far you're willing to go for the people you care about. That's all I need to know to be sure that I could eventually trust you. And don't try to convince me that your loyalty lies with Nylah just because she's family. You told me you were okay with me killing your brother before you killed your father a few hours ago."

I'd already blocked that from my memory. How I'd overpowered Ryne. I'd made sure to *not* use my supernatural abilities, just so I could prove that I never needed them, and then stabbed him in the chest fourteen times.

Something whispered that I should feel a slight bit of guilt for what I did, but no part of me listened. How could I feel remorse after everything he'd done to me for the last eight years?

"That shouldn't be enough for you. I haven't even apologised for what I've done."

People typically wanted something in return for an act of kindness. While this was mutually beneficial for us, she held all the power and yet she hadn't asked for a damned thing.

She should have forced me to my knees, forced me to beg for her forgiveness, or asked me to sell my soul or to put my sister up as collateral. If she demanded me to, I would do three out of those four things without hesitation.

"No, you haven't and you won't. I don't want you to apologise for putting your sister's safety above that of a stranger to you." Caeli cut me off, and there was something I couldn't understand in her eyes.

"Look, by reviewing your past actions, I know that you'd work well with Vince and I because you already have. On top of that, you were willing to face what was left of Templum by yourself so the rest of us could get to safety. That wasn't just for your sister, it was for Vince and I as well or you would never have told me to leave."

"But-"

"And you told me you trusted me, which I believe was the truth. I also believe that feeling of yours hasn't changed. Now that I know who you are, I also realised that a lot of the other stuff you told me was the truth as well. It's easy to tell what were facts and what were lies now that I have all the information."

Maybe I hadn't given her enough credit. Maybe she would have actually helped me had I told her everything at the beginning of this. But telling her wouldn't have helped ease the risk that Templum could have heard it. They would have killed Nylah if they had proof I'd betrayed them. It was the reason I'd been docile until now.

"I can tell it's hard to gain your trust, but you gave it to me and I don't take that lightly," she said softly. It warmed something in my chest to know that she wouldn't just throw what I'd given her back in my face. It was rare that I trusted people, because the few times I had they immediately showed why it was a mistake.

"Apparently it's even harder to gain yours..." I trailed off, and she smiled.

"I'm just extremely protective of what's mine." She ran her fingers through her hair, her fingertips rubbing her scalp. "Trusting too easily risks the people I care about, and I've been forced to learn that lesson multiple times. Now, I'm not saying you're one of mine yet, but I would be open to the idea of you working towards it. You only have to agree if the idea of learning what's *beneath my silver armour* appeals to you."

Why did she have to use the words I'd said when she begrudgingly agreed to work with me? Or, rather, when she agreed to work with *Hunter*? I'd hoped she'd forgotten every sly tactic I'd used, every attempt I'd made to break down her walls, and every time I'd tried to let her see what I truly needed from her.

"If that appeals to me?" I asked as I leaned forward in my chair to be a little closer to that intoxicating scent of hers. "I would say it does, *yes*."

"Good." Her bright eyes flashed with excitement. "Now, first call of action is finding somewhere to lie low for a while. Second will be making sure Nylah and I have complete control over our powers. The third will be finding some work. We need money since Paititi was a bust on that front."

"I could help with all three points if you'd like me to. I had to study custos and truci magic since Templum wanted me to steal all the power I could. They always planned on having you as my *battery*," I explained. She nodded in response.

While she hadn't asked me to, I would try to prove that trusting me and allowing me to continue working with her was a good decision. I'd do whatever it took in order to prove that I could be a worthy ally.

"Okay, and what about point one? Do you know where we could stay?" She asked as she hopped off the table and retrieved a laptop from her bag.

"Well, I have more than an idea. I have a place. My mum

inherited a family home in Costa Rica. I inherited it from her, but changed my name on the contract when I got it sorted a few years ago," I explained as she sat on top of the table once more and set the computer on the surface just in front of me.

"What name is it under?" She asked, her eyes fixed on the computer screen. I knew she was listening, even if she didn't look at me. She wanted to learn all she could about me and wouldn't let the opportunity go to waste.

And maybe I could have pulled on the ground rules we'd set when I was Hunter and used them to my advantage. She'd asked about my past, so that meant I could ask about hers... but it was probably best to not push the generosity she'd already shown me. There would be time to learn everything I could about her, and I wanted her to share it without the need for the 'rules'.

"Hunter Dawson," I answered, and watched as her eyes shifted to meet mine.

Had she sat on the table so I had to look up at her for once? I restrained the smile that wanted to tug at my lips, because I was damned sure that's why she was on the uneven piece of furniture.

"Dawson was my mother's maiden name. Hunter is the name she wanted to give me but couldn't because of Ryne. He specifically wanted to name me Samael after they ran the test that proved I was a conduit."

"So that's where that name comes from..." she trailed off as she processed the information I'd handed her. "Does

Black have any significance as well, or was it just the first surname you came up with?"

"It was Daniel's last name. Nylah has Mum's surname because they wanted her to have the same last name as me since we're siblings. Back then I was Samael Dawson, not Eldridge, because Mum got us out of Templum when I was a toddler." Mentioning Mum always caused my chest to tighten a little; it brought back memories of that time of freedom and joy.

Fuck, I missed her and Daniel.

Caeli nodded slowly as her eyes turned back to the computer screen. I assumed she was looking for something we could steal in Costa Rica, or anything else we could do that would get us some quick cash.

"Well, I think there's a choice you need to make then," she said. The sound of her fingers tapping the keyboard was rhythmic and helped to ease that pain in my chest.

I'd worked through the worst of my grief at losing Mum and Daniel already, but sometimes the echo of it still hit me. I couldn't let now be one of those times—not in front of Caeli at least.

"What choice would that be?" I asked, and she looked back at me with those hypnotising eyes.

"What you want your name to be," she replied. "From here on out, it's up to you. You can decide to go with Samael or Hunter, Dawson or Eldridge. It's completely your decision as to who you want to be known as." I mulled over the choice for a moment as Caeli returned to typing on her laptop.

I'd spent some time now pretending to be Hunter, and while it was the name Mum wanted to give me, it wasn't who I was. Unfortunately, I'd always been Samael—an embodiment of the angel of death and king of demons. And the way Caeli said it in her perfectly gravelly voice was another incentive for me to keep it.

But Eldridge? I no longer had to have that connection to my father, or my brother, who we hadn't seen the last of. No, I didn't have to be a part of that family anymore. I could go back to how it was when I'd been in New Orleans with Mum and Daniel and Nylah... I could share the same last name as my sister again; the one sibling I actually felt was my family.

"I might stick with Samael, but shift to Dawson," I said. I could tell by the way she smiled at me she approved of my choice.

"Well, it's nice to meet you, *Samael Dawson.*" I smiled in response to her reciting my name and rubbed the back of my neck as my entire body flooded with warmth.

While I couldn't explain the draw I felt to her, or why she made my body act in strange ways without my approval, I knew it would be stupid to ignore it completely. And now, with our new working relationship, I could maybe push the boundaries a little again. I could test just how much opposition I would face from her.

There was no way it could just be me feeling like this...

"You could call me Sam though, *Princess.*"

A light laugh left her lips, and it was a melodic sound I could listen to endlessly. Her eyes focused on mine, and the silver burned with something other than anger. I wanted whatever that something was to be injected directly into my veins.

"I don't think I'll be calling you that anytime soon. If you keep calling me *Princess*, then I'm going to keep calling you *American*." Well, there was an easy solution to that problem.

"If you'd told me earlier that all it would take for you to call me by a nickname was to come up with a new one for you, I would have done it days ago, *Caels*."

Her eyes widened for a moment, before she tilted her head to the ceiling and let out a deep sigh. Was that not what she'd wanted her nickname to be? It was too late now, because Caels was locked in whether or not she liked it.

"You are an absolute dullard, Samael."

The troupe will return in 'To Break a Shadow' coming in 2024

ABOUT THE AUTHOR

R. A. Mayes is in the process of chasing her dream to be a full-time author. She holds a Bachelor of Arts, majoring in creative writing and sociology, and uses both to create stories that she hopes people can feel seen in. While she dabbles in a handful of different genres, her stories will always hold relationships in high importance (romantic or otherwise)—everyone deserves someone who understands them and is willing to go to the ends of the earth for them. You can trust that every one of her stories will (eventually) have a happy ending.

She loves the nuances of morally grey characters and entwining themes of mental health throughout her stories.

Her favourite tropes include enemies-to-lovers, forced proximity and 'who did this to you?' (especially combined) and many others.

You can follow her on TikTok or Instragram (@r.a.mayes_writes) to get news on future works.

ALSO BY R. A. MAYES

THE SHADOW SERIES
[a new adult, contemporary romantic fantasy series]
Rise of the Shadow
To Break a Shadow [coming soon]

STANDALONES
Hyde and Seek
[a second chance action-romance]